Readers love ANDREW GREY

The Good Fight

"As per his normal, Mr. Grey has created great characters, used vivid descriptions, a fast pace, a well-scripted plot and all the emotional turmoil I could handle."

—Literary Nymphs Reviews

"I get a glimpse into the lives of people living very differently from me and it's never condescending or boring. He brings them to life by cutting through all the labels and bringing out their humanity, both the good and the bad. They never live in an ideal world or fit into some preconceived stereotype. I love that!"

—Reviews By Jessewave

An Isolated Range

"This is a great story about personal independence, love found and lost, and what it really means to be a loving, supportive parent. Another wonderful character-driven novel in the style we have come to expect from the story-telling mind of Andrew Grey. Enjoy."

—Mrs. Condit and Friends

A Foreign Range

"If you are looking for a quick romantic read about some emotionally guarded but hunky cowboys then saddle up and take a ride on the Range series."

—Guilty Indulgences

Legal Tender

"Buy the book and have an engaging, enjoyable day of reading."

—Randy's Book Bag Reviews

Novels by ANDREW GREY

Accompanied by a Waltz
Dutch Treat
In Search of a Story
A Wild Ride
Three Fates (anthology)
Work Me Out (anthology)

ART SERIES
Legal Artistry • Artistic Appeal • Artistic Pursuits • Legal Tender

BOTTLED UP STORIES
Bottled Up • Uncorked • The Best Revenge • An Unexpected Vintage

CHILDREN OF BACCHUS STORIES
Children of Bacchus • Thursday's Child • Child of Joy

GOOD FIGHT SERIES
The Good Fight • The Fight Within • The Fight for Identity

LOVE MEANS… SERIES
Love Means… No Shame • Love Means… Courage • Love Means… No Boundaries
Love Means… Freedom • Love Means … No Fear
Love Means… Family • Love Means… Renewal • Love Means… No Limits

SENSES STORIES
Love Comes Silently • Love Comes in Darkness

SEVEN DAYS STORIES
Seven Days • Unconditional Love

STORIES FROM THE RANGE
A Shared Range • A Troubled Range • An Unsettled Range
A Foreign Range • An Isolated Range• A Volatile Range

TASTE OF LOVE STORIES
A Taste of Love • A Serving of Love • A Helping of Love • A Slice of Love

Published by DREAMSPINNER PRESS
http://www.dreamspinnerpress.com

Novellas by ANDREW GREY

A Present in Swaddling Clothes
Organic Chemistry
Shared Revelations
Snowbound in Nowhere

FIRE SERIES
Redemption by Fire • Strengthened by Fire • Burnished by Fire • Heat Under Fire

CHILDREN OF BACCHUS STORIES
Spring Reassurance • Winter Love

LOVE MEANS… SERIES
Love Means… Healing • Love Means… Renewal

WORK OUT SERIES
Spot Me • Pump Me Up • Core Training • Crunch Time
Positive Resistance • Personal Training • Cardio Conditioning

Published by DREAMSPINNER PRESS
http://www.dreamspinnerpress.com

STRANDED

ANDREW GREY

Dreamspinner Press

Published by
Dreamspinner Press
5032 Capital Circle SW
Ste 2, PMB# 279
Tallahassee, FL 32305-7886
USA
http://www.dreamspinnerpress.com/

Stranded

Cover Art by Reese Dante
http://www.reesedante.com

ISBN: 978-1-62380-658-3
Digital ISBN: 978-1-62380-659-0

Printed in the United States of America
First Edition
July 2013

To Jane: Thank you for everything.

CHAPTER
ONE

HE FIDGETED in his seat in the Dolby Theatre, gripping the armrest and holding his breath as the music sounded and the presenters walked out on stage, the starlet in an incredible gown that must have cost more than his parents' house, and the star in a tuxedo that actually shone a bit under the lights. They glided out to the podium and did their short shtick before getting to the business at hand. By this time, he figured his heart was two seconds from giving out. The man moved a tad closer to the microphone. "And the nominees for Best Actor are...."

A year or so earlier....

KENDALL MONROE rushed offstage and into the wings just after the lights faded. He had two minutes to change and get ready for his next entrance. He'd already pulled off his shirt, and his shoes had been kicked off, with one of the runners picking them up. He hurried behind a screen and shoved his pants down, then stepped out of them and into another pair already waiting. He was handed his shirt, and as soon as he walked out, the shirt was buttoned and his tie placed around his neck and tightened. His collar was fixed, and he shrugged on his coat. Shoes were already in front of him as if by magic, and he slipped them on. They were tied for him, and one of the wardrobe people gave him a good once-over, nodded, and Kendall walked back toward the wings to await his cue.

He stepped out of the wings and met his costar in the center of the stage, where they did their final scene together, she in his arms, and he guiding her through the final dance number. The music built, he kissed her, and then the stage opened up and the rest of the cast joined them, adding their voices to the stars' as the music, lyrics, and dance all built to a crescendo that ended with everyone taking their final pose and waiting for the curtain to drop.

As soon as the fabric hit the floor, Kendall breathed a sigh of relief. Everyone hurried off the stage, and the curtain rose again. Cast members rushed back out on stage for their bows, and at the very end, Kendall and Joyce held hands and walked back on stage. The applause grew, echoing thunderously off the walls of the theater. They bowed together, and then the rest of the cast came together around them. Kendall clasped hands with Jeffrey, like he always did in this choreographed display of fake spontaneity, bowed again, blew kisses to the audience, and then bowed one more time before stepping back and letting the curtain come down for the last time.

As soon as he walked offstage and down to his dressing room, it hit Kendall that this was the last time he'd play the handsome, dashing, and sometimes bumbling Stone. The run was over—not because they weren't selling tickets, but because the producers hadn't been smart enough to leave their options open when they'd negotiated with the theater, and another show was booked and ready to start rehearsals.

Kendall changed out of his final costume and into his street clothes. A knock sounded on his door. "Come in," Kendall called, and Joyce stepped inside.

"Can you believe we're actually closing?" she asked, flopping down on the sofa.

"No," Kendall said, sitting next to her. One of the things they'd discovered when they'd begun working together months ago was that neither of them wanted the crush of people that always seemed to appear after a show. So either she came to his dressing room or he went to hers, and they hid until things quieted down and they could leave in peace. Most of the others in the cast and crew respected their need for quiet and a chance to decompress. "Even my agent hasn't been looking very hard because he thought the producers would come up with a way for the show to continue. We've sold out for weeks, but there aren't any available theaters right now, so...."

"I know," she said. "I was really hoping this engagement would be extended for another few months."

"Have you heard any more about doing that reality show?" Kendall asked as he got up. He pulled a bottle out of the mini refrigerator and popped the cork. "I know we don't normally do this, but I thought we deserved to celebrate a bit." Kendall poured two glasses of the champagne and handed one to Joyce. "Here's to you," he said, raising his glass. "I've loved every day working with you."

"Me too," she said, and they clinked glasses. "I'm to start filming the *Housewives of Massapequa* in a few weeks." Joyce chuckled and then burped a little. "I never thought I'd do one of those shows, but I'm looking forward to it." She held up her hand. "I promise not to take the whole thing too seriously." Kendall sat back down and closed his eyes for a second as he let the bubbling wine slide down his throat. "I'm going to miss dancing with you eight shows a week." She sipped from her glass. "Do you realize you're the first partner I've had who's never stepped on my foot or given me bruises on my ankles?"

"You're kidding," Kendall said and downed the contents of his glass before pouring another. He topped hers off as well.

"Nope," she said with a grin. "You remember I was in *Mamma Mia* before this. I came home after each performance with a new bruise. My dance partner always figured my feet were part of the stage." She took another drink, and Kendall listened. There was still noise coming from outside, but the sounds were diminishing. Joyce finished her glass and then stood up. Kendall did the same and hugged her tight. "I'm going to miss you."

Kendall nodded. "Please call me and let me know how the show is going."

"And you be sure to let me know where you land," Joyce said, heading for the door. "I just know there's something great waiting just around the corner for you." They hugged again, and then she left.

"I certainly hope so," Kendall said to the empty room as a sort of prayer before gathering his things for the last time. He packed up everything he'd kept there for the run of the show. It took two bags but eventually he had it all, and once he was sure he'd left nothing behind, Kendall opened his door and stepped out in the hallway. He walked down to where he knew he'd be able to find the director. The producers were with him.

"Kendall," the producer who seemed to do all the talking said as he approached. He hadn't wanted to disturb them by interrupting their conversation. "We're all sorry about the way things worked out, and both Jerry and I hope to work with you again in the future. You brought life and fun and more depth to Stone than we thought possible."

"Thank you," Kendall said, shaking hands with Roger and Jerry before offering his hand to Gregory, the director. He accepted the envelope that would contain a statement of his final payment for the show; the check would go to his agent, Sal. After saying good-bye one more time, Kendall turned and left the theater. As soon as the stage door closed behind him, he turned and looked at it, having the strangest feeling that things were about to change in a big way.

He'd been working in Broadway theater for almost fifteen years, and he was a star. He'd risen from the chorus to small parts to understudy, and then finally to the lead of his first show, which had run for five years. After that, the theater world had been his oyster and he'd been able to pick his roles, just like he'd decided to do the role of Stone. But in this economy there weren't a lot of roles available, and for the first time, he wasn't able to move almost immediately from one role to another. Granted, it wasn't the money he was worried about. He'd lived fairly frugally, knowing that in theater there were ups and downs. He just hadn't expected the downs to come like this—a smash hit that ended before anyone expected it would.

Kendall took a final look at the nondescript door and then walked toward the sidewalk. The after-theater crowd was still out and about, heading to bars and restaurants before going home. Kendall had done the eating and partying after shows a few times, but his waist and pocketbook had paid the price, so he hadn't done that in a while. He'd learned his lesson quickly. Thankfully, out of costume, he was rarely recognized, so Kendall headed for the subway station and descended underground.

He caught a train and found a seat. The doors slid closed and the train began to move. Instantly, the weariness from being onstage and active for hours caught up with him. But he didn't dare close his eyes, not on the subway. He'd made that mistake once, and it had cost him the bag he'd been carrying. He didn't make eye contact with anyone, and at his stop, he jumped off and walked down the platform to the exit. He climbed the stairs and exited the station before walking down the familiar sidewalk to the west side midtown brownstone he called home. Kendall let himself into the building and climbed the stairs to his second-floor apartment.

"You're home," Johnny said as Kendall closed the door. They kissed in greeting, and Kendall dropped his bags on the floor. "How was it?"

"Everything was fine until the second act. Then it seemed to hit everyone that this was the last night. We did a good show, but I think some of the energy was just different. It's hard to explain, but things were off. Not that the audience knew, but we did." Kendall knew he should take care of his stuff, but he was tired and didn't have the energy. Johnny, however, glared at the bags more than once until he picked them up and carried them into the bedroom. "They can wait for now," Kendall said, hoping Johnny would come sit beside him and commiserate a few minutes.

"I'll just go ahead and do it," Johnny said.

Kendall heard him moving around. He should have known Johnny wouldn't settle until everything was just where he wanted it. The television was on, and Kendall began watching a program about the Ice Age or some crap like that, and soon his eyes closed. He felt Johnny sit down at one point, but he was too tired to move and made no effort to curl next to Johnny. The gesture probably wouldn't be welcomed anyway.

"Kendall, are you going to fall asleep?"

"Probably," Kendall muttered.

"Then go to bed," Johnny said, and Kendall cracked his eyes open. He did notice that Johnny didn't say "come to bed," or even offer to take him to bed, the way he used to. Kendall definitely noticed that, but he wasn't sure what to do about it. He stood up and shuffled into the bathroom. He made sure to clean up well, and brushed his teeth before leaving the bathroom. In the bedroom, he stripped down and got under the covers.

After a few minutes of listening to the muffled sound of the television, Kendall got up and opened the bedroom door. "Johnny, are you coming to bed?" He wanted to be held, to have someone be with him on a night like this. Something he'd worked on for months was over and he didn't want it to be. He was at loose ends and hurting a bit.

"Not for a while," Johnny said. Then the light and sound from the television ended as Johnny turned it off. Kendall sighed and returned to bed; the last sounds he heard before falling asleep came from the keyboard as Johnny typed at his computer.

Kendall woke a few hours later. Johnny was snoring softly next to him, and Kendall was a bit cold, so he snuggled up to his partner of almost a decade and closed his eyes again. The warmth, comfort, and contentment from Johnny's skin against his was just what he needed, but as he was about to fall asleep, Johnny began tossing and turning and then used his weight to roll Kendall back to his side of the bed. Johnny's warmth then disappeared as he went back to his side of the bed. "I'm cold," Kendall groused softly.

"Then get a blanket," Johnny told him, and within seconds the soft snoring began again. Kendall sighed, pushed back the covers, and got out of bed. He went to the small closet, got an extra blanket, and spread it on his half the bed, careful not to put it over Johnny or he'd be too warm. Kendall then got back into bed and closed his eyes. Johnny hadn't stirred, and Kendall, warm now, drifted back to sleep.

WHEN Kendall woke, it took him a few minutes to remember what day it was and that he didn't need to go into the theater. Sunday—Johnny should be home, and there was no place they should have to go. He heard movement in the living area and slipped out of the bed, then pulled on a pair of old sweatpants and a threadbare T-shirt that was the very definition of comfort. He quietly opened the bedroom door.

Johnny sat on the sofa, typing at his computer, an endearing expression of relaxed concentration on his face. Kendall didn't make a sound and just stood where he was, watching with a smile on his face.

"Are you trying to make me nervous?" Johnny asked, barely looking up.

"I was just watching you," Kendall said, and he walked to the sofa and sat next to Johnny, then rested his head on his shoulder. "Actually, I was thinking, it's Sunday and we don't have anyplace to go. I don't have to go to the theater, and you don't have to work, so maybe we can go to the park or just get some coffee somewhere."

Johnny paused from his work. "I have a lot I need to get done." Johnny slipped off the glasses he used for close work and set them on the coffee table. "I have a deadline. I promised Lynn that she'd have this manuscript by the end of the week, and she's counting on me."

"I know," Kendall said as Johnny leaned forward once again, picked up his glasses, and went back to work. Slowly Kendall rubbed Johnny's back. "I just want to spend some time together. I'm always busy, you work a lot, and I thought one day for just the two of us would be nice."

Johnny sighed as though Kendall had asked him to walk over hot coals with his bare feet, and rather than push it further, Kendall stopped rubbing and shifted to the far end of the sofa. There was no use in asking again, he knew that, so he left the room and went to the bathroom. He brushed his teeth, shaved, and then showered before returning to the bedroom to dress. When he was finished, he returned to the living room. Johnny hadn't moved and was once again immersed in his work. Rather than try to make breakfast and have to listen to more dramatic sighs and the occasional complaint about the noise, Kendall grabbed a jacket and left the apartment, heading for his favorite coffee shop.

Once there, Kendall got in line and waited his turn. He'd ordered his usual chai latte and was sitting at one of the tables, trying to relax, when he heard someone say, "Where's Johnny?"

He smiled up at Gina and motioned for her to sit down. She lived in the neighborhood, and he'd run into her numerous times over the years, so they'd become friends. "He's on a deadline, so he's home working, and I decided to step out for a while to give him some peace."

Gina squinted at him slightly and then sipped from her cup. "Things aren't going so well?" she asked, and Kendall nodded in resignation.

"Can't hide anything from you," Kendall said.

"Nope. But I figured it was either that or your show closing." Gina yawned once and then drank some more of her coffee. She worked just down the street at a deli and was most likely on her break. She was Kendall's age, but had had a much tougher time of it. Young when she'd gotten pregnant, Gina had a fourteen-year-old daughter, Chelsea. Gina worked at the deli on weekends to help make ends meet. It hadn't been easy for her. Kendall had heard all the stories over the years, just like Gina had heard all the trials and tribulations he'd gone through when he'd been starting his career. "Johnny's rarely around when you are, and…." She paused. "I remember when the two of you were inseparable and you finished each other's sentences."

"We're going through a tough patch right now. But we'll be fine. Once he's through with his manuscript, he can relax, and I'll have some time until I get another job, so we'll be able to reconnect," Kendall said, acting more positive than he felt. The truth was that he wasn't sure how he felt about his relationship with Johnny. It wasn't as though there was anything wrong or that they were fighting. They just seemed to be growing apart. Kendall knew some of that had to do with their schedules, which he hoped would even out soon. "I've been thinking about seeing if he wanted to take a cruise or something in a few months. Give us a chance to get away."

"I think you have more than a chance," Gina said, and then she sipped from her cup. "Johnny's a nice man, and think about it, both of you have spent how many years building your careers?" She set down her cup, and Kendall paused with his cup near his lips, wondering what her point was. "How many years have you done eight shows a week, mostly in the evenings, with one day off a week?"

"A long time. I did my first show at eighteen," Kendall said, remembering the small part he'd had. He hadn't had many lines, but the part required a lot of stage time, and Kendall had had a ball hamming it up in the back of the scenes.

"Exactly, and you met Johnny ten years or so ago. Your entire relationship you've had this weird schedule, and now you don't. But he's built his life around your weird schedule. He worked full time and wrote in the evenings. Now his books have taken off and he's come into his own."

"I know. I see them in the windows of all the bookstores," Kendall agreed.

"But have you read one of them?" Gina asked. "Other than his first ones, have you read them?" Kendall swallowed and finally shook his head. He hadn't had the time to read them all. "Then maybe you should start there. You can't expect him to be all lovey-dovey with you if you aren't involved in his life."

"God," Kendall said. "I didn't know I was being a real dick." He gulped his cooling coffee and swallowed hard.

"You haven't been, just busy. Just like Johnny probably wasn't at the closing performance last night. You're both busy, or were busy. But you aren't now. So if you want things to change, that probably needs to come from you," Gina said, checking her watch. "I need to get back." She stood up, and Kendall did as well. They hugged, and then she hurried toward the door. Kendall watched her go and then sat back down and finished his coffee.

On the way back to the apartment, he stopped at Zabar's and bought some cheese, fresh fruit, and other goodies he knew Johnny liked before walking the four or five blocks back to the brownstone.

Inside, he found Johnny seated in the exact same place, still bent over his computer. He was typing to beat the band, and Kendall knew to make as little noise as possible. If things were flowing, then he didn't want to interrupt. He put away the groceries and then went into the bedroom, where he scanned their bookshelf for one of Johnny's books. He plucked out one he hadn't read, opened the window to let in fresh air, and settled on the bed to read.

"You're home," Johnny said with a bit of surprise when he came into the room.

"Yeah," Kendall said, looking up from his book. "I brought you some of the Gouda you liked and some berries." He marked his page and closed the book. He caught Johnny's gaze and scooched over on the mattress, hoping he'd join him. "Is the writing coming?"

"Yeah," Johnny answered excitedly. "It's been flowing fast." He stepped toward the bed and leaned over, giving Kendall a light kiss.

Kendall wrapped his arms around Johnny's neck and pulled him in for more, but he stiffened and only lightly kissed Kendall again. "I've got to get back to work." Johnny straightened up. "Do you want to make dinner tonight?"

"Sure, I can cook," Kendall said, and Johnny nodded, then left the room. Soon Kendall heard the almost frantic tapping of computer keys once again. Sighing softly, he got up and went into the kitchen to get a can of soda and some crackers before returning to the bedroom. This time he settled in the chair and put his feet up, taking as consolation that if he couldn't spend time with Johnny, at least he could spend time with his stories.

He must have read for a few hours. Time seemed to fly as he got into the book. Johnny wrote adventure stories around the search for famous objects or bits of knowledge. When they'd met, Johnny had still been in graduate school finishing up a master's in history. He'd planned to go on for his doctorate and then teach at the university level. A few months after they'd moved in together, Johnny plopped a sheaf of computer printouts on the table and asked Kendall to read them. It was the first half of his first novel. He'd started it on a whim during a break from school, and by the time he had his master's degree, the book was done. He'd made the mistake of showing it to one of his professors, who had deemed the work trite and beneath a true historian. Johnny had almost given up, but Kendall had pushed him, and by the time Johnny had started his course work for his doctorate, he had an agent, and by the end of the first semester, a contract. Once the book was released, it took off, and Johnny Harker became a sensation. He wrote two books a year that regularly hit all the bestseller lists. As he read one of Johnny's books for the first time in a while, Kendall understood why.

"Sal wants you to call him," Johnny called from the other room. Kendall hadn't heard the phone. "He called while you were out, but it slipped my mind until now." Johnny said nothing more, and the soft tapping on the keyboard commenced again. Kendall clenched his fists in frustration. He sat up and walked to the bedroom door, ready to yell at Johnny, but he stopped himself. It wouldn't do anything except get Johnny upset and then he'd lose his train of thought, which would have him stomping and pacing the living room until he got his ideas straight again. "Sorry," Johnny said again and continued typing. Kendall snatched the phone off the bedside table and dialed his agent, checking the time on his phone.

"Sal, it's Kendall," he said when the rather gruff man answered the phone. He was one of those old-time agents who smoked, ate, and drank too much, but knew every single person in town.

"'Bout time you called me back, kid. I was about to pass this opportunity on to someone else." Sal always said crap like that.

"Yeah, sure you were, and I was about to see if I could get myself a real agent. Now that the pleasantries are through, what's up? And why are you in the office on a Sunday? Isn't it about time for you to be visiting the cemetery to pick out your plot?"

Sal laughed heartily. "No, but you'll be picking out yours if you don't learn some respect." Of course the indignation was fake. Kendall loved Sal almost like a father—he was the best, and had guided his career with dexterity, making sure Kendall only took the right parts. Of course they'd fought on occasion, but Sal was usually right. "So how's that partner of yours? Is he in the middle of writing another bestseller? Ethel reads every one of his books."

"I'll be sure to tell him, and yes, I hope so. He's on a deadline, and the world could stop and he wouldn't realize it unless it somehow stopped his computer from working. So what really has you working on a Sunday?"

"You, kid. It seems word has finally sunk in that your show has closed and that you're free. I've been fielding calls for days, and we have some offers, big offers. You could have chosen between the Phantom or one of the fathers in *Mamma Mia.* But I told them all no."

"Sal!" Kendall said with surprise. "You're killing me."

"No, I'm not. You're beyond that stuff now. You originate roles, you don't follow others. Of course, there are no new roles right now. Things are pretty stagnant."

"Okay, so you've made me so I can't work. Is that what you're saying?" Kendall kept his voice low because he didn't want to interrupt Johnny, otherwise he'd have been yelling at the top of his lungs.

"Don't get your knickers in a twist, or whatever kind of drawers you gay boys wear. I was holding out for something really good, and I got the call this morning." He seemed to be building up to something.

"Call from who?"

"Hollywood," Sal said. "One of the units of Disney has a script they've been sitting on for a while because they haven't been able to find the right person to play the lead. See, it takes someone with looks, but also someone who can bring an in-depth character to life and display a variety of emotions in less than two hours. I convinced them that what they really needed was a stage actor, someone with presence and the ability to hold an audience with the crook of a finger or the lift of an eyebrow. And that's you. They loved the stuff I sent them and they loved your stage presence."

"Okay, but I've never worked on film before. I've only done live theater—you know that," Kendall said, his stomach roiling in a mixture of excitement and fear.

"Yeah, and so do they. This isn't some big-budget blockbuster. It's a smaller film, but it has the potential to become huge. They also need someone who can carry a scene alone, because a lot of the film will be just you."

"So what's this film called?"

"*Stranded.* They overnighted a copy of the script, and I'm having a copy made and messengered over to you this afternoon. I really think you should do this. If you don't like doing films, then you can always come back to Broadway, but this is the next step for you. There are only so many roles here, and the community is only so big."

"Tell me about it—it's almost incestuous," Kendall agreed.

"Yes. So see the rest of the world. They want you in Hollywood in a week, and you start shooting in two. It should take about three months to shoot the entire film, and by then, if you want, there will be plenty of roles available here if you want them."

"I'm not sure about this," Kendall said. "I don't have to work. I can simply wait here for a few months." He and Johnny could spend some time together.

"No, kid. You know you're either working or dying. Do this— it'll be good for you," Sal said in his gruff way. When Kendall hesitated, Sal continued. "Look, I've seen you on stage, remember? You have to play to the back row, but you always put those little things into your performances for the front row. Well, that's what they want. Those small gestures you always included are what will be seen and remembered. Take a chance, kid, for God's sake. Because if I were in your place, I'd be on a plane so fast...."

"Okay, Sal, you made your point. Let me look at the script."

"Fine, get back to me Monday morning. That's when I need to know. Say hello to Johnny for me and look for that package. I'll expect your call." Sal hung up, and Kendall stared at the phone for a second before tossing it on the bed and walking into the living room.

Johnny had his arms over his head, shifting his body from side to side, most likely in an effort to work out the kinks. But in seconds, an image came to Kendall of a younger Johnny making that same movement, but instead of getting out the kinks, he was writhing on the mattress, pleading and moaning while Kendall drove into him without mercy. Damn, Johnny had been beautiful—hell, he still was, and when his shirt rode up, Kendall was tempted to walk right over to Johnny, tug it over his head, and remind Johnny of just how much fun they could have together. "What did Sal want?" Johnny asked, bringing his arms down and positioning his fingers on the keys, ready to start again.

"He called to tell me about an offer," Kendall said.

"So which show is it, and when do you start?" Johnny asked and began typing again, intent on his screen.

"Well, actually, it's called *I'll Strip For You* and I need to get naked on stage and ride around on hobby horses while pretending to have sex with them. Sort of *Equus* meets *The Full Monty*."

"That's nice," Johnny said, continuing to work.

"Johnny," Kendall snapped, and finally Johnny stopped typing. "You weren't listening." Kendall walked over and sat next to Johnny on the sofa. "First thing, you really should get a better place to work." Johnny rolled his eyes and made a little hurry-up motion with his finger. "Secondly, Sal called with an offer, but it isn't a show. They want me to do a movie. He's messengering the script this afternoon, and I need to let them know by tomorrow." Not sure how Johnny would react, Kendall held his breath. "I can hold out for a show here in town, instead. There should be some openings and opportunities in the next few months—there just aren't any now," he explained in a rush.

"I think you should do it," Johnny said. "Read the script first, to make sure it interests you, and then go for it." Johnny turned back to his computer, but didn't start typing right away. "When do you leave and how long do you think you'll be gone?" Johnny asked, the same way he'd inquire when Kendall would be back from the grocery store. Kendall wasn't sure how he felt about that.

"They want an answer by tomorrow, and I'd need to fly to LA in a week, probably, to work through the business stuff. Shooting is scheduled to start a week later, and I'd be gone about three months." Kendall took Johnny's hand. "You could come with me. I'd have a trailer, and you could work there."

Johnny shook his head. "I need to be here. The research libraries I'm familiar with are here, and I have access to the libraries at Columbia. Out there, I'd be away from everything I need to work. It would only be three months and then you'd be back. By then I would have my next book outlined, researched, and mostly written. I could be ahead, and we could take a vacation or something, maybe." Johnny turned back to the computer. "I've always thought you should do movies. You're good enough, more than good enough." He turned back to him, and Kendall saw a hint of the excitement they'd shared after he'd gotten his first big part. Of course, that evening's celebration had ended in the bedroom, and they'd been loud enough to be the talk of the stairwell the following morning. Somehow he didn't think that would be happening tonight.

"Will you come out to see me while I'm there?" Kendall asked, and Johnny pulled his hands away from the keyboard.

"Of course I'll come visit once or twice while you're out there. But I suspect they're going to have you busy most days until all hours. But I'll definitely come." Johnny smiled at him and then stood up, pulling Kendall into a hug. "There are great libraries out there I can visit for research purposes."

Kendall returned Johnny's hug, but his heart wasn't in it. "Thanks, I think," he muttered.

Johnny was quiet for a few seconds. "I didn't mean it the way it sounded. I just thought that while you're working, I could go to some of the libraries and things to get some research done."

"I've been with you long enough to know what you meant." Kendall stepped back. "It's just that I'm going to be gone for months, and you don't seem disappointed."

Johnny sat back down. "But it's not going to be that different. I work during the day and into the evening. You go to the theater in the afternoon and work until late six days a week. We don't actually see each other all that often now. Sure, I'm going to miss you, and you'll miss me. But like I said, you'll make your movie and I'll finish another book, and then we can take a vacation." Johnny got that faraway look that meant his characters were speaking to him. "Hon, I really need to get this done. Then tonight we can spend some time together."

The door buzzer sounded. Kendall hated to leave, but he knew it was probably the messenger, so he turned and left the apartment, then took the flight of stairs to the main level. Sure enough, he saw a bicycle messenger waiting outside the door. He took the package and gave the kid a tip before making sure the door closed tightly and then going back to the apartment. Johnny was back at work, immersed in his story, and Kendall knew he needed to let him work.

He opened the envelope and pulled out the screenplay for *Stranded,* then threw away the wrapping. Then he sat in one of the chairs, the clacking of computer keys his accompaniment as he began to read.

He hardly moved for almost two hours as he read the script from cover to cover. By the time he was done, he had an excellent idea about the story.

"So, what do you think?" Johnny asked. The lid of his computer was closed and Johnny handed him a glass of iced tea. "I figured you could use something to drink."

"Yeah, I think so," Kendall said as he took the glass and drank down half of it. "This is…." Kendall swallowed. "I think this could be very powerful, but I don't know if I can do it." He opened the script and found the pages he wanted. "The main character gets stranded in a car. You know I'm claustrophobic, and they want to handcuff me in a car for hours on end." Kendall could already feel the sweat threatening to break out all over at the thought.

Johnny read for a few minutes. "Hey, think about it. The car will only be parts of a car, because they have to film it. So while it'll look like you're stuck in a car, you won't really be." Johnny handed him back the script. "I think you're trying to psych yourself out so you won't have to do this." Johnny sat next to him. "Here in New York, you're a big fish. Everyone knows who you are, and yes, you can get almost any part you want. But this would be like starting new. You should be excited, not afraid."

"Are you trying to get rid of me?" Kendall asked.

"No. I'm only returning the favor. You encouraged me with my first book, and now it's time for me to do the same for you. You need to spread your wings." Johnny lightly patted his leg and then leaned in and kissed him softly. Kendall hoped for something a little warmer, and attempted to pull Johnny closer, but he pulled away. "I have an appointment with one of the librarians at Columbia." Johnny glanced at his watch. "I'll only be gone for a couple of hours, and when I get back, we can have dinner together. I promise."

"On a Sunday afternoon?" Kendall asked, but Johnny was already up and going. He grabbed a light jacket and hurried out of the apartment. Kendall didn't know what the hell to do, so he went back to the bedroom and opened the book he'd started earlier. But he couldn't concentrate.

A cell phone ringtone sounded, and he snapped the book closed and located Johnny's phone. He answered it to stop its incessant ringing. "Hello," Kendall said tentatively.

"Johnny?" a young male voice asked.

"No, this is Kendall, can I help you?"

The line was quiet for a few seconds. "No, that's okay. I'll see him later." The call disconnected, and Kendall stared at the blinking number. He set the phone on the coffee table and was about to go back to his reading, but instead, he picked up the phone again and brought up the call history. While there was no name in contacts, Johnny had been getting calls from the same number every few days for at least the past month or so. Kendall closed the phone and placed it back where he'd found it.

He needed something to do, so he decided to start dinner. He chopped vegetables and got them ready to cook. He seasoned the beef he'd bought earlier and let that sit to build up some flavor, and peeled potatoes before getting them ready to boil. The entire time, Kendall found himself staring every few seconds at Johnny's phone, and finally he allowed himself to voice what he was fearing: *Is Johnny having an affair?* At least that would explain the complete lack of interest. God, he didn't want to think so, and his heart ached. He still loved Johnny, and he needed him. Johnny was his anchor, his rock—he always had been.

They had been growing apart; he could see that. But maybe it was just a product of their busy lives and months or years on very different schedules.

His phone rang, and Kendall hoped it was Johnny. No such luck. "Hey, Sal," Kendall said when he answered.

"Did you get the script?"

"Yeah, and I read it," Kendall said.

"Good. I wanted to make sure. They need an answer tomorrow," Sal told him, and Kendall nodded.

"I know, and you'll have it. I need to think things over. I know how you feel, and I'm giving this a lot of thought," Kendall said as he wandered over to the window, peering out at the relatively quiet street below. "I have to be honest that I'm nervous about doing it."

"Of course you are," Sal said. Kendall settled on the bench and watched the people and cars as they navigated the narrow street. "This is going to be different with all new people, but I know you're right for this part. I've represented many people who've gone from Broadway to

Hollywood over my career, and rarely have any of them received a vehicle as perfect for them to make the transition as you have."

"But, Sal, they're going to lock me in a car," Kendall said as he half watched out the window.

"I know. Isn't it wonderful?"

"Sal!" Kendall yelled.

"Don't take that tone with me. I know how you feel about enclosed spaces, but that's why it's perfect for you. Use that fear in the movie. Let them see what that does to you and your character. Don't run from it—embrace it. Trust me," Sal said, and Kendall sighed softly. "I told you it was perfect."

"If you say so," Kendall said as a cab pulled up in front of the building. "As I said, I'll be sure to call you Monday morning." The cab door opened, and Johnny got out. "I need to go. Johnny just got home from the library, and I need to get dinner ready."

"You two have a big celebratory night planned?" Sal asked.

Kendall's smile at the thought lasted until he saw another man lean out of the cab. He appeared to be speaking to Johnny. The other man disappeared from view back in the cab, and Kendall saw Johnny lean inside the vehicle for a few seconds and then back out once again. Johnny closed the cab door, and Kendall could have sworn he saw a huge smile on Johnny's face before he disappeared from view.

"Kendall, are you there?" Sal asked.

"I'm here," he said. "Tell the people in Hollywood I'll do it." Kendall said. Maybe three or four months on his own to explore a bit and figure out what he really wanted wasn't such a bad idea, after all.

CHAPTER TWO

A WEEK later, Kendall said good-bye to Johnny, who, to Kendall's slight relief, appeared sad at his departure. Kendall had noticed a few mysterious calls Johnny received during the day and he always rushed out right afterward with some excuse about needing to get to the library for an appointment he'd forgotten. Kendall hadn't said anything, because even though he was becoming more and more convinced about the reason for these calls, he hadn't wanted to force the issue right before he left. Kendall also knew it was because he kept hoping he was wrong. After all, he'd been away most afternoons for most of their relationship. Maybe this was a regular routine that the research for Johnny's books involved.

Johnny had taken him to the airport, and they'd arranged for Johnny to come out for a visit in a month or so. After a hug that, to Kendall's relief, lasted longer than was necessary, he got in line at LaGuardia, and after waiting, going through security, and then more waiting, he boarded the plane and winged across the country on his way to Los Angeles. The flight itself was long and boring, but Kendall had his copy of the script, which he spent some additional time with, as well as a copy of one of Johnny's books. "I read that," the lady in the seat next to him said at one point. "It's really good."

"I'm enjoying it," Kendall said. "It was a gift from the author."

The woman's eyes lit up and she almost bounced in her seat. Because of their public lives, neither of them had been vocal about their relationship. Their friends knew, but neither of them marched in parades or anything. "Yes. He's a special friend," Kendall said, leaving it at that. Johnny had always said that readers were readers and he didn't want to piss any of them off, so there was nothing about Kendall in the printed bio, just like there was nothing about Johnny in Kendall's *Playbill* bio. They had both agreed a long time ago that their private life was just that—private.

Kendall returned to his book, and was rewarded for keeping his mouth shut when the woman pulled her own book out of her bag—one of those "self-help through prayer" books. Kendall smiled at her and nodded, continuing to read until he finished the book about the same time the flight attendants were readying the plane for landing.

He'd been told that a car would be sent for him, and once they landed and he took the escalators to the baggage claim, a man in limousine livery stood waiting with his name on a small sign. "That's me," Kendall said.

"Very good," the chauffeur said. "I'll help you with your luggage and take you to your hotel." Kendall nodded and headed over to the luggage carousel. He got his luggage, and the driver put the bags on a cart and led the way outside. Another man, smartly dressed, stood beside a stretch limousine. The door was opened for him, and Kendall climbed in back. The seats were plush and comfortable after the hard-as-a-board plane seats. There was a stocked bar and soft lighting, and music if he wanted it. He heard his luggage being placed in the trunk and the lid closing. After a few moments, the vehicle began to move, and Kendall settled back and closed his eyes. The flight had been long and he'd heard all about Los Angeles traffic, so he settled in for a while. He knew he should rest, but instead spent the time staring out the windows as palm trees and greenish-brown hills dotted with homes passed outside as they inched down the freeway.

Eventually, they exited the freeway and made a series of turns that left Kendall feeling completely turned around until they pulled under a hotel portico. The door was opened by one of the drivers, and Kendall got out, instantly wishing he had sunglasses. "We'll bring in your luggage," the smartly dressed man said.

"Thank you," Kendall replied and headed into the hotel. He wasn't sure what he'd been expecting. The hotel was nice, but this was

Hollywood, and he'd been expecting a grand entrance hall, chandeliers, maybe even starlets walking through the lobby in glittering gowns, not a nice but ordinary hotel with normal people walking around everywhere. "Kendall Monroe," he said to the desk clerk.

"Of course, we've been expecting you," she said with a smile and nodded to one of the bellmen, who took Kendall's luggage from the drivers. "I'll just need a credit card for incidentals," she explained, and Kendall handed his over.

"We'll be waiting for you, sir," the driver said very softly. "The producers and director are expecting you at the studio in"—he checked his watch—"two hours."

"Thank you…." Kendall extended his hand.

"Juan," he said, shaking Kendall's hand. "I'm one of the director's assistants," Juan explained. "Well, actually, I'm the assistant to Mr. Davidson's assistant."

"It's good to meet you, Juan," Kendall said.

"You too, Mr. Monroe."

"Kendall, please," he corrected and turned to the desk clerk, who had things for him to sign. He did where she indicated, listening as she explained everything. Kendall took his keys and card, and the bellhop and Juan followed him to the elevator.

"What room are you in, sir?" the bellhop asked, and Kendall told him the number. They stepped off at their floor, and the bellhop led them to the room, then took Kendall's key and opened the door for him. He carried in the luggage and set it on the stands, explained where everything was, and opened the curtains. Kendall was immediately enthralled with the view—the city all laid out in front of him, stretching as far as he could see.

By the time he turned around, the bellman was gone and just Juan stood near the door. "Let me get my things unpacked and we can head over. I'd sort of like to look around if I could before I have to go to the meeting." Kendall motioned Juan toward one of the chairs and began to unpack. The task didn't take long, and Kendall noticed that Juan watched him closely. "Is something wrong?" Kendall asked as he closed the drawer.

"No," Juan said. "It's just that we still have time." Juan stood up and moved closer. "You're a very handsome man," he added, his accent now coming through. "I was told to do anything I could to help make you comfortable." Juan stepped even closer, entering Kendall's personal space. He placed his hand on Kendall's chest. "Like I said, you're very handsome."

"Juan," Kendall said, placing his hand on Juan's and then slowly removing it.

"You aren't gay?" Juan asked, stepping back.

"It isn't that," Kendall said. "I have someone in my life." He wasn't sure what he and Johnny were to each other at the moment. While he might have an inkling that Johnny was cheating, although he didn't have proof, he wouldn't cheat. Even if Juan's deep brown eyes and the hint of young, virile muscle beneath his light, flowing white shirt were damned tempting. "You're a handsome man too, Juan, and I'm very flattered, but this isn't the way I want to start things out here." God, this was not at all what he'd been expecting.

Juan shifted his gaze to the floor. "I'll wait outside until you're ready."

"That isn't necessary," Kendall said, getting the last of his things together. "We can leave now." He tried to act as though nothing had happened. After all, there were worse things than being propositioned by a young man with deep eyes and a body that moved with a dancer's grace. They reached the elevator and rode down in silence.

"Do you want me to ride up front again?" Juan asked, and Kendall rolled his eyes.

"No," he said, getting into the back of the limousine. Juan followed him, and the driver closed the door. "So what's supposed to happen once we get to the studio?"

"Well, you're supposed to meet with the producers and director. If there's time, I can show you around the lot a bit. Part of the film will be shot on a soundstage, but from what I've heard, the car scenes will be shot out in the desert west of here. There was some talk of you spending some time with Mr. Davidson, scouting out locations, but I don't know if anything has been decided yet."

"Okay," Kendall said and turned to look at the scenery passing outside the window. "How am I supposed to know when I'm supposed to be where? I've only done theater, and that stuff is very easy. They tell us what time to show up, and we do. It's always the same theater, day in and day out."

"God, that must be boring," Juan said with a hint of a smile. "The production team will keep you informed, and of course the director will, as well." Juan shifted slightly in his seat. "You'll do just fine. The thing is, don't let them rattle you."

"About what?" Kendall asked and Juan shifted a bit closer.

"See, there seems to be a… difference of opinion about you. So various people might try to rattle you to see what you're made of."

"Sort of like playing tricks on the new guy?" Kendall asked. He remembered the jokes the cast sometimes played on first-timers. They weren't malicious, just a bit of teasing. He'd expected that sort of thing.

"Yeah, probably," Juan said seriously, and Kendall got the feeling that whatever was going on was a lot bigger and would probably go a lot deeper than harmless pranks. "Like I said, don't let them rattle you."

"I'll do my best," Kendall said. He'd spent the past fifteen years around serious theater people with their squabbles, egos, and petty requirements. He figured he could handle whatever these people threw at him. But from the doubtful expression on Juan's face, the assistant's assistant didn't think so. "Don't worry. I spent years dealing with temperamental directors and costars on Broadway."

"If you say so," Juan said and then reached to the seat next to him. He opened an app on his smartphone. "Like I said, you're meeting with the producers and the director. Later, you have an appointment with wardrobe so they can take all your measurements. After that, we'll stop by makeup so they can get a look at your face and skin tone. After that, it's cinematography, where we'll get you in front of a camera so they can see the lighting, filters, and other effects that work best for you."

"Is there some sort of screen test on the schedule? I sort of figured they'd want to see me in front of a camera before they actually hired me."

Juan looked at him askance. "They did. As I understand it, you did a television special a year ago to promote one of your shows. From what I saw, the camera loves you."

"Okay," Kendall said, trying to remember that appearance. It hadn't been more than five minutes, and all he'd done was talk to one of the hosts and perform one of the songs from the show. It seemed to him they were basing a lot of decisions on a very few minutes, but then again, these people knew what they were doing. At least he sure as hell hoped they did. The car pulled to a stop, and Kendall peered out. They appeared to have stopped at a gate.

"We're entering the studio," Juan said, and after a minute they pulled forward and along what appeared to be a road, but most of the traffic seemed to be golf carts. They traveled slowly, probably stuck behind one of the carts. Eventually they stopped. The door opened, and Kendall stepped out of the large vehicle, followed by Juan. A few people stopped to look, but they quickly moved on. "They're checking to see if you're someone."

"What?" Kendall asked.

"They're checking to see if they recognize you. Many of the people around are studio personnel or extras, and they sometimes stop to see if they recognize someone famous."

Kendall obviously didn't warrant their attention for very long, because everyone moved on. Juan walked around the car and spoke to the driver. Then he walked back to where Kendall was waiting and craned his head to look at everything around him. There was surprisingly little to look at—mostly what he surmised were soundstages, large buildings that all looked the same, painted the same shade of off-white. "I expected it to be more… interesting," Kendall said, and Juan laughed.

"Here, the magic happens on the inside, and there are more interesting areas. Some of the studios still retain their backlots, like at Universal, and they rent them out for various movies. It's all a business, and everything is here to make movies or television shows, which hopefully make money." Juan chuckled. "We have some time. I can show you around a bit if you like." Juan began walking, and Kendall followed. "If you see filming, just keep quiet, and whatever you do, stay out of the shot." They wandered down the street of soundstages until they came to the back. "That's the backlot."

"It looks sort of like a hollow city," Kendall said. *Of course, what else would he expect?* "They're like stage sets, only larger."

"Exactly. The front is dressed for the movie, and no one but the crew ever sees the back, so that's left as it is. Most of what you see as buildings in the movies are just sets on a framework. Most shooting happens on soundstages because it's so much easier to control everything. There aren't weather issues, and the light is just the way you want it. But sometimes it isn't possible, so then films are shot on location. For *Stranded*, there have been people scouting locations for a month or more now. But Mr. Davidson needs to okay them."

Kendall nodded, and they walked back the way they'd come. "It's a bit warm," Kendall remarked, and he moved into the shade of the large buildings, where it was cooler. He didn't want to be a sweaty mess for the meeting.

"Sorry, I should have been paying attention," Juan said and then stopped. "Look, you won't tell Mr. Davidson about what happened... you know, at the hotel. He'd probably fire me... not that he really knows who I am, but still."

"Juan, I promise. If things had been different, I'd probably have taken you up on your offer," Kendall said. "But don't sell yourself short. You deserve more than...." Kendall swallowed, then said, "Than what you were offering." He didn't want to presume anything, but Kendall had an idea that he wasn't the first guy Juan had propositioned like that.

"What more is there?" Juan asked with a wicked grin, the grown-up version of a kid on Christmas morning.

"Love," Kendall said. "Someone who's yours, and yours alone." He paused and thought about Johnny, smiling at a mental image of him bent over his computer, staring intently at the screen. Then Johnny looked up and smiled at Kendall, the smile that was only for him. It had been a long time since he'd seen that look. Kendall was trying to remember exactly how long when Juan softly cleared his throat. "Lead on," Kendall said, and followed Juan back.

"Go on inside," Juan said. "They should be expecting you."

"Aren't you coming?" Kendall asked as he walked toward the door and Juan stayed back.

"God, no. I need to get back to my boss, and for this one, you're on your own." Juan chuckled, and Kendall pulled open the door, walking inside what appeared to be a small office area.

"Can I help you?" the receptionist asked as she looked him over and then returned to her computer screen. Obviously she didn't think he was entitled to her attention. "If you don't have an appointment, you can have a seat and they might get to you today, otherwise...." She never looked up.

"I'm Kendall Monroe, and I believe I'm expected," Kendall said in his best New York haughty accent. He'd encountered more than his share of self-important functionaries in his career.

"Oh," she said, her eyes widening. That obviously got her attention. "Please make yourself comfortable. I'll let them know you're here." She stood up and hurried away through a door behind her desk. Kendall looked around. The place seemed more like mobile home chic than Hollywood grandeur. Kendall wondered just what he was getting himself into. Was this some movie they were making on a shoestring? With the money Sal had said was being offered, he hadn't thought so, but who knew. She returned, and Kendall heard a heated discussion drift in.

"I don't care. I didn't ask for him," a commanding voice said, and then the door closed, cutting off any more.

"They'll be just a minute. Can I get you something? Coffee, Perrier?" she offered, her change of tone complete.

Kendall stood up. "No, thank you...." He held out his hand, and she stared at it for a second.

"Cassandra," she finally supplied, taking Kendall's hand. Kendall had discovered a long time ago that the assistants, secretaries, and receptionists in the entertainment business wielded their own sort of power—access. More than once, Kendall had gotten a leg up on the competition simply because he knew and was on friendly terms with a producer's assistant. He'd also found it took very little effort to be kind and to see people others tended to overlook.

"Although from the argument I heard, a belt of something might be in order before I get thrown to the lions." He chuckled and Cassandra did the same as she sat back at her desk.

"They're all bark and no bite," she said as she took her seat once again. Then she leaned across her desk. "You seem like a nice guy, so whatever you do, don't let them push you around."

Kendall shook his head just a tad. He'd met two people so far, and both of them had told him that. "Thanks," he said, and Cassandra answered the phone and then hung up again without saying a word.

"You can go on back," she told him, motioning toward the door. "Good luck."

"Thanks," Kendall said and pulled open the door to a conference room. Three men stared at him when he entered, and once he'd closed the door, they stood up.

"Kendall," one of the men said, walking around the table. "It's a pleasure to meet you. I'm Robert Starr, and this is Barty Lippert. We're the producers of *Stranded*." He took Kendall's hand and shook it warmly. "Barty and I saw your last show when we were in New York," he said as he looked at the other man, "two, three months ago. It was fabulous, and when we heard it actually closed, we knew we had to snap you up before someone else did." He smiled, seeming to bounce with so much energy that Kendall couldn't help smiling too. Then they turned to the third man in the room. "And this bundle of joy is our director, Lyman Davidson."

"It's good to meet you," Davidson said without a hint of sincerity. He also didn't offer his hand. Robert motioned him to a chair, and Kendall sat down.

"You've read the script?" Robert asked.

"Yes. I received a copy from my agent."

"Then you've read it?" he repeated, and Kendall nodded, settling back in his chair. "What did you think of it?"

"Parts of it were interesting," Kendall said honestly, and all three men looked at each other. "I really like the idea of exploring Parker's emotions as he's locked in the car." His leg shook under the table at the thought of being locked in a car, but yeah, as he'd examined the script on the plane, he'd realized Sal was right and he could use that fear in the character.

"Look," Lyman snapped as he leaned on the table. "I believe in putting the cards on the table, yeah," he said in an Australian accent. He'd have been cute were it not for the fire coming out of his eyes. "They're the producers and they chose you for this role. I get that. But this is my movie and you will do as I say. I'm the director, and it's my vision for the film that will get it to the screen, not some dancing pansy from Broadway."

Kendall looked at the other two men, who had gone silent, their praise and fluff withering on the vine. "You're just a bundle of sunshine, aren't you?" Kendall said, and he leaned forward on the table. "I think we need to get something straight. I've worked with all kinds of directors. Some who were easy to get on with, and some of the biggest assholes in the business, and there's one thing I know: the shows directed by the assholes all closed fast, because their assholeness made it onto the stage. Or in your case, the film. See, my agent told me who the director was, and I spent the last week watching every one of your movies." Kendall saw Lyman smile. "And they were interesting, because they're a reflection of you. The assholeness came through, big-time. Your characters were all angry even when it wasn't necessary." Kendall met the director's stony gaze with one of his own. "The directors who worked with their cast and pulled the best performances they could from the ensemble? Those shows ran for years."

"Robert, Barty, I just don't think this is going to work," Lyman said to the other two men, and Kendall stood up.

"That's perfectly fine," Kendall said. "Just pay me and I'll be on my way."

"Pay you?" the producers said.

"Oh yes, read the contract. I did. It states on page eight the amount I will be compensated for this movie, with the first two hundred thousand payable on the first day. I'm here, I'm working, this is the first day. So write me a check and I'll go back to New York." All three of the men went white. "Yeah, see I'm from New York, and I might look like I'm fresh from the farm, but I'm not. I'm a professional, and I give each role the very best I can. I also treat everyone with respect,"

Kendall said, turning his gaze to Lyman. "So if you want to work together, then treat me with the same respect you want from everyone else, and we'll make a great movie." Kendall sat back and let his gaze shift from one man to the next.

"This is going to be perfect," Robert said with more enthusiasm than he'd had before. Then he stood up, along with Barty, and they left the room. Obviously they were expecting a directorial explosion and wanted to be out of the room when it happened. The door clicked closed, and Lyman stood up, glaring over the table.

"How dare you?" he yelled. "Those films...."

"Were just what I said. They were good and I enjoyed each of them, but I told you the truth," Kendall said, standing up as well, meeting the director glare for glare. "You didn't even meet me. You made assumptions about me and had already made up your mind before I ever got in here."

Lyman huffed through his nose. "So what's your point?"

"I was hired because I can bring this character to life, and I will, if you let me." Kendall softened his tone but kept it firm.

"We'll see," Lyman said without breaking Kendall's gaze. "There's some revisions being made to the script. I'll make sure a copy is messengered to you tonight."

Kendall nodded. "Tell them to pay extra attention to pages fifty-six to eighty. The dialogue came off as particularly stilted and plays on some assumptions that aren't strong enough. I can give you the exact lines if you need them." They finally broke gazes, and Kendall sat back down.

"I think we're done here," Lyman said, and he walked to the door. "I'm reserving judgment, but I'll see you tomorrow morning. We're leaving to go on location at eight tomorrow. My assistant will send a car." Lyman opened the door, and the two producers came back inside. Kendall said good-bye to the three men and left the room.

"You still with us?" Cassandra asked, and Kendall smiled.

"I think so," he answered and left the office. The car was still parked outside, and the driver opened the door so Kendall could climb inside.

"Back to the hotel, sir?" the driver asked.

"Do you have to be somewhere?" Kendall asked the driver.

"No. I'm at your disposal for the day," he answered.

"Then could you—" Kendall began, but he was interrupted by a knock on the window. Kendall opened the door and saw Juan standing outside. Kendall motioned him inside and then turned back to the driver. "Could you show me around town?"

"Certainly, what would you like to see?" he asked, and Kendall turned to Juan.

"Take us to Hollywood," Juan said, and the driver turned around and the car began to move. "How did it go?" Juan asked.

"I'm not sure," Kendall answered, and Juan looked like he expected Kendall to say more. "Did you get everything done you needed to?"

"I guess," Juan said, pulling an iPhone from his pocket. He answered a text and then shoved it back into his pants.

Kendall's phone rang, and he fished it out. "Hi, Sal," he said.

"I heard you made quite an impression," Sal told him without any of his usual pleasantries.

"The director was being a total ass, so I used the leverage we talked about. I really owe you one for that," Kendall said. "I think we've come to some sort of understanding, even if it is a cold war. At least he knows I won't roll over or kiss his boots." Kendall glanced at Juan and saw him hanging on every word. "How did you find out already?"

"Barty and I are old friends. He found the two of you interesting," Sal explained. "Watch out for those two. Robert does all the talking, but it's Barty who has the money and the real power. You impressed him. So, well done, but remember you need to work with Davidson, and he can be a vindictive bastard when he wants to be."

"I understand," Kendall said as the limousine stopped momentarily for a light. "I'm supposed to look at locations tomorrow morning. So I suspect I'll find out then."

"I suppose you will," Sal said and then hung up. Kendall disconnected as well and placed his phone back in his pocket, then looked out the window and watched the scenery slide by.

The driver stopped on Hollywood Boulevard, and Kendall jumped out of the limousine. Juan took care of the arrangements with the driver, and then they wandered up and down the Walk of Fame. Kendall couldn't help reading all the names on all the stars embedded in the sidewalk. At one point he pulled out his phone and dialed Johnny. "Guess what, I'm standing right next to Lucille Ball," Kendall said as soon as the connection had been made.

"Johnny, I must have picked up your phone," he heard a strange man say, and Kendall's heart plunged into his stomach.

"Hello," Johnny said.

"Who was that?" Kendall asked a little more snappily than he intended.

"Just a research assistant from Columbia," Johnny whispered. "Did you get there okay?"

"Yes," Kendall answered. "I met with the director and producers today. Tomorrow I'm supposed to go with the director to look at locations." He wanted to say that he missed him and needed him, but couldn't, the nagging doubts inside stopping him. "I didn't want to call too late."

"I'll be up working for most of the evening," Johnny said. "Have a good trip scouting locations, and I'll talk to you real soon."

"Okay," Kendall said and hung up the phone. When he did, he caught sight of the time. It took him a few seconds to remember that the clock on his phone had reset to local time. He did some quick math and realized it was eight thirty back home. "Research, my…."

"Is something wrong?" Juan said from behind him.

"No," he lied, placing his phone in his pocket. "Do you think we could get something to eat? I'm hungry, and then I want to go back to the hotel. This time change has me all out of sorts, and I need to be ready and awake in the morning." Everything told Kendall that he needed to be at the top of his game around the director.

"You don't want to eat and then go to some of the clubs? Sunset Boulevard is just a few blocks away, and there are some of the best clubs in the city," Juan told him.

"No, thanks. They're sending over the revised script, so I'll have work I need to get done." What Kendall needed was some time alone to think, not a loud club full of strangers. "Maybe another night, though." Kendall looked up and down the boulevard, and as the sun sank behind the surrounding mountains, the lights from the signs added a garish quality to everything around him. "Can we go to a place that's quiet where I can get a good cut of beef?"

"Okay," Juan said skeptically and called for the car. It arrived a few minutes later, and Juan gave the driver the information about dinner as Kendall settled back in the plush seat. They arrived at a restaurant and had a nice dinner. He and Juan chatted a bit. "Johnny would love this place," Kendall said at one point and then quickly steered the conversation in another direction.

After dinner, he rode back to the hotel and said good night to Juan. "The car will be here at seven," Juan reminded him. Kendall thanked him for all his help and then walked into the hotel. He stopped at the desk, where he was given a large envelope, and then headed up to his room, where he settled on the sofa with the script.

After an hour he found it hard to concentrate and realized what it was. Always when he read a new script, he settled on the sofa at home, curled near Johnny while he worked. There was nothing he could do about that now, and he wasn't certain he would have a Johnny to go home to. Pushing his fears and doubts from his mind, Kendall concentrated on the script so he could be ready in the morning.

CHAPTER
THREE

KENDALL tossed and turned for most of the night. The bed didn't feel right no matter which way he lay, and more than once he rolled over to put an arm around Johnny and only came up with an empty bed. Of course, he woke at that point and tried to get comfortable again. But his mind would start running through his suspicions and he'd end up wide awake once again. Once during the night he even went so far as to pick up his phone to call Johnny, just to hear his voice and to ask what he needed to know. But he didn't. The time change allowed him to sleep in a bit, and he was downstairs waiting when the car arrived.

He joined Juan in the backseat and rode, half asleep, to wherever they were meeting the director. Kendall had suspected they were going to the studio, but the limousine pulled into a diner parking lot. Kendall got out and saw Lyman standing with another man near a huge SUV. Kendall was relieved he'd dressed in older clothes when he saw the other man. "That's the cinematographer, Guy Reynolds," Juan said when he got out as well.

Kendall nodded. The two men seemed deep in conversation around a map, and he didn't want to interrupt them. "Do actors usually go when they scout out locations?"

Juan shrugged. "I don't really know. Every director does things their own way, but my guess would be no."

"Wonderful," Kendall muttered, resisting the urge to fan himself, sweat breaking out on his skin. It was hot already, and from the strength of the sun, it was going to get even hotter. The others looked up from their conversation, and Kendall walked over.

"Excellent," Lyman said as Kendall approached. "We have the necessities in the back." Lyman handed the map to the other man who folded it. "Kendall, this is Guy, he'll be our chief cinematographer. Guy Reynolds, this is our lead, Kendall Monroe."

They shook hands. "It's nice to meet you," Guy said and then turned to the director. He seemed to have the same question Kendall had.

"This is going to be a very involved role," Lyman said to both of them. "The desolate landscape and harsh conditions will play almost as big a part in the movie as the characters, so I want Kendall to really experience it before we start shooting." That seemed to satisfy Guy, and they all headed for the vehicle. "We'll be back here about seven," Lyman told Juan, who nodded and headed back toward the comfort of the air-conditioned limousine. Kendall walked toward the SUV and climbed in the backseat. The others got in as well, and soon they were barreling down the highway.

"We've already had people scouting these locations, and Guy has seen most of them," Lyman said as they rode. Kendall noticed the director's accent seemed to come and go, and he wondered how much of it was an affectation.

"So you need to see them and make a final decision," Kendall supplied.

"Exactly. Guy's narrowed down the list to five places. We'll see three of them today. The other two are farther away and would be more costly to use. So if we don't see anything right today, Guy and I will wrap this up tomorrow."

"Aren't you leaving this a bit late?" Kendall asked.

Lyman sighed. "Everything on this film seems a bit late. But once the money got approved and the checks written, we needed to move. So today and tomorrow we check out the locations. Then we'll make final preparations, and next week we'll start the studio work while the road teams get everything ready at the location."

Kendall nodded and sat back, listening as the two men talked about the kinds of shots they'd need and the feeling they wanted for each one. He tried to pay attention, but couldn't follow a lot of what they said, so he stared out the window. After five minutes, the scene outside the window held no further interest. He pulled out his phone and was surprised to see he still had service. He dialed Johnny's number, but the call went to voice mail, so he left a message. "Hi, it's me. I just wanted to talk to you. I'll be scouting locations today and I don't know how long we'll be in cell range. I hope the writing is going well. I miss you." Kendall added the last part quickly and then ended the call. The conversation up front hadn't stopped, and since they weren't paying any attention to him, Kendall settled back on the seat. His thoughts instantly turned to Johnny, a younger Johnny.... He and Johnny had met at a friend's holiday party. Kendall closed his eyes, and he could see Johnny as he walked in, the embodiment of the poor college student.

JOHNNY had worn his best clothes to the party, but they'd definitely seen better days. The party had started in the afternoon and would probably go well into the wee hours of the morning, but Kendall had a show to do in a few hours, so he drank Diet Coke and talked to people. Kendall saw Johnny as soon as he walked into the room. Tall, with a shock of blond hair that seemed to go everywhere at once, bedhead before bedhead was fashionable. He appeared lost and out of sorts as he moved through the other people, not making eye contact with anyone, and he would have passed Kendall if he hadn't accidently on purpose stepped in his way. What Kendall hadn't been planning on was Johnny knocking him onto his butt.

"Oh, God, I'm sorry," Johnny had said, taking Kendall's hand to help him to his feet.

"It was my fault," Kendall said honestly as their hostess quickly mopped up. Thankfully, his glass had been nearly empty. "I'm sorry," he said to June as she finished up.

"No problem, sweetheart," she said. June called everyone "sweetheart" or "darling" in the cutest Hungarian accent. God, he loved the diversity of this city. "Johnny, you made it," she said, throwing her arms around the shocked man. Kendall would find out

later that Johnny's family hadn't been demonstrative in any way and those kinds of displays had always shocked him. Sometimes they still did.

KENDALL smiled as he rode in the SUV, but didn't open his eyes.

"HAVE you met Kendall?" June asked with a naughty giggle. "He's a real sweetheart and is currently on Broadway in some show I can never remember, but he's brilliant." She smiled at both of them and hurried off.

"So you're brilliant, huh," Johnny said and smiled a smile Kendall would remember always.

"If she says so," Kendall replied. "I don't think she's ever actually seen the show. But take it from me—I'm brilliant." He added the last part in June's accent, and Johnny nearly snorted his drink out his nose.

"You're not supposed to be funny when I'm drinking," Johnny told him, and Kendall grabbed a napkin and wiped Johnny's shirt. He even wiped spots that weren't there, and by Johnny's chuckle he knew it too. "Tell me about this show of yours," Johnny said as he threw the damp napkins in the trash. Kendall regaled Johnny with stories about the show and his part in it. Then Johnny told him all about his graduate work in history, specifically the Renaissance, which moved them into a discussion of art, something they both loved.

Before Kendall knew it, the afternoon was nearly gone. He set down his glass. "I have to go right now," Kendall said in a bit of a panic, "or I'm going to be late." He said good-bye to Johnny and June before hurrying out of the apartment and down the stairs.

"Kendall," Johnny called from the stairs as he hurried down, stumbling and catching himself as he reached the landing. "Can I call you?" he asked nervously.

Kendall pulled out his wallet and got out one of his cards, fishing in his coat pocket for a pen. He wrote his home number on the back and handed it to Johnny. "I think that would be very nice," Kendall said and then reluctantly raced out into the cold. He nearly tripped on the sidewalk as he ran to the subway. He made it to the theater just in time. After the show, he stripped off his makeup and changed his clothes before leaving via the stage door and heading out into the night. As he passed in front of the theater, he saw Johnny buried in his coat, collar turned up, gangly legs carrying him closer.

"What are you doing here?" Kendall asked, a bit startled.

"June told me what time you got out and where to meet you. I hoped I could walk you home, if that was all right," Johnny offered, and for the second time that day, Kendall saw the bright, hopeful smile that reached all the way to Johnny's eyes.

"That would be...." Kendall was a touch speechless. "... wonderful." Johnny caught up to him, and they walked side by side beneath the flashing marquee lights. Along the way they stopped for hot chocolate, and when Kendall reached the doorstep of his building, Johnny leaned forward, and they shared a gentle, chocolate-flavored kiss. "Are you okay to get home?" Kendall asked as the snow, which had been coming down lightly all evening, got thicker.

"I'll be fine. I'm just a few blocks," Johnny said as he pulled up his collar once more, then shoved his hands into his pockets. Kendall watched as Johnny quickly moved away, the snow falling harder and harder, quickly swallowing him up.

THE SUV began to bounce, and Kendall opened his eyes to the sun's harsh glare off the desert. He opened his sunglasses case and put them on.

"We're almost at the first location," Guy said and then turned off the main road, traveled a short way, and stopped. "This is federal land, but we have permission to shoot here if we want," Guy said and then opened his door. Blast-furnace heat blew into the vehicle, and Kendall had to remind himself to breathe.

"There are golf umbrellas in the back," Lyman told Kendall as he stepped out of the backseat. "The sun is brutal, and I don't want you sunburned. It'll ruin our early shots."

"Gee, and I thought you were turning into a humanitarian," Kendall quipped, and Lyman gawked at him while Guy began to laugh.

"Come on, you have to admit that was good," Guy told the director. Kendall didn't see Lyman's reaction as he pulled up the back liftgate and took out three golf umbrellas, then handed them out. Kendall put his up and was immediately relieved of the heat from the intense sun beating on him. "This location is great from a cinematic point of view," Guy said. "There's that scene when Kendall here realizes he's truly all alone. He's in the car looking out, and when we pan the camera high into the air the car gets smaller and smaller as the land gets bigger. We'd actually put the car about a half mile over there and we'd need to shoot that angle before the ground is disturbed. We could use the air from the chopper blades to simulate the wind blowing away the tire tracks and erasing the signs of his passage."

"I think that could work. And for the close-up shots, there would be a lot of room to maneuver," Lyman said and turned to him. "What do you think?"

Kendall pulled himself out of the initial throes of fear that threatened to grip him at the thought of being enclosed in the car for that scene. *It's only a car,* he told himself; he'd been in plenty of those with no problem. "I've never made a movie before, but I don't feel it," Kendall said, and both of the other men rolled their eyes. "It's too open," Kendall said, ignoring the stares. "You can see for miles in every direction here. A car or anything out of the ordinary would stand out like a sore thumb because there's nothing else. The script says he spends almost four days in the car, but here it would be too easy to spot, especially from the air. There should be camouflage, something to disguise the shape of the car." Kendall figured they had probably expected him not to have an opinion, but Lyman had asked, so he offered.

Guy seemed impressed and nodded slowly, but Lyman humphed and headed back to the SUV. He climbed in and shut the door without another word. Guy shrugged and opened the rear hatch, then grabbed a cooler from the back. They collapsed their umbrellas and placed them inside. Kendall added Lyman's, which he'd leaned against the side of the vehicle, and Guy closed the liftgate.

Kendall opened the door and climbed into the backseat. "I guess someone never learned to put their toys away when they're done," Kendall said to Guy as he placed the cooler on the seat next to him. Kendall saw that Guy was trying not to laugh as he closed the door. Kendall wasn't about to pick up after Lyman again. He opened the cooler and passed out cold bottles of water to everyone. Guy retraced their path back to the main road, and they continued on.

"What's in there to eat?" Lyman asked after a few minutes, and Kendall opened the cooler again. He'd expected sandwiches, not plastic containers of tapenade, brie, and assorted cheeses, as well as regular and red pepper hummus. Kendall peered over the backseat and found a bag of biscotti, brioche, baguettes, pita quarters, and a loaf of french bread. He handed Lyman what he wanted and did the same for Guy before tearing into the olive tapenade with a vengeance.

"The next location," Guy began after he swallowed, "has a more rugged terrain, but it's going to be harder to film because of the obstacles. It could work, but it'll have its challenges."

They rode and ate in near silence for almost an hour, with Kendall handling the food, until Guy once again turned off the road and wound through a few miles of rough road before pulling to a stop at the bottom of a dry canyon about twenty feet deep. They got out of the SUV and stood in its shade, looking out over the monochromatic landscape.

"Is this hilly enough for you?" Lyman asked sarcastically.

"Actually it's pretty cool, but would you film down here? You could never do that wide shot you were hoping for. It's too restrictive," Kendall said to Guy.

"The color is great, though," Lyman said as he looked up at the canyon walls. "The hard thing about desert filming is that everything is so monochrome. This would allow us to break that up." Lyman looked at both of them. "But filming would be a royal pain in the ass," he pronounced. "And the light would suck for most of the day."

"So I take it this one is a no," Guy said.

"Afraid so," Lyman admitted, and they headed back to the vehicle, then once again stashed the umbrellas in the back. Kendall noticed that this time Lyman took care of his own. Once in the vehicle, they all drank more water. Kendall couldn't believe how thirsty he was after being out in the desert for only half an hour. The air seemed to suck all the moisture out of him.

"The next site isn't far, only twenty minutes or so," Guy explained as he carefully backed the vehicle out of the canyon and wound his way back to the main road. "We're just about to cross into Nevada," Guy explained. A small sign a few miles later was the only indication that they'd changed states. Just across the border, Guy turned south, and they rode for a ways until Guy turned off onto an even smaller road. "How did you ever find this place?" Kendall asked as he peered out the window.

"We started with topographical maps, and the scouts work with local people to try to find potential spots. It's a real art that they're amazing at," Lyman answered just before the vehicle pulled to a stop. Kendall got out and popped the liftgate, grabbed a golf umbrella, and headed away from the SUV. There were hills, but not too high, and what looked like plenty of room to move. He could see Guy being able to do the shot he'd talked about earlier because, from the air, the hills would even out, but up close, they'd provide a place where the car could be hidden.

"Well?" Kendall asked Guy, who had a smile on his face. Even Lyman seemed happy.

"I take it you agree?" the director asked him.

"This feels right," both Kendall and the cinematographer said at the same time.

"It's federal land and not restricted, so we have permission as long as we return the land to the state we found it," Guy said as he consulted his notes. Kendall wandered around one of the small hills and was surprised at how he instantly felt alone. He couldn't see or hear anything but the desert and the wind. It was like the rest of the world had disappeared. This was the feeling the script was trying to convey. At least he thought so. Kendall walked a bit, figuring he'd just go around the hill, but he didn't see the SUV, and the desert went on and on. Wondering if he'd turned when he shouldn't, he did an about-face and followed his footprints, thankful the air was still.

"There you are," Lyman said with a bit of exasperation.

"We were afraid we were going to lose you," Guy said.

"Nope, but behind that hill might be what you're looking for," Kendall said, and Guy tramped off, returning ten minutes later with a grin on his face. "Did I lie?" Kendall asked.

"No," Guy said. "It's perfect. It's between two hills, but wide enough for all the equipment and cameras. The hills even dampen the outside sound somehow. It's super quiet." Lyman didn't appear to buy it. "Go take a look for yourself, but be sure to turn around and come back the way you came. The valley seems to lead off somewhere and doesn't bring you back like you think it will."

Lyman walked off, and Kendall turned to Guy. "How long have you known him?"

"We've worked together before. He's not a bad guy, just a colossal pain in the ass when he thinks he's right, even when he's not," Guy said. "But you seem to have his number."

"I don't know about that," Kendall said.

"Sure you do. Think of him as a kid who's used to always getting his own way and always needs to test the boundaries. He'll push and push until you push back. It's part of what makes him a good director, but also what makes him a bastard, because he's always pushing for something and he doesn't know what it is sometimes."

"I've worked with people like that before," Kendall said as he saw Lyman making his way back. "The last one we sent sailing off the stage and into the orchestra pit," Kendall said, keeping a straight face. "It was a beautiful, perfect arc until he crumpled like a rag doll." Kendall turned and headed back toward the SUV.

"You're full of shit," Guy called.

"Maybe," Kendall said, making a smooth sailing motion with his hand, and Guy began laughing again.

Kendall got back in the SUV, leaving the door open while the other two huddled beneath their golf umbrellas talking earnestly as they swept their arms over the landscape. He could make out their tones and some of their words, but not enough to follow the conversation, though that really didn't matter. They had their work to do, and in his mind Kendall began building the character for the movie. After a good ten minutes of talking and gesturing, the others returned to the SUV, and after stowing everything, they climbed inside. Guy turned the key, and the SUV started and then immediately died. He tried again, and the vehicle did the same thing.

Heat was already building up in the interior, and Kendall closed his eyes and prayed for the stupid engine to start. It didn't. Guy got out, walked around to the front, and lifted the hood. Kendall opened the door on the shady side to let some of the heat out. Then he opened the cooler, thankful there was plenty of water. He took one and handed another to Lyman. "Fucking piece of crap," Kendall heard Guy swear from outside. Then he stomped to the back and lifted the gate. "Thank God I keep tools with me," Guy mumbled, and Kendall heard the rattle of a toolbox.

"Is there anything I can do?" Kendall asked as he looked over the backseat.

"No," Guy said as he hefted the toolbox out of the back before walking around to the front again. Kendall turned to Lyman, who shrugged and huffed softly.

"He should have it fixed pretty quick," Lyman said. Kendall wanted to believe that, but he wasn't feeling hopeful. After a few minutes of banging and a bit more swearing, Kendall grabbed a bottle of water and wandered around to the front.

"I think I've almost got it," Guy said. "Wasn't getting enough air—damned dust." He banged what seemed to be the air filter, and a cloud of crap filled the air and then blew away on the wind.

"Here." Kendall handed the water to Guy and took the filter, hitting it gently to dislodge the dust. Guy upended the bottle and then set to wiping out the inside of the filter housing. "It looks better," Kendall said, not really sure what he was doing, but getting that junk out should be good.

"There's something that's letting the dust in. I'll have to tell the studio people when we get back. But cleaning this out should be enough to get us home," Guy explained as he began to put everything back together. "I appreciate the help," he added once he had the cover on the filter housing. "Try to start it," Guy said, and Kendall climbed into the driver's seat and turned the key. The engine started immediately and stayed running. Guy ran to the back, the tools thunking and clanking as he set down the box.

Kendall moved to the backseat, and Guy slid into the driver's seat. They all closed their doors, and Guy turned onto the side road.

"Well, that was a bit of an adventure," Lyman said. "I tried to get some help, but there was no signal."

"That's why I always have tools on these trips. I also left word with your office with exactly where we were going and when we'd be back. There's no one out here and the nearest town, once we get to the main road, is Las Vegas." They bounced around for a while before reaching the main road and finally the highway. Kendall had never been so grateful to be back on smooth pavement in his life.

Kendall sighed as worry about the vehicle having further troubles became less urgent. The other guys talked and reviewed what they'd seen. Kendall was pretty sure Lyman had liked the third location, but the final decision would be his. All Kendall could do was offer his opinion. They crossed back into California and continued driving. After about twenty miles, they came to a combined gas station, convenience store, and restaurant at a turnoff. Guy pulled in and got gas. Lyman headed inside, and Kendall went inside to use the restroom. He was getting a soda when his phone chimed. He pulled it out of his pocket and saw a message from Johnny. "Miss you too." Kendall smiled and sent a quick reply before heading into the tiny bathroom. He'd hoped for something else from Johnny, but no further messages came. He did his business and washed up, passing Guy as he left the bathroom.

He wandered through the small store, which had a Burger King in one corner with a few booths, shelves of basic necessities, food, soda, candy, and, of course, a section with condoms and aspirin, as well as a large area of auto repair supplies.

"Can I get you anything?" the woman behind the counter asked. Kendall ordered a soda and paid for it before sitting across from Lyman at one of the booths. Lyman didn't seem to be in the mood to talk, so Kendall sat quietly, waiting for Guy, who got something to drink as well and joined them in the booth.

"This was productive," Guy observed, and Lyman nodded once.

"I think we can cancel the trip for tomorrow. We have what we need," Lyman said and pulled out his phone. He began a texting conversation that seemed manic for a few minutes; then he looked up at Kendall. A few seconds later, Kendall's phone rang.

"Hello?" Kendall asked when he saw the strange number.

"Hi, it's Juan. Are you going out again with Mr. Davidson tomorrow?" he asked frantically.

"No," Kendall answered, and Juan sighed softly.

"I went ahead and made appointments with all the departments for you tomorrow. They're anxious to get their hands on you," Juan said with a snicker.

"Fine, I'm all yours. You'll be able to show me where to go?" Kendall asked, suddenly worried he would have to find his way around the labyrinth of studio buildings.

"Of course. I'll meet you at your hotel in the morning," Juan said and then hung up.

"Looks like I'm booked for tomorrow," Kendall said to the group, and Lyman nodded.

"There's another script revision coming on Friday," Lyman said matter-of-factly. "We were to start shooting on Monday, but I think it will—No… no… no," Lyman blustered as he gave up texting and dialed the phone. He stood up and headed toward the door. Kendall assumed that meant they needed to go and got up to follow.

Once they were on the road, Lyman spent most of the time on the phone. "I need a date," he said emphatically at one point and then lowered his voice. Kendall checked his phone once again, but there were no messages. He thought about calling, but Johnny was probably working. He got comfortable, and it wasn't long before he began to feel sleepy, so Kendall rested his head back against the seat.

KENDALL hurried to get ready for his date. Johnny had called the morning after walking him home from the theater and had haltingly asked him out for dinner. "It'll have to be Sunday because I only have a matinee, or Tuesday, because that's the day the show is dark," Kendall had said.

"Okay, then, this Sunday?" Johnny asked, and Kendall agreed. "Should I meet you at the theater?"

"My apartment would be better," Kendall said. He figured that way he could shower and change before Johnny saw him. So now Kendall expected Johnny at any minute, and he'd just stepped out of the shower five minutes earlier. Kendall pulled on his pants and shirt, relieved that he'd had the foresight to lay out his clothes before going to the theater. He'd pulled on his socks and one shoe when the buzzer sounded. Kendall hopped into the other shoe as he walked the few steps to the door. "Johnny?" Kendall said into the intercom

"Yes, it's me," Johnny said, and Kendall buzzed him in before checking himself out in the mirror near his bed. He looked okay, and opened the door as he heard Johnny's footsteps. "You look nice," Johnny said, and Kendall smiled as he stepped back to let Johnny into his studio apartment. "This is really nice," Johnny said, looking around.

"It's tiny, but it doesn't take me forever to get to work," Kendall said. He shut the door, and Johnny moved close. "I kept thinking about you all week."

"Me too," Johnny said, and Kendall angled closer and kissed him. There was no chocolate this time, just Johnny, and Kendall liked it better. "I kept thinking about that kiss."

"No chocolate this time," Kendall said, and Johnny kissed him again.

"I almost didn't call," Johnny admitted when he straightened up again. "I couldn't figure out what an interesting guy like you could see in me. I'm boring and spend my days researching dead guys."

Kendall chuckled as he shook his head. "You're intense and you're passionate about your subject, which isn't boring." Kendall hoped Johnny might eventually throw a bit of that passion his way, and he shivered with excitement. "The subject might be boring, but passion never is." It took Kendall a second to realize what he'd said. "Not that I think what you study is boring," he added hastily. "I didn't mean that...." God, he'd really stepped in it.

"It's okay, I know what you meant," Johnny said with a grin that included a soft chuckle. "You're cute when you're flustered."

Kendall turned away so Johnny wouldn't see him roll his eyes at the cute comment. Cute was the dating kiss of death. He didn't want to be cute. Dashing, yes, handsome, hot, even adorably sexy would work, but cute....

"You should get your coat," Johnny said, pulling Kendall out of his woolgathering.

"Is it still snowing?" Kendall asked as he pulled his heavy coat out of his closet. He also found his nice scarf and gloves.

"Yes, but not too hard, and the wind died down, so it's pretty," Johnny told him. Kendall bundled up and turned off the lights. They left the apartment, and he locked up. Once they'd descended the stairs, they stepped out into a Christmas card. Fresh snow glittered in the lights around windows and from the pine trees in small pots. "I always wondered what a Winter Wonderland looked like," Johnny commented softly and turned to Kendall.

"It is pretty with the fresh snow and lights," Kendall said.

"Yes, it is," Johnny told him without breaking his gaze. Kendall instantly warmed, and Johnny kissed him there on the street. A car honked as it passed, and Johnny moved away and then guided them down the sidewalk.

"Where are we going?" Kendall asked as he licked his lips, trying to get the last taste of Johnny left on them. "I'm not really hungry yet." It always took a while after the excitement of a show for his appetite to kick in.

"Perfect," Johnny said, and they began walking toward the center of the city, where he hailed a cab. "Take us to the park, please," Johnny instructed, and the driver began moving once they were in.

The ride didn't take long, and the driver let them out at the south corner of Central Park right near the Plaza Hotel, which was all decked out for the holiday. "I thought we could go for a ride," Johnny said, and he engaged one of the horse-drawn carriages. Kendall almost shook his head, thinking those were for tourists, but he got in. The driver handed them a thick blanket to put over their legs and started the horse moving. "I always wanted to do this on a date," Johnny told Kendall in a whisper.

"You've never done this before, then?" Kendall asked, and Johnny shook his head slowly.

"I haven't been on many dates," Johnny confessed. "Have you?"

Kendall didn't know how to answer and decided on the truth. "I've been out with guys, but on very few dates," Kendall began, and Johnny moved closer, putting his arm around Kendall's back. "And certainly no dates like this," Kendall added, looking up at the trees covered with snow, flakes falling and melting on his face.

"So this was a good idea?" Johnny asked.

"This was a magical idea," Kendall told him and snuggled closer. What a way to sweep a guy off his feet. The snow seemed to be letting up, and the car-horn blares and engine revs faded into the distance as they traveled the park road, leaving most of the world behind and entering a world of snow-covered lampposts and lawns turned to blankets of white. In the morning it would be trampled and messy, but right now, from a slow-moving carriage, everything was pristine and unspoiled.

The ride lasted almost an hour and then the driver pulled up where they'd started. Kendall blinked a few times as he stepped out of the carriage. They'd been in a cocoon for the past sixty minutes, and the harsh world had suddenly invaded once again.

"Our restaurant is within walking distance," Johnny said, and they walked with the holiday shoppers and New Yorkers rushing home for the evening. Johnny led him down Fifth and then up one of the side streets to a small bistro. They stepped inside from the cold into a room filled with warm scents that seemed to surround Kendall. A server led them to a table, and Kendall took off his coat and draped it over the back of the chair.

"This is perfect," Kendall said as Johnny sat down, and they shared a smile. "Did you plan this whole thing?"

"Of course. I put in my order for fresh snow as soon as you said yes," Johnny quipped, and Kendall grinned. "I did know about the carriage rides and I made the reservation, but the rest just sort of happened." The weather had conspired to provide a romantic evening. At least it felt that way to Kendall. Everything was perfect. And of course perfection never lasted. The waiter brought menus, and they ordered hot chocolate and then placed their food orders. The hot chocolate tasted like it came from a can, just like the whipped cream and later the soup. Kendall's chicken was overcooked, and Johnny's beef nearly raw. The only things that were right were the salads, which probably came out of a bag, but at least they weren't mushy or brown. The manager apologized when Johnny complained, and their plates were taken away.

"I'm sorry," Johnny said, and Kendall leaned over the table while they waited.

"I barely noticed," Kendall said as their gazes met again. He would have eaten chicken-flavored shoe leather if it meant he got to spend time with Johnny. This sweet, gentle man was quickly stealing his heart. Their replacement food arrived, and they ate. Kendall hardly tasted anything.

At the end of the meal, Johnny paid the bill. They bundled back up and left the restaurant. "I should get a cab to take us home," Johnny said, walking toward the Fifth. Kendall caught up.

"It's okay," Kendall said. "We can walk. They'll be skating at Rockefeller Center, and the tree will be lit. The buildings will be decorated."

"If you're sure," Johnny said, and they began walking down the avenue. They watched the skaters for a bit and then continued on, cutting across town and continuing away from the commercial areas. Kendall was shivering a little when they finally reached his building, and he knew Johnny had to be cold as well.

"Come up and I'll make you something to get warm," Kendall offered. He opened the door, let them both inside the building, and then led the way up to his apartment. Once in the apartment, Kendall hung *up their coats and went right into the kitchen, where he heated some milk to make proper hot chocolate, which he brought to where Johnny sat on the sofa. "This should do it," Kendall said with a grin.*

"Little marshmallows," Johnny said happily and sipped from his mug. Kendall did the same, the smooth sweetness warming him all the way down.

"Are you warmer now?" Kendall asked, and Johnny set his mug on a coaster. He took Kendall's mug, placed it next to his, and then leaned close.

"I'm getting there," Johnny said and kissed him softly at first.

Their kisses had been chaste up till now, but Johnny deepened it, and Kendall moaned softly, wrapping his arms around Johnny's neck. Kendall felt Johnny's weight shift, and then he was pressed back onto the cushions. Intensity built quickly in the touch of their lips, but there was no urgency, no need to rush. Their fires were banked, and for now Kendall was content. He'd rushed into things with too many guys, and all it had gotten him was sex and a quick "see you later" as the guy rushed out the door.

"I'm warm now," Johnny said.

"I'll say," Kendall said before tugging Johnny into another kiss. "I think you taste best covered in chocolate." Kendall licked his lips, and Johnny smiled and sat back up. Kendall swallowed hard and straightened up as well. They picked up their mugs again, and Kendall leaned against Johnny, soaking up his warmth.

"I do, huh?" Johnny said.

"The chocolate tastes sweeter when it's on your lips," Kendall said and angled for another kiss, which he got. "Is this okay?" Johnny turned to look at him, seemingly a bit puzzled. Kendall continued, "I mean, this is nice, but I mean... well... you know... without sex right away."

"There goes that cuteness again," Johnny told him. "There's no rush. This isn't about sex, or maybe I'm hoping it's about more than that." Kendall shifted closer, rested his head on Johnny's arm, and softly hummed his agreement. He certainly hoped so. Kendall turned on the television. A Christmas Story *was on. Kendall reached for the remote, but Johnny stopped him.*

"I always liked this as a kid and haven't seen it in years," Johnny told him. The two of them laughed through Ralphie's antics as he schemed to get his "Red Ryder BB gun with a compass in the stock and this thing that tells time."

"YOU still with us back there?" Guy asked, and Kendall lifted his head off the back of the seat. Housing developments and strip malls dotted the side of the road as they approached the edge of the city.

"I'm fine, just thinking," Kendall said. Lyman was on the phone, and Kendall wondered if he'd stopped talking since they'd come back into cell range. He checked his phone, but there wasn't a message. He decided to call before it got too late, and Johnny answered.

"How was the trip?" Johnny asked, sounding tired.

"I think it was good," Kendall said, catching Guy's eye in the rearview mirror for a second before he looked away. Kendall knew to be careful about what he said. "The director seems pleased, so that's good. Tomorrow I have a million appointments at the studio."

"'Hurry up and wait' type stuff?" Johnny asked.

"I hope not. From what I'm told, I'm booked back-to-back with the various departments all day," Kendall explained, but he didn't want to talk too much about movie stuff where he could be heard, so he changed the subject. "How is the book coming?"

"I made my deadline, but just barely, and now I'm starting on a new project." Johnny sounded excited.

"Does this one require a lot of research?" Kendall probed.

"Nope. For this one I know all the material I need. But I'm researching some ideas for the next story that's working its way into my head." For a second Kendall wondered just what kind of research Johnny was doing with the guy who'd answered Johnny's phone and with the guy from the cab. He was starting to get paranoid.

"When do you think you can come out for a visit?"

"I'm not sure. This book is flowing pretty quickly and I don't want to break the rhythm," Johnny said.

"You can work from out here," Kendall told him.

"I know. Why don't you see what your schedule is going to be like? And when you think you might have a break, I'll make arrangements to fly out."

"You don't have to come if you don't want to," Kendall said quietly, and Johnny sighed.

"It isn't that," Johnny said. "I don't like to travel much, you know that. And if you're going to be busy, there's no use in me coming out if I'm not going to be able to see you. I'll only end up sitting around waiting for you to come home."

"It just feels wrong being apart like this," Kendall said.

"It's not going to be forever, and when you're done, you'll come back here. We've been together for a long time, and yes, this will be the longest we've been apart, but you'll make it, and so will I." Johnny paused. "I do miss you. This place just isn't the same without your clothes falling on the floor of the closet and shoes left everywhere."

"Okay, I get it," Kendall said as he felt the tender moment slip away. "I'll let you get back to work."

"Call and let me know how it goes," Johnny asked, and Kendall agreed before hanging up. He noticed there was no "I love you" or any other sentiment at the end of the call, and he tried to remember when those had disappeared, but he couldn't. He'd just now realized they were gone and had been gone for quite a while. Kendall missed them. He also knew it wasn't Johnny's fault any more than it was his. They'd let those things slip away, along with some of the intimacy in their relationship, and Kendall wondered if it was too late to get them back.

Lyman finally hung up, and their small group rode in near silence until they got close to the gas station where they'd started their trip. The limousine was waiting, and when they stopped, Kendall got out and shook hands with both men. "Thank you," he told Lyman. "This was an eye-opening experience, and I think it helped me build the character in my mind."

"Very good. We'll talk later this week or early next week about how you see your character and how I see your character. Then we'll come to an understanding going forward," Lyman said with as much camaraderie as Kendall had heard all day. "Let me know if you have any trouble getting everything done tomorrow. I know there's a lot going on, but we're crunched for time."

"It's fine. I've been through this before," Kendall said. "Not with a movie, but I understand the urgency." Lyman nodded a bit, and Kendall thought he might be seeing the beginnings of a touch of respect from him. When he didn't say anything more, Kendall walked toward the limousine and found it blessedly empty. He climbed into the back and asked the driver to take him to the hotel. As he rode he called Juan.

"I need some help," he said after they'd exchanged greetings. "I'm going to need a small place to live while I'm here as well as a car of my own. Can you help me?"

"Of course," Juan said. "Let me make some phone calls to see what I can find."

"Thanks. I don't want some huge showy place; just a small secure apartment for a few months will do." He was used to making do with a small space and that suited him.

"But what if you decide to stay?" Juan asked, and Kendall paused. Leaving New York had never occurred to him. "Okay, I'll see what I can do."

"Thank you, I appreciate the help," Kendall said.

"No problem. I'll see you in the morning and help you get to all your appointments," Juan said.

"Thanks." Kendall hung up the phone and slid it into his pocket. He was exhausted, and tomorrow promised to be long, as did most of the days ahead. He was used to long days, but he was also used to coming home to Johnny every night, and he really missed that, especially once the driver had dropped him off and he took the elevator to his solitary hotel room.

CHAPTER
FOUR

KENDALL never knew four weeks could fly by so damned fast. Juan had found him a nice furnished apartment through his studio connections. A car proved more problematic, but he finally managed to lease one for six months. Granted, he wasn't expecting to need it that long, but it was the shortest duration he could find. "They're ready for you on the set," a runner said, and Kendall didn't even get a chance to turn his head before he was gone. He understood speed, but everyone here seemed to exist in hyperdrive.

As he headed out to the set, he was handed an updated script for the scene he was about to shoot. "Thank you," Kendall said with a smile and began looking it over. He noted the change and committed it to memory. When they were ready for him, he took his position.

"Okay," Lyman said from his position just off camera. "You got the change?"

Kendall nodded and stepped into position. He did the scene as written with the feeling and enunciation Lyman had said he wanted, but it felt off to him.

"Cut," Lyman said at the end and waited for the playback. "It's what we said, but…."

"Can I try it again?" Kendall asked, and Lyman nodded and then called for everyone to move back to their places. They did the scene two more times, with Kendall making minor changes, but Lyman still wasn't happy. Finally, on the fifth attempt, Kendall played the scene the way he thought it should have been played all along.

"Perfect," Lyman called and then watched the playback. "That's exactly what we needed. Let's get one more and we'll wrap this set." Kendall did the scene, and when Lyman cut and said they were done, everyone breathed a sigh of relief.

"God, I thought he was going to keep us here half the night, like he did yesterday," one of Kendall's costars, Barbara Hamill, said softly to the woman next to her.

"I would have if it wasn't for Kendall," Lyman said in his booming voice to let Barbara know she'd been overheard. Yes, Kendall knew many things were new to him about making movies, but being a good actor wasn't an issue. That came naturally, and Kendall was a hard worker and always made sure he knew his lines and blocking. It came from the discipline the stage required. Movies were forgiving in a lot of ways; live theater was not. "We have a lot to do tomorrow, so everyone finish up and go home. Rest well, because you're all going to need it." Lyman said something like that at the end of every day, and it was usually true. Of course, it hadn't taken Kendall long to realize that long after they'd all left, Lyman was still up planning the shoots for the next few days. Barbara hurried over to him as soon as they broke up. "No, you don't look like you have a brown nose," she sniped.

"This isn't high school, Barbara," Kendall retorted. "Act like a professional rather than a prom queen and you'll get a lot further." He stopped the next comment that threatened to come out by turning away and walking toward his dressing area.

"What do you know?" she asked as she stormed after him. Kendall continued to his dressing room, and she followed him inside and closed the door. Kendall could tell she'd worked up a good head of steam, but he wasn't about to take any crap from a glorified cheerleader.

"Plenty. You don't do eight shows a week with your name on the marquee without learning a few things. One, always know your lines inside and out; two, it's about the show and the audience, not you; and three, treat people the way you want to be treated, because someday you'll have to work with them again." Kendall kept his voice level but firm. "Do you think the people you've pissed off are going to want to work with you again? The Broadway community is small and word gets around. Suddenly you don't get called back, no matter how high you can kick it." Kendall actually kicked his foot well over his head. "No one will hire you. And I'm sure the community here is just as cliquish and word spreads just as fast. So cut the dumb blonde act— Marilyn Monroe is dead."

Barbara's mouth hung open. "Am I really that bad?" she asked, a bit horrified.

"Not yet, but you could be." Kendall sat down and began removing his makeup. "I headlined shows in New York, big ones, and I always have work lined up." Sal was lining up offers and opportunities for Kendall as he spoke. "People like to work with me, so I get to work with the best people." He turned around in his chair. "You want to make a career of this? Or are you just looking to be famous? Because if you want a career, then do your best every day, and the fame and everything else will come. But if you want to be Paris Hilton, and the butt of everyone's jokes, then you could be well on your way."

"You don't pull any punches," Barbara said, moving toward the door.

"Nope, but I will say I wouldn't have bothered to tell you anything if I didn't think you were worth it," Kendall said, watching her in the mirror. "The last thing you want is people writing tell-all books about you. Become good at what you do."

"Is that what you did?" Barbara asked, stopping near the door.

"You better believe it." Kendall turned back to her. "Because when you have a theater full of people all watching you, and you flub something or screw up, all those people will know and they'll tweet it and tell their friends. Then when the show closes, so does your career, and you're back to waiting tables at Ruth's Chris for tips." He went back to removing the last of his makeup.

She giggled. "You must be doing something right. I certainly don't get flowers."

Kendall looked around and saw two pink roses resting on one of the chairs. They'd been showing up every now and then in his dressing room or on the seat of his car. At first he'd wondered, or hoped that Johnny had been sending them, but that wasn't Johnny's style, and when they started showing up in his locked car, Kendall had gotten nervous. He began carrying his keys everywhere with him or hiding them when he was on the set. None had shown up in his car since, but now they showed up in his dressing room more often. "Please take them," Kendall said as he reached over and lifted the flowers, then handed them to her.

"You're serious?" she asked as she accepted them.

"Of course. Enjoy." Kendall smiled, and Barbara left his dressing room, closing the door behind her. He finished up and grabbed his things, making sure he had everything and that nothing was missing. Then he left the soundstage with the actors and crew and headed for his car.

"Hey, Kendall." He turned and saw Guy striding toward him. "I was wondering if you'd like to go out for a drink or something."

Kendall smiled. "Can we make it another night? I'm really tired and want to eat, shower, and fall into bed." Kendall tried to think. "What day is it, anyway?"

"Thursday," Guy said.

"Then how about Sunday afternoon? There's nothing scheduled, and Lyman needs to give the crew a day off." They could all use a day to recharge.

"All right. I'll call you," Guy said, and Kendall continued on toward his car. He got inside and drove out the studio gate. His apartment was only five miles away, but it took fifteen minutes for him to get home. The building had a locked parking garage beneath the building, and Kendall's apartment came with its own parking space. The gate slid closed behind the Mustang, and he pulled into his space.

Kendall took the elevator up to his floor and let himself into the apartment. After setting down his bag, he flopped into a chair and called Johnny. His call went to voice mail. Kendall left a message and then began making a quick dinner.

THE Sunday following their ride through the park, Johnny was coming over for dinner. Kendall stood in his kitchen, wondering what in hell he was going to do. He didn't cook much, and had gotten food he thought was too simple to mess up. His apartment had this tiny stove and oven that was perfect for mouse-sized meals. Kendall opened his small refrigerator and stared at the groceries he'd bought. He could cook the steaks, that wasn't a problem, but the rest of it.... In desperation, he picked up his phone, dialed, and waited.

"Mom, I need your help," Kendall said as soon as his mother answered.

"What's got you so frazzled?" she asked.

"I need to cook dinner and I'm not sure what to do," Kendall whined, and his mother laughed hard and long. "What's so funny?"

"You sing and dance in front of thousands of people every day, but making a meal for someone—I'm assuming there's a guy involved—tips you over the edge? That's so funny."

"Mom!" Kendall said indignantly. "It's not the same."

"I know, honey. So I take it this meal is sort of special," his mother said.

"Yeah, it is." Kendall told her about meeting Johnny at the party and about the carriage ride. "We've only kissed."

His mother gasped dramatically; Kendall came by his theatrical talent honestly. "So this is a big deal." His mother was familiar with his carousing ways. "What do you have?" she asked, and Kendall ran down the menu of steak, potatoes, green beans, and salad. "Honey, there's nothing to it. Season the steaks with some salt, pepper, and garlic, if you have it, before you cook them. Put some water on to boil to cook the beans, and about fifteen minutes before you're ready, microwave the potatoes. Do you have butter and stuff?"

"Yes," Kendall said as he fished around in the refrigerator. "I have a bottle of red wine too."

"Good. Don't panic and take your time. You'll be just fine," she said.

"But how long do I cook the steaks?"

"It depends how thick they are, but three minutes a side is usually good to start. Cut into the one you'll eat to make sure it's done if you have to, and serve the good one to your guest." His mother chuckled

again. "You are planning to bring this young man out to visit soon, aren't you?"

"I will," Kendall promised and hung up. He set the phone on the counter and filled a pan with water before setting it on the stove to boil.

The door buzzer rang, and Kendall jumped, nearly scattering the bag of beans he was pulling out of the refrigerator all over the floor. He set them on the counter and verified it was Johnny at the door before buzzing him in. Kendall opened the apartment door slightly and returned to the kitchen.

"Hello," Johnny greeted him as he pushed the apartment door the rest of the way open.

"I'm in here," Kendall called, staring at the unsnipped beans. "I have to warn you, I'm not much of a cook."

Johnny chuckled and took off his coat, draping it neatly over the back of one of the chairs before joining Kendall in the kitchen. "I'd say so," Johnny said. "You need to take off the ends before you wash those."

"Maybe we should go out," Kendall said, ready to open the wine and say to hell with the rest.

"Or maybe we should cook together," Johnny suggested. "I'll clean the beans for you, if you like."

Kendall felt so helpless. His mother was an amazing cook, but he'd never spent much time in the kitchen. Now he wished he had. Although with his usual diet of protein shakes, chicken, and salads, getting something to eat had never been a particular problem. The bodega around the corner also had great take-out food, so cooking had never been a priority. "Thanks. I need to season the meat and clean the potatoes." He figured this would be a simple meal, and he knew Johnny liked beef from their meal at the restaurant the week before, so he'd played it safe. He had no idea cooking the stuff would feel like brain surgery. Kendall got out the steaks and pulled out the salt and pepper. He also found some powdered garlic he hadn't known he had and set that on the counter as well.

"You don't want to go too heavy," Johnny told him, and Kendall began to sprinkle the seasonings. "A little bit more salt, and you can add the pepper and garlic." Johnny watched him as he snipped the

beans. *"That should be good, now rub the steaks a bit so the seasonings stick, and turn them over to do the other side."*

Johnny bumped him with his shoulder, and they shared a smile. Once the steaks were seasoned, Johnny had him set them aside.

"Are the beans ready to go in?" Kendall asked.

"Just about," Johnny said. *"Do you have minced onion?"* Kendall shook his head. *"Then add some salt to the water."* Johnny washed the beans, and once he deemed the water ready, he put them in to boil and turned down the heat. *"I can cook the steaks if you want."*

"Thank you," Kendall said. *"I feel bad about putting you to work."*

"Then you can pay me," Johnny said with a wink, and he leaned a bit closer. Kendall was happy to oblige, and he kissed Johnny lightly at first, but deepened it quickly.

"That was just the down payment," Kendall whispered after they broke the kiss, and Johnny's eyes widened. Kendall grinned his best mischievous grin, knowing Johnny must be wondering just what he had in mind.

Kendall got out the potatoes to clean. Once they were ready, he put them in the microwave and started it. He then began getting out the stuff for salad. He and Johnny worked for the next ten minutes or so in his tiny kitchen, occasionally bumping into each other, but it was a good kind of bumping, and Kendall was pretty sure some of it was on purpose.

Johnny volunteered to fill plates, so Kendall took a minute to set his tiny table, which was just big enough for two. Then they sat down across from each other. To say the table was tiny was an understatement. In an apartment this size, space was a premium, and the table usually doubled as a computer workstation. They began to eat, and anytime either of them moved, their knees rubbed together. It was rather intimate in an almost comical way. The food, on the other hand, was amazingly good. Johnny spoke first. *"I love to cook. I don't get a chance to do it very often, though. My place is even smaller than this, and I have it crammed full of books and research material."*

Kendall took a small bite of steak and chewed slowly. *"You can cook for me anytime, and I'll definitely return the favor, somehow."*

Johnny's hand rested on the table, and Kendall reached across and placed his on top. "I've thought about you a lot this week," he admitted.

"Me too," Johnny said. "I mean, I've thought a lot about you too."

"Now who's the cute one?" Kendall said as Johnny blushed a bit. "Do you have plans for the holidays?"

"I'm supposed to go see my family." Johnny didn't seem very excited about it. "They give me no end of grief whenever I'm there. All my dad does is ask me what kind of job I'm going to get studying history, and my mother keeps shoving girls in my direction." Johnny reached for the wine bottle and topped off their glasses. "They know I'm gay, but refuse to talk about it. They're in denial and they're not happy about it, although...." Johnny swallowed hard. "Who knows? This could be my last visit. The last time I talked to them, they told me it was high time I forgot whatever foolish New York big-city notions I had in my head, settled down, and got married." He shook his head slowly. "How about yours?"

"You think they'd disown you?" Kendall asked, nearly dropping his fork. That was so far from his own experience he could hardly fathom it.

"Dad can out-stubborn a mule," Johnny told him flatly. Then he began eating again, and Kendall figured Johnny might not want to talk about it.

"I didn't come out of the closet, I tap-danced, belted show tunes, and kick-turned my way out of the closet," he said.

Johnny chuckled, and his smile reached his eyes.

Kendall momentarily lost his train of thought when he saw that smile. "There was never much doubt, and my parents accepted me and encouraged me and my talent. They're pretty amazing, and I'll spend the holidays with Mom and Dad out on Long Island."

"What does your dad do?" Johnny asked.

"He was an investment banker turned hedge-fund manager. He made more money than he and Mom need, so now he and Mom do volunteer work with children's charities and travel. After Christmas, they'll head to Florida for the rest of the winter. When they're down

there, Dad helps build houses for Habitat for Humanity and stuff like that." Kendall *took a bite of his salad.* "He likes to keep busy, but now he can do what he loves to do."

"Sounds ideal," Johnny *said softly. They continued eating, the conversation shifting to books and then on to art and other topics. When they were done eating, Kendall cleared the table and set the dishes in the sink.*

"It sounds to me like you're doing what you want to do," Kendall *said from the sink.* "You're passionate about history and the lessons it has for us today." *He walked back to the table and picked up the rest of the dishes, leaving the wineglasses.* "That's plain in the way you talk. I saw that the first time I met you."

"But what if my dad's right and I'm never able to get a job?" Johnny *said, and Kendall watched as he picked up his wine glass.*

"Then make your own job," Kendall *suggested.* "Take the skills you have and carve out a niche for yourself. Other people get a history degree to teach, right?" Kendall *ran the water to start the dishes.* "So find a way to teach people other than in a classroom."

"Sure," Johnny *said indulgently.*

Kendall *rolled his eyes.* "My dad told me that he hated working on Wall Street. He was good at it, so he and his clients made a lot of money, but after he'd done the deal of his life and made a ton of money, he left, and now he's happier than I can ever remember him being when I was a kid. He said if he had it to do over again, he'd skip the whole Wall Street thing entirely and he'd build houses for a living." Kendall *began washing the dishes, and Johnny stood up, then carried his wineglass to where Kendall was working.* "And I think I can agree with him. There are few things more important than loving what you do."

"Do you really mean that?" Johnny *asked with a touch of skepticism.*

"Of course I do. I love what I do and hope to grow old and one day, after my performance, go back to my dressing room after the bow and die… at a ripe old age, of course." Johnny *laughed.* "It's been done," Kendall *added.* "Irene Ryan had a stroke during a performance of* Pippin *and died a few days later. That's the way I want to go—doing* *something I love." Kendall put the last dish in the drainer and let out the water. "If you could die happy doing something, what would it be?"*

Johnny thought for a few seconds and then set his glass next to the dish drainer. He pulled Kendall into his arms and kissed him hard and full on the mouth. "You did ask," Johnny whispered when they came up for air, before kissing him once again.

Kendall couldn't think much after that, not that he particularly cared. Thinking was definitely overrated when being held and kissed like that.

Johnny gently guided him out of the kitchen area, and soon they fell and bounced on the bed in the corner. It was only a twin, but Johnny held him so close they only used part of it. "You're very special," Johnny whispered, kissing him again.

Johnny stroked his hands along Kendall's side and tentatively slipped under his shirt like he was waiting for Kendall to object. Instead, he moaned softly as soon as Johnny touched his skin. "You're pretty special too." Kendall groaned when Johnny lightly plucked at one of his nipples. He loved being touched like that, and Johnny kept it up. With each gentle pluck, Kendall moaned a little bit louder, pleasure building with each touch.

"Dang, you're responsive," Johnny whispered.

"You have no idea," Kendall came back, a bit breathlessly.

"But I fully intend to find out," Johnny retorted, and Kendall stilled as Johnny tugged on the tail of his shirt, lifting his weight off and pulling the shirt over Kendall's head. Johnny tugged off his own shirt as well and then pressed him back into the mattress. Skin to skin, Johnny's heat set him on fire.

"You do?" Kendall pressed, and Johnny kissed him hard, erasing both the ability to speak and to think. After that Kendall had no thought of teasing. Johnny divested him of his shoes and the rest of his clothes with kisses and touches that left Kendall tingling. He would have begged for more, but his mouth was otherwise engaged, so he simply held on and returned Johnny's kisses until they were both naked. Chest to chest, lips to lips, hip to hip, sliding his straining cock along Johnny's skin, each movement brought a new round of cock-throbbing

joy. He'd had sex, plenty of it, but none of those experiences had felt like this, and no one had taken the care Johnny was. "Johnny, please," Kendall begged. The pressure inside had built to the point that little flashes of light twinkled behind his eyes, and yet he didn't want it to stop.

Johnny broke their kiss and slowly slid down Kendall's body, laying kisses along his skin as he went. Johnny stroked Kendall's chest and belly, trailing his lips after his hands, adding warmth to warmth. There was no sex talk, no swearing or cursing. It wasn't needed; none of it was. Johnny's touch and taste said a hell of a lot more than words could ever express. And when Johnny ran his lips along Kendall's length, Kendall nearly thought his time had come. Shortness of breath, tightening of the chest, tingling in his arms—Kendall figured he must be having a heart attack until Johnny swallowed him deep, sucking hard, and then he didn't care. Nothing else mattered except the warm heat around his cock and Johnny's gentle caresses of his leg.

THE insistent dinging of the microwave pulled Kendall out of his daydream. He blinked and looked around, expecting to see Johnny sitting on the sofa, bent over his computer, but he was alone, very much alone. Kendall opened the door on the microwave and pulled out the pasta with meat sauce he'd been heating up and sat at the table. He opened his copy of the script and tried to review the scenes for the following day, but he could hardly concentrate. He closed it and pushed it back, unable to stop thinking about that first Christmas together.

Johnny got into an argument with his parents three or four days before Christmas, and they basically told him not to come home. At least that was what Johnny had told him. He'd been so upset he could barely speak. Johnny had called to tell him, and Kendall had told him to come over right away. He had hot chocolate waiting and ended up adding some additional fortification. "If I can't live according to their expectations, then I'm not welcome under their roof," Johnny had told him and then broken down in tears. Kendall had held him and let him cry. Then he'd taken him to bed and continued holding Johnny all night long.

In the morning, Kendall had called his mother and told her there would be one more for Christmas. Johnny had tried to stop him, but Kendall wouldn't hear of it, and as soon as he hung up with his mother, she apparently went shopping, because she called him four more times that day asking all kinds of questions, including sweater sizes. On Christmas morning there had been tears in Johnny's eyes when he realized some of the presents under the tree were for him.

Kendall's mother still went all-out each Christmas for both of them. He simply wished they'd remembered to continue to go all-out for each other. He ate the rest of his meal and then took care of the dishes. Once he was done, he grabbed the script off the table and sat in the one comfortable chair in the apartment, attempting to concentrate.

People occasionally passed his door as they walked down the hall, and Kendall barely noticed them until he thought he heard someone stop. Kendall paused and tensed, listening, and sure enough, a few seconds later he heard footsteps move away from his door. Kendall got up and hurried to the door. He pulled it open and saw two pink roses just outside the door. Kendall leaped over them and raced down the hallway toward the elevator. The elevator was heading down already, and Kendall ran back down the hall to the stairs and took them two at a time as he hurried toward the lobby. Whoever it was would have to go out that way, and Kendall was determined to find out who in the hell was stalking him and, more importantly, why. He banged through the door, charging into the empty lobby, but there was no one there.

Kendall moved out of sight, leaned against the wall, and watched the elevator display as the car descended. The door opened and an older lady he'd seen in the hallway multiple times gingerly stepped out. "Hello," she said with a smile. "Waiting for someone?"

"Sort of," he said. "Did you happen to see anyone in the hall as you were getting on the elevator?"

"I think a young man passed me as I was getting in, but I didn't see which way he went. Was he a friend of yours?" she asked with a smile. "I heard you were making a movie. You're definitely handsome enough for it."

"Thank you," Kendall said, smiling back. "And yes, I'm making my first movie. I've done shows on Broadway since I was a teenager, but this is my very first film."

"I was in films when I was younger and worked with Bette Davis on a film. She was incredible. But that was a long time ago, and things have changed so much with all the special effects and computer graphics stuff. Now you don't know what's real and what was dreamed up on some computer screen. In my day, actors had to really act or the film was flat. Today, the people sometimes seem like wood, and they fill in around them with all that fancy stuff so no one notices."

Kendall smiled. "I suppose you're right. The movie I'm working on doesn't have much in the way of special effects."

"Well, good," she said and began walking toward the front door. "Let me know when you're done, and I'll be sure to go see it."

"I will," Kendall promised and pushed the elevator call button. The doors slid open and Kendall rode back up to his floor. When the doors opened again, he stepped out and strode down to the apartment. The flowers still sat on the floor, and Kendall noticed a piece of paper under them. Kendall picked up the flowers and the paper and carried them inside. Then he shut the door and locked it, listening for anything unusual, but heard nothing. After taking and releasing a slow, deep breath, he carried the flowers into the kitchen and dumped them in the trash before opening the folded piece of computer paper.

I saw you gave my flowers to Barbara the Bitch, so I thought I'd replace them.

That was all the computer-printed note said, and Kendall shivered. Whoever this was, he wished they'd either come forward so he could talk to the person, or simply leave him alone. Kendall reached for his phone and called Johnny, not giving a damn what time it was. "Johnny, I need to talk to you," Kendall began when the call went to voice mail. "Please call me back when you get this. I need your advice and I want to talk about when you can come to see me." He'd feel a lot better when he wasn't alone. Kendall carried his phone with him to his chair and set it next to him so he could grab it when Johnny called back. He still had plenty of work to do before tomorrow, and he forced himself to concentrate on the script.

An hour later, his phone rang and Kendall snatched it up. "Johnny," Kendall said as he answered it and then checked the time.

"Sorry I didn't call earlier, I'm just getting home," Johnny explained. It was after midnight in New York. "I lost track of time at the university library and then stopped to get something to eat on the way home. Is something wrong? You sounded a bit frazzled when you left the message."

"I was wondering when you were going to come out for a visit."

Johnny paused, and then Kendall heard a sigh. "Will you even have time to spend with me?"

"I'm going to be busy, but there's only a few weeks until we go on location and it probably won't be practical then. I was hoping you could come out the week after next. I'm only scheduled to be on set for three days that week, and the rest of the time we could do things together." Kendall's excitement ramped up. He was looking forward to seeing Johnny and having the chance to rekindle their relationship.

"That's a long way to travel for just a few days," Johnny said slowly.

"If you don't want to come, then just say so," Kendall snapped.

"It isn't that," Johnny told him. "I do want to see you and I miss you every day. But the book I'm working on is coming together faster and better than I ever imagined, and I can't take a break or I'll lose the train of thought."

"It must be flowing, what with all the research you're doing," Kendall observed, trying to keep the skepticism out of his voice.

"For this book I have all the research I need. I'm working with a student at Columbia to research some ideas for my next book. He's been a huge help in a lot of ways."

"I'll bet," Kendall muttered very softly.

"It isn't a really good time right now, and you're not going to have time for me anyway. Your schedule will change, and I'll be sitting alone while you're working all day. I can sit alone here and work."

"Fine. Whatever you want to do is fine," Kendall said quietly. "I just miss you." God, he sounded needy. If Johnny didn't care enough to come out and see him, then there was nothing he could do about it.

"I know, and I miss you too. But I need to get this done, and you need to get your work done," Johnny told him, repeating the same thing he'd said all along.

"Johnny, I didn't know how hard it was going to be to be out here alone," he admitted. "You're there in New York, where all our friends are. I really don't know anyone out here, and…." Kendall swallowed. "I think I may have a stalker."

Johnny laughed. "Don't you think you're being a bit dramatic? You haven't finished the movie yet. How can you have a stalker?"

"Well, thanks for the vote of confidence," Kendall shot back.

"You're serious," Johnny said, the mirth disappearing from his voice. "What's been going on? Have you been followed or threatened?" At least Johnny seemed to care. Kendall had been beginning to wonder.

"I keep getting flowers, roses, delivered. At first I thought they might have been from you." When he'd gotten the first ones, he'd actually smiled and gotten warm all over because of Johnny's thoughtfulness. "I was about to call you and thank you, but the next ones I got were left inside my car, which I knew I'd locked. Now I hide stuff or keep everything locked up. The flowers keep showing up in my dressing area, and tonight someone left flowers and a note outside my apartment door. It's beginning to freak me out," Kendall said.

"Maybe it's just an admirer or something," Johnny said. "They haven't threatened you, have they?"

"Not really, I guess. But I feel like someone's watching me all the time and like no place is safe," Kendall said.

"Have you told anyone?" Johnny asked, sounding more concerned but still not convinced of the threat.

"Only you, so far," Kendall admitted. "At first it seemed so innocuous and innocent, but it's like whoever they are is telling me that they can get to me no matter where I am." Kendall paused. "I know you think I'm being stupid, but I'm not. And I've been afraid to tell people in case they think I'm just causing trouble and stuff. I'm finally beginning to earn people's respect, and I don't want to blow that. After all, you laughed when I told you," he said indignantly. "Why would they believe me when you didn't?" Kendall huffed a bit through his nose and waited for Johnny to say something.

"I'm sorry," Johnny said softly. "I know you're upset, and you should take this seriously, but I don't have any advice for you." Johnny paused. "Except maybe you should tell the studio. They must have dealt with this kind of thing before. I mean, they have huge stars and famous people working there all the time. They have to have seen this before. Maybe they can help."

"Thanks. I'll think about it," Kendall said and sat quietly. "I'll let you get to bed. Talk to you tomorrow." Kendall hung up and set the phone aside. At least Johnny hadn't said he was crazy, but he'd come damned close. Kendall shook his head and went back to his script. It was looking more and more likely that once this movie was over, there might not be as much to go back to New York for as he'd always thought there would be.

CHAPTER
FIVE

GUY did call, and by Sunday afternoon Kendall was looking for something to do. He got directions to a small bar off Colorado Boulevard. Kendall met Guy there, and to his surprise, it seemed that Sunday afternoons were for karaoke. Kendall slid into the booth across from Guy and looked around the place. It was brighter than he expected a bar to be, and cleaner. "This is nice," Kendall said as a server walked over. They each ordered a beer.

"It's sort of a hangout place, and the owner decided years ago that he didn't want to own a dingy bar. So he spruced up the place, and the drunks disappeared, but the locals began to come," Guy said as he lifted his glass. People began taking turns on the small stage singing along with the recorded music. Kendall tried his best to keep from grimacing at some of the clunky notes. They finished their beers and ordered another round. "Go on and have a go," Guy told him.

"I don't think so," Kendall said, but Guy urged him on, so he got up and looked through the book to see what they had. He found the old standard "New York, New York" and couldn't resist. When his turn came, he cued up the song. Every head turned as soon as he began to sing. Mostly people had been polite, but the room seemed to stop as he sang. When he was done, people applauded, and Kendall smiled and sat back down.

"Did you sing on Broadway?" Guy asked.

"Yeah. I just finished a musical." Kendall sipped his beer. "I can dance too, but don't tell anyone." He and Guy laughed, and others got up to sing. After a while, they ordered some snacks, and when they were done, Kendall convinced Guy to take a turn. He wasn't half bad, and Guy convinced Kendall to have another go. It was a great afternoon, and Kendall had definitely needed some fun.

THE next three weeks turned out to be hectic as hell, but they were really productive too. At least that was what Lyman had told him. Filming seemed to be going very well, with most shots only requiring one or two takes. Lyman seemed to be flying high, and the entire cast and crew was running on high energy and excitement. As Johnny had predicted, Kendall's days off had evaporated because the filming schedule compressed as the scenes clicked by one after another.

"Okay, listen up everyone," Lyman had said a few days earlier. "We're moving along very well, and I've asked the location team to be ready for us to show up Monday. They've assured me they'll be ready, and so will we. I've revised the shooting schedule, and we should finish these last studio scenes this week." Everyone had listened politely. "The location shooting schedule will make the one we've been using seem like a piece of cake because we'll need to shoot around the heat, wind, and sun." Lyman paused. "So let's finish up this portion of the film." Lyman walked back to his place behind the camera to signal he was through talking, and Kendall got into position for the next shot.

"He wants to see you," Juan told him a few minutes later, and Kendall walked to where Lyman sat making notes.

"I need you to stay tonight. We're going to need some publicity stills, and they want to do some here. We'll need some on location as well." He looked up from his pages. "Sorry for the short notice."

Each night for the rest of the week, Kendall ended up staying for photos. Sometimes it was just him, but most of the time it was with other cast members too.

By the end of the week, Kendall was exhausted. They'd been filming full-on for weeks on end, and he'd had very few days off.

Lyman was a bit of a slave driver, but Kendall could also see what he was trying to do.

"Get some rest," Lyman told him when they were finally done with the last scene on the shooting schedule before heading to location.

"I will, I promise," Kendall said and then went to his dressing room. The place was a shambles, with his things strewn everywhere. The mirror had been shattered, and shards of glass covered the dressing table and floor. Everything made of glass in the room was in pieces, including makeup containers.

"What the hell happened?" Lyman demanded from the doorway as Kendall turned around.

"I don't know," Kendall said and looked through the room. Sure enough, a pair of pink roses sat on the seat of the chair. They appeared to be the only things to have escaped the carnage. "Everything was fine when I arrived on the set, and I've been in the studio all day."

"What's with the roses?" Lyman asked, and he stepped into the room, glass crunching beneath his shoes.

"Don't," Kendall said, and Lyman turned around. "I've had someone leaving me flowers for weeks now. Mostly here in the dressing room, but a few times at my apartment and once in my car. They'd sort of stopped for the past ten days or so, and I was hoping whoever it was had given up."

Lyman pulled out his phone and made a call to security. "These guys won't mess around. They're professionals, not rent-a-cops. They might be able to help."

Kendall surveyed the wrecked room. He hadn't kept anything personal in his dressing room other than the clothes he changed out of when getting into costume. Of course they were covered in broken glass, and when he looked closer, Kendall saw they'd actually been ripped to shreds. Kendall let go of the fabric and stepped out of the dressing room. Lyman came out right after him, and a few minutes later, two huge, brutish men strode over. They were like walking walls in dark clothes. "You reported an incident," one of the men said in a remarkably deep voice. Kendall almost suspected he was auditioning for a part rather than responding to a call for assistance.

"Yes. Over here." Lyman took charge, and for that Kendall was extremely grateful. "Someone broke into this dressing room while we were filming. Kendall has apparently been having a bit of trouble with a stalker." Lyman's Australian accent was out in full force. "And things seem to have escalated a bit."

The men peered inside. "Did anyone hear or see anything?"

Kendall looked around. "I wouldn't know. Most of the cast and crew had gone by the time I returned. I certainly didn't hear anything, and I suspect Lyman didn't either, or he would have paused shooting because of the noise."

Both men pulled out notebooks. "When were you here last?"

"Just after lunch. I had a wardrobe change to make, and since then I've been occupied on the set. I spent much of the day either on camera or waiting for shots to be set up," Kendall explained. Many of the other actors went back to their dressing rooms between takes, but Kendall had found he was fascinated with the movie-making process and liked to watch the set changes being made. "I suppose someone could have gotten in here during that time. It would have been noisy with people coming and going." Kendall looked at Lyman, who nodded in agreement.

"We were making some set changes this afternoon, and that would probably have covered the noise," Lyman said.

"Shouldn't we be calling the police?" Kendall asked, and all three of the other men stared at him.

"No publicity," Lyman said, turning to Kendall. "This kind of thing can doom a film fast." The other two men nodded their agreement. "No one was hurt, after all."

"We'll take a look around and see if we can find anything," the deep-voiced guard said, and Kendall turned away, wondering what he was going to wear home.

"I've got some extra clothes in my office," Lyman offered, and Kendall thanked him. "They'll be a bit big, but they should do to get you home." Kendall followed the director out of the soundstage, and they got into a golf cart and were driven across the lot to the small office where Kendall had first met Lyman and the producers. Lyman gave him a pair of old pants and a shirt. Kendall changed in the restroom and gathered up his costume.

"I'll take care of those for you," Beverly, Lyman's administrative assistant, said when he came out. Kendall looked around, wondering where Lyman was. "He had an appointment, but before he left he asked me to make sure there's security while you're on location. I'll also make sure that your trailer has a lock and only you will have a set of keys."

"Trailer?" Kendall asked.

She smiled. "Yeah. You're going to be in the middle of nowhere. Think of it as your private dressing room. We're booking you into hotels in Las Vegas, but that's an hour away, so it isn't like you'll be able to run there to get a soda. We've arranged for trailers that will provide you some privacy." She sat down at her desk and began gathering her things. "Don't worry, everything will be fine." She had a strange expression on her face, and for a second Kendall thought she might be his stalker, but that was ridiculous.

"Thanks for your help," Kendall said, checking to make sure he had all his things. Then he left the office. Kendall walked across the studio to where he'd parked his car. Before getting in, he checked it over and then carefully drove home. Kendall kept checking his rearview mirror the entire time to make sure he wasn't followed. He was pretty sure he wasn't, but he made a few extra turns just in case before turning into the drive and opening the gate to the underground parking. He realized this action was useless as soon as he parked: the stalker already knew where he lived.

Once he'd parked, Kendall carefully looked around the garage and then made his way to his apartment, jumping at every sound. When he approached his door, he sighed when he saw nothing waiting for him—no roses or notes, or bunny carcasses. His imagination was definitely running away with him at this point. Kendall unlocked the door and peered inside. Everything looked normal and he didn't hear anything. He went in and closed the door, then checked over every room before returning to deadbolt the door. He put on the chain as well, then hurried through the apartment making sure all the windows were locked, as well as the balcony door. It didn't matter that he was on the third floor—Kendall needed to feel safe.

Once he was sure no one could get in, he sat down and called Johnny, but the call went to voice mail, so he did what any red-blooded American man would do—he called his mother. Her phone went to voice mail as well. Kendall didn't leave a message, figuring he'd only worry her.

For a while he sat on the sofa, staring at the walls and listening for any unusual sounds, but he heard nothing, and eventually his heart stopped pounding in his ears and his breathing returned to normal. The next time his heart raced like that, he hoped it was for something a hell of a lot more fun, preferably involving lips, hands, and being naked. Eventually he got up off the sofa, deciding that whatever this crazy freak had going on in their head, he wouldn't let the person dictate his life. He walked toward the kitchen and opened the nearly empty refrigerator, trying to figure out what to eat before he went to bed.

The sound of the call button made him jump nearly to the ceiling. Once he restarted his heart, he pressed the intercom. "Who is it?" He hadn't been expecting anyone.

"It's Juan."

Kendall buzzed him in and then instantly wondered if that was such a good idea. Juan could be his stalker. After all, Juan had propositioned him that first night and Kendall had turned him down. Maybe Juan had been sending him the flowers, and it would have been easy for him to get Kendall's keys and access to his dressing room. Juan also knew where he lived because he'd helped him get the apartment, and Kendall hadn't told anyone else where he was living, not even Lyman, who wasn't above suspicion either. He hadn't seen Juan on the set today, but that didn't mean he hadn't been there and wasn't the person who'd trashed his dressing room. Kendall was relieved he didn't jump when Juan knocked on the door, but he did look around for a weapon. Of course, there wasn't one.

Kendall peered through the peephole in the door and saw Juan shifting from foot to foot. "I can hear you in there," Juan said, almost laughing. "I'm not your stalker."

"How do I know that?" Kendall asked, beginning to realize he was being a complete idiot. He opened the door, and Juan stepped inside.

"I heard about what happened and figured you'd be pretty freaked out, so I wanted to make sure you were okay," Juan told him. "I also sort of figured you didn't have anything in the house, so I stopped and picked up takeout." Juan lifted the bag he was carrying and chuckled a bit. "I'm not going to hit you with it," he added when Kendall stepped back. "This has you jumping at your own shadow, doesn't it?"

"Yeah, I guess," Kendall admitted. "Whoever it was trashed my dressing room during production today. They knew enough about how things work to get in and out of there without being seen or at least rousing suspicion. That's pretty scary, don't you think?"

"Yeah, it is," Juan agreed, and he began unpacking the white plastic bag of take-out containers. "I hope it's okay I came here," he said after a bit of hesitation, and Kendall motioned toward the table. "You're always so nice to everyone. Most of the stars don't give the people around them the time of day, but you've been nice and treated everyone with respect and kindness. You don't deserve to be treated like this. Heck, you even got Barbara to be nicer to everyone, and she was the queen bitch supreme." Juan handed him a plastic container. "I got you a salad with mixed greens, nuts, Craisins, chicken, and apples. It's some sort of harvest salad, but it looked good."

"Thanks, Juan, I've been...." Kendall let his voice trial off. The emotions coursing through him were too muddled and irrational to explain.

"Let me see," Juan said, pausing with a second salad container in his hand. "You're feeling violated because someone went through your stuff, and you're scared because you don't know who's doing this." He set the second container on the counter. "You're also here away from the people you know, so everything is a bit amplified." Juan sat down at the table across from him.

"Can you read my mind?" Kendall asked, opening the container. The salad was huge, but it was fresh and smelled amazing. Juan passed over some dressing packets, and Kendall chose one. Juan apparently hadn't been sure of what Kendall liked—he seemed to have gotten one of everything.

"Nah, it's just how I'd feel if I were in your place." Juan grabbed one of the dressing packets and began squeezing ranch dressing on his salad. "So I figured I'd come keep you company. It didn't occur to me until I was standing outside your door that you might think I was the stalker." Juan's cheeks got a definite red tinge to them when Kendall smiled. "God, that first night I was such a doofus." Juan blushed further.

"Actually, I was flattered," Kendall said honestly. "It's been a while since I've felt... desirable to anyone." God, he shouldn't be talking about this stuff, least of all with Juan. "Things with Johnny and me have been... I don't know. The spark seems to be gone."

"Well, he's in New York and you're here. That's bound to make things difficult. I mean, the equipment doesn't reach." Juan kept a straight face for about two seconds before losing it, and Kendall went right behind him. He laughed so hard his sides hurt. "So try something else—maybe phone sex."

Kendall laughed again, but for a different reason. There was no way he could see Johnny talking dirty on the phone. He barely talked dirty during actual sex. It was funny—he was a man who made his living with words, but in the bedroom, words always seemed so far away. "It isn't that. Things between Johnny and me got... comfortable. The passion cooled, and we didn't do much to try to rekindle it. We had different schedules and we were still intimate occasionally." Kendall sighed softly. "The thing is, I still love Johnny, very much. He's the other part of me, and I can't see my life without him. But I don't know if I'm the other half of *him* any longer." Kendall took a bite of his salad to give his mouth something to do other than talk. He swallowed and figured, what the hell. Juan was listening to him and he was a good guy. If Juan was his stalker, then Kendall had bigger problems. And damn it, he needed a friend right now, someone who wasn't a continent away.

"If you tell anyone about this conversation, I'll hunt you down," Kendall said, and Juan snorted.

"Please. The papers would pay me a fortune for what I know about famous people. You learn pretty fast to keep your mouth shut, or you won't have a job for long," Juan told him. "So don't worry."

"I think Johnny might be having an affair. He's got some grad school assistant he's 'doing research' with, but... I don't know. He won't come out here to visit because I'm not going to have time to spend with him. And he's probably right, but it would be nice to have him here with me for a few days." Kendall put down his fork. "I can't get back there to see him because this shooting schedule is so brutal. I know I wouldn't get to see much of him, but just having him here would help me feel safer and not so freaking alone."

"Doesn't he work?" Juan asked.

Kendall continued eating. "Yes, he works. Johnny is a writer." Pride welled up inside him. "Johnny Harker."

"*The* Johnny Harker? No way! I love his books." Juan nearly vibrated out of his chair. "That's so cool. His stories are so great." Juan settled in his chair, but just barely. "You should tell Lyman. I bet he'd give his eyeteeth to make movies of those books."

Kendall chuckled. "He probably would, but Johnny won't allow it. He's had offers over the years, but after what he's seen done to some other books, he's always said he'd rather just have the books." Kendall returned to his dinner. "He's back in New York right now, working on a manuscript." His momentary excitement faded, and Kendall continued eating, losing himself in his own thoughts and suspicions.

Juan kept talking through much of the rest of the meal. He told Kendall about the famous people he'd seen. "I don't get to work with many of them. Mostly I'm running errands for someone when the big stars are around." Kendall wished he'd been better company. He wasn't really concentrating much on what Juan was saying, even though he tried.

By the time they were done eating, Kendall was exhausted. Juan gathered up the trash and threw it away. The apartment got quiet, and Kendall heard footsteps approaching his door. He signaled for Juan to listen too. His nerves ramped up instantly, and he waited until the footsteps passed his door before peering out to check that nothing had been left.

"You really are jumpy," Juan said softly once Kendall closed the door.

"Yeah. Whoever is doing this has been here before." Kendall locked the door once again and threw the chain for good measure.

"Do you want me to stay?" Juan asked. "I mean, on the couch."

Kendall wanted to say yes. He wasn't interested in spending the night lying awake, jumping at every noise. "You don't need to do that," he said.

"It's okay. You have a busy schedule and you need to rest. I'll sleep on the sofa, and then maybe you'll be able to sleep."

"Okay. Thank you," Kendall said. He was already tired, so he got an extra blanket and pillow for Juan and placed them on the sofa. Kendall then went to his bedroom and got ready for bed. He cleaned up and popped his head into the living room. "I set out some towels and stuff for you in the bathroom."

"Thanks," Juan said. "And don't worry. I'll be out here if anything happens. Try to get some rest."

Kendall nodded, went back to his room, and turned out the light after making triple sure the curtains were closed. Then he climbed into bed. Kendall stared at the ceiling for a long time.

HE AND Johnny had been dating for months, seeing each other almost every Sunday and Tuesday. When an actor in one of the secondary roles had quit the show, Kendall auditioned for the role and got it. That had been three months ago. His schedule hadn't changed, but it had meant a raise in pay, and he'd been saving for something special.

It was late June and the weather had been perfect. Kendall had just finished up his show on Monday and didn't have to be back to the theater until after noon on Wednesday. "Are you going out?" Kelly, one of his costars, asked as Kendall hurried back to his dressing area.

"Not tonight, thanks. Johnny and I are going away, and he's going to meet me at my place in"—he checked his watch—"fifteen minutes."

"Have fun," Kelly said, and Kendall rushed to change out of his costume and get his makeup off. He did all of it in record time, grabbed his things, and headed toward the theater exit. Once on the sidewalk, he raced to the corner and hailed a taxi. Luck was with him and he caught one right away. He gave the driver the address, and the taxi pulled up to his building just as Johnny was coming down the sidewalk. Kendall paid the driver and hurried to where Johnny waited.

"What's all this about?" Johnny asked.

"I have something for you," Kendall said as he unlocked the door. They climbed the stairs to Kendall's apartment, and he let them inside. Once they were inside, Kendall closed the door and tugged Johnny into a deep kiss.

"Is that my present?" Johnny asked once they broke apart.

Kendall giggled. "No. That's just the appetizer." He set down his stuff and took Johnny's hand, leading him to the sofa. He'd been tempted to lead him directly to the bed, but if he did, they wouldn't do much talking and he had things he needed to say. "I know my schedule is really crazy and makes things hard on both of us. So I really wanted to do something special. I know your classes don't start again for a week or so." Johnny nodded. "I figured we could go someplace together."

"That isn't necessary," Johnny said.

"I know that now. So instead of going away, I thought we'd stay here." Kendall jumped up, hurried to the kitchen area, and pulled open the refrigerator. "I got all your favorites, including mint chocolate chip ice cream. Tomorrow night I made reservations at a nice Belgian restaurant in the village." Kendall closed the refrigerator door. "I have some movies, and I ordered dessert from the bakery you like." Johnny was grinning at him. "What's so funny?"

"Nothing. I'm thrilled you went all out, but what's the special occasion?" Kendall joined Johnny back on the sofa.

"There isn't an occasion yet," Kendall said and sat back on the sofa. "I have something I want to tell you, and I want it to be special." Kendall took a deep breath and released it slowly. "What I really wanted was to take you to a fancy hotel, maybe in Bucks County or in the Adirondacks, but...."

Johnny silenced him with a light stroke on his cheek, and Kendall leaned into the caress. "You don't have to take me anywhere. Being here with you is what's important. We both have weird schedules. So spending time together is more important than spending money on fancy hotels. Here we have everything we need with the whole city just outside."

Kendall nodded and tried to speak but couldn't at first. "See, I've been with other guys, you know that. Before I met you, I dated and... well, hooked up. But other than sex, it didn't really mean anything, and when I met you I so wanted it to be different."

"You mean it wasn't?" Johnny asked, his expression becoming pained.

"No," Kendall said. "Wait, this isn't working the way I wanted. I mean, it is *different with you. I began to realize that the first night we met, when you walked me home from the theater." Kendall chuckled. "Do you remember walking me home that night? I remember it well. It was snowing and cold, but I was warm on the inside the entire way." Kendall moved closer to Johnny and took his hand. "I'd sort of run through what I wanted to say in my head, but it isn't going like I wanted, so I'm going to say what I wanted to say." Kendall took another deep breath, then said, "I love you."*

Johnny stared back at him, blinking a few times, but he didn't say anything at first, and Kendall figured he'd really made a fool of himself. This was the first time he'd ever taken the plunge and told anyone other than his folks that he loved them. Kendall glanced away as Johnny stared at him with his mouth open. He was about to try to backpedal when Johnny grabbed him and pulled him close, hugging Kendall like his life depended upon it.

"God, I love you too," Johnny whispered, and Kendall tried to lift his head away from Johnny's chest so he could kiss him, but Johnny held him too tight. Eventually Johnny loosened his grip, and they shared a kiss that seemed to stop their hearts. "I'm sorry," Johnny whispered between kisses, over and over again.

"Why?" Kendall asked, cupping Johnny's cheeks in his hands. "What do you have to be sorry for?"

"I should have told you. I...," Johnny said. He had tears running down his cheeks. "After what happened with my folks, I was afraid to say anything because...." Johnny gasped. "They should have loved me no matter what and they didn't. If my own parents can't love me, then I wondered how anyone else could." He swallowed and wiped his cheeks with the back of his hand.

"Hey." Kendall lightly kissed Johnny. "I've known what I felt in my heart for a while, but it took me time to be ready to say the words. You're the most lovable person I know, and if your parents don't understand that, then it's their loss and my gain, because I have you and they don't." Kendall kissed him again, this time harder and more demanding. "I get to know the wonderful person you are." Johnny had been hurting since Christmas. Kendall knew that, but because Johnny never wanted to talk about it, Kendall hadn't known just how much. Johnny had done his best to hide it.

"But...," Johnny began, and Kendall silenced him with a kiss and then another, followed by more.

It took them hours before they ever made it to the bed. Kendall refused to let Johnny move away from him for a second. Somehow they managed to divest each other of their clothes. The sofa wasn't very wide, and soon the back cushions ended up on the floor, added to the pile of strewn clothes.

Johnny pressed him into the cushions, lips to lips, belly to belly, and thigh to thigh. Kendall could barely contain his excitement as they kissed. He stroked up and down Johnny's broad back with long fluid movements, extending his hands to caress as much of Johnny's skin as possible.

"I want you, Johnny," Kendall whispered as he reached for the drawer in the coffee table. He hadn't planned on making love on the sofa, but he'd stashed the condoms there because he had been in a hurry. Kendall got the drawer open and found the package. He dropped it on the floor, and Johnny paused at the sound. He peered at the package and arched his eyebrows slightly before kissing him again. Kendall wrapped his legs around Johnny's waist, offering himself, letting Johnny know what he wanted. "Please, Johnny, I...." Kendall's words turned to a soft moan when Johnny ghosted his fingers over his opening. Kendall shuddered.

Johnny brought a finger to Kendall's lips and he sucked it in, wetting it. Then Johnny slowly pulled it from between Kendall's lips. He gasped and groaned when Johnny lightly tapped his opening before teasing him there. When Johnny slid the spit-soaked finger into him, Kendall sighed and slowly gasped for breath. "I love you, Kendall. You're everything to me." Johnny stroked him slowly, rubbing his *finger over the spot inside him, and Kendall nearly came unglued. Johnny knew exactly how to touch him; he had almost from the first. Kendall clamped his eyes closed, clutching Johnny's back to steady himself so he didn't completely fly apart.*

"I love you so much," Kendall repeated over and over until Johnny's finger slid away and he stilled.

"I got a test a few weeks ago and—" Johnny said, and Kendall kissed him, cutting off the words.

"So did I," Kendall said, and they both smiled. "I want to feel you and only you."

"Me too," Johnny said and kissed him once again. "Is there stuff in the drawer?"

"Yeah. I meant to put it away but forgot," Kendall explained, and Johnny pulled open the drawer and found the small bottle. He snicked it open, and Kendall watched with rapt fascination as Johnny slicked himself. Johnny began kissing him again while he pressed to Kendall's opening, slowly increasing the pressure until Kendall's muscles gave and Johnny entered his body with nothing between them for the first time. "I've never done this before," Kendall admitted.

"Not used a condom or made love?" Johnny asked, stilling.

"Both, I guess," Kendall said.

Johnny smiled beatifically, the smile reserved for him, and then kissed him hard as he pressed deep into his body. Johnny made love to him long and slow, each movement tender, each caress meaningful, and each kiss magical. Within minutes Kendall floated on Johnny's love, unable to think, just feel. His entire body tingled. Kendall was on fire—a little more sensation would send him over the edge, but Johnny held him off, building the intensity one layer at a time. His movements became erratic and Kendall reached for his cock, but Johnny shook his head and sped up. Kendall moaned softly at first and then louder, with more intensity. Johnny seemed to come apart, shaking, mouth open, eyes wide as he came inside Kendall.

Kendall gasped as he realized the significance of what they'd just done and the trust both of them had shown. Johnny stilled and then slowly, pulled out of Kendall with a small sigh as their bodies separated. Johnny smiled and crashed their mouths together before kissing and nipping down Kendall's neck, chest, and stomach before sucking Kendall's cock deep into his warm mouth. Kendall was too far gone to control himself. He bucked and thrust hard and fast. Within seconds his release careened into him and Kendall came in a fountain of joy, passion, and love.

It took a few seconds for the room to stop spinning, and by that time, Johnny had him in his arms. Kendall whispered, "I love you," into Johnny's ear and held on as well, basking in the glow of truly being head over heels in love and being loved back.

KENDALL woke and slowly opened his eyes. He quickly realized that he was wet and he knew exactly why. He hadn't had a wet dream since he was a teenager, but he'd had one now, remembering making love for the first time. Kendall got out of bed and quietly walked to the bathroom, where he wiped himself up and got a drink of water.

The bedroom seemed huge and isolated when he returned, the bed cold and uninviting. Instead of getting back in bed, Kendall opened the bedroom door and heard Juan snoring softly. Then Juan rolled over, making the couch springs squeak slightly. Juan began snoring again almost instantly. Kendall stepped closer and stood watching Juan sleep. He was tempted to wake him and bring him to his bed. At least the bed wouldn't be so big, and he'd have someone to hold him. In some ways, Juan reminded Kendall of Johnny, or at least the way Johnny had been a long time ago, with the same energy and caring heart. Kendall took a step closer, then stopped. He couldn't do this. Even if Johnny was having an affair, they had to talk things over. He wouldn't cheat on Johnny, even if Johnny might be cheating on him.

Kendall thought about going back to bed, but walked to the front door. He peeped out and then cracked the door open without undoing the chain. Sure enough, on his doorstep lay two pink roses tied with a bit of what Kendall realized had been the shirt from his dressing room.

"Is everything okay?" Juan asked from the sofa.

"They've been here," Kendall said and closed the door. He unlatched the chain as Juan came closer. Then he opened the door. The roses were there tied with the bit of fabric and they rested on a red cutout of a heart.

"There's something written on it," Juan said, and Kendall gently lifted the flowers off the paper. "You're mine," Juan read aloud, and Kendall began to shake. "Go on back to bed. I'll take care of the flowers."

"Okay," Kendall agreed. "But save the cloth and the note." Juan bent down to pick up the flowers. "Wait," Kendall said, and he grabbed his phone and snapped a picture of everything as it had been left. "Okay. Get rid of all of it." He wondered again if he should call the police, but figured he'd talk to Lyman, like he'd been asked, before he did.

Kendall went back inside and Juan joined him a few minutes later. He closed the door and locked it. "Have you told your landlord that someone is bothering you? If they know, they could have the access changed," Juan said, and Kendall shook his head, flopping into one of the chairs. "What I'm really worried about is being on location."

"Yeah," Juan sighed and walked back over to the sofa. "You should also see if there's a camera in the lobby. If there is, you might be able to see if there's anyone you know coming into the building." Kendall shuddered. It was easier to think of a stranger doing this than someone he knew and maybe even liked. "Go on to bed and get some rest. I'll be out here."

"Okay," Kendall said. He got up and went into his bedroom, then climbed beneath the covers. Hours later he was still staring up at the ceiling and only fell asleep an hour or so before his alarm sounded.

THANKFULLY, the next few days were quiet. No new presents were left either at the studio or at his apartment. He'd spoken to the landlord, who had agreed to change the locks on the front doors. Of course Kendall had had to pay for it, but he'd done it gladly. He at least felt safer in the apartment. He either carried his keys with him or gave them to Juan, who also watched over his cleaned-up dressing room. On Friday, they wrapped up shooting about noon to a round of applause, and Kendall gathered all his things as they prepared to vacate the soundstage.

"You were really good," Kendall told Barbara after they wrapped up the last scene.

"Thanks." She beamed, giving Kendall a light hug. "I think I'm really feeling it, you know?"

"It's great when that happens, isn't it? And for the record, you were right to play that scene slightly bitchy. It's what the character calls for," Kendall said, and she glowed. The only hitch that day had been a difference of opinion between Lyman and Barbara. Kendall had argued Barbara's case when Lyman pressed it, and in the end the scene was better once Lyman let them have a bit of freedom.

"He's such an ass sometimes," Barbara said.

"Well, maybe, but he believes he's right and he's the director. That doesn't mean you're wrong, but that we need to make our case sometimes," Kendall said.

"That's right," Lyman said from behind him, and Kendall jumped a bit, turned, and glared at the director. "You were both excellent," Lyman said with excitement. "Babs"—Lyman's nickname for Barbara, which she hated with a passion—"we'll see you in a few weeks." Kendall could almost see her grinding her teeth. "Kenny"—an equally hated nickname that had made an appearance lately—"I'll see you Monday." Kendall figured Lyman was trying to be an equal opportunity hemorrhoid.

"I'll see you in a few weeks," Kendall said, and Barbara hugged him again and then hurried off.

"By the way," Lyman said from behind him, and Kendall jumped again.

"Would you stop that?" Kendall said, turning around. He'd been jumpy for days, and it was only getting worse.

"There will be security while we're on location. Special security, in addition to what we usually have, and they've been informed about the problem you're having. I've been promised you'll be looked after." Lyman didn't breeze out the way he usually did, and to Kendall's surprise, he closed the door. "Look, it was no secret I wasn't convinced you could do this picture, but I was wrong. You've been a godsend.

Barbara is a real pain in the ass, everyone knows that. But you have her eating out of the palm of your hand, something everyone on the set is grateful for. You've been professional, on time, and always ready with your scene. I couldn't ask for more from anyone."

"Thanks," Kendall said as brightly as he could. "It's been an experience, and I'm assuming it will continue while we're in the desert."

"I won't kid you. This is going to be the hardest part of this film. It's going to be hot, miserable, and the days long. But I need you to keep your eyes open. I have been, but I haven't seen anything. I also asked a few of the senior people to keep an eye out without telling them why. I made up some story about receiving a vague threat." Kendall wasn't sure how he felt about that, but there was nothing he could do, and Lyman was trying to help. "Have a good weekend, maybe go out and see something, have a bit of fun. I've worked everyone really hard, and the next month is going to be as bad or worse, depending upon the weather."

"Thanks. I'll do that," Kendall said, and Lyman opened the door and left the dressing room. Kendall closed the door to finish changing and immediately heard a knock.

"It's me."

"Give me a minute, Juan," Kendall said, and he finished changing before opening the door.

"Here's the stuff you asked me to hold for you," Juan said, and he handed Kendall his keys and wallet. "It's been quiet on the freak front," Juan said. That's how they'd begun referring to the stalker incidents.

"Let's hope it stays that way. Since everyone isn't going on location, maybe whoever it is will be left behind," Kendall said as he shoved his wallet in his back pocket. "Thanks for everything," he said. "I was wondering if you have plans for—" A knock on his doorframe cut him off, and he turned to where Guy stood, smiling.

"I was wondering if you'd like to get some dinner or something? Maybe have a beer and watch a game," Guy offered.

"That'd be great," Kendall said hesitantly. "But I was about to ask Juan if he had plans. He's been helping me learn my way around, and I wanted to thank him. Do you mind?"

"Not at all, that's cool," Guy said, and his phone rang. He raised his finger and answered it, talking quickly before hanging up. "I gotta go, but I'll call you later." Guy hurried off, and Kendall got the rest of his things.

"I don't know about you, but I'm ready to get out of here," Kendall said.

"I still have work to do," Juan explained. "Do you want me to come to your place?"

"That would be great. There are some cool places near the apartment, we can probably eat at one of them," Kendall suggested, and Juan nodded and smiled. "Sounds great. I'll stop by this evening." Juan hurried away, and Kendall grabbed his things and headed out to his car, moving as fast as he could without actually running.

On the drive home, he could have sworn he was being followed. He kept seeing the same red car even after he made more than one turn. So instead of going to the apartment, he stopped off at the Glendale Galleria, parking with the valet. As he got out, he looked around carefully for the red car, but saw nothing. Feeling a bit foolish, he headed inside and wandered around the mall for a while. At one point he grabbed a small bit of lunch. Afterward, he stopped by a bookstore with a display of Johnny's books in the window. He browsed for a bit and then continued on. He stopped in a small store filled with displays of rocks and fossils. Kendall was fascinated and looked at everything before buying Johnny an ammonite. The sales girl wrapped it and placed it in a bag. Kendall paid for it and left the store with a smile on his face. Throughout their relationship they'd had to travel separately, which Johnny hated, but they always brought back little gifts for each other, and he wanted to have something interesting for Johnny.

Kendall sat down on one of the benches, his bag resting next to him, and without thinking he pulled out his phone. "How are you?" Kendall said when Johnny answered his call.

"Really good. The book is coming along well, and I should be done in a few weeks. How much longer will you be out there?" He sounded more excited than he had since Kendall left.

"About a month. I may have to come back after that if they need me to fix things. We're starting the location work on Monday. I don't know if I'll have cell phone coverage during the day, but I'll call when I get back to the hotel at night." Johnny made an agreeable sound but didn't say anything. "Is something wrong?"

"No… well, maybe yes. But I…. It's not really important," Johnny began.

"What isn't important?" Kendall asked.

"Nothing. I'm just a bit lonely," Johnny admitted, and Kendall grinned.

"So am I," Kendall said, and he heard some noise in the background. "What's that?"

"Jeremy's here. We're going over the things he found and having dinner," Johnny said, and Kendall wanted to reach through the phone and throttle whoever this Jeremy was. He should be the one there having dinner with Johnny.

"I'm tired of this whole thing and want to come home," Kendall said. "I've been working for months, and everyone I know except for Juan and a few others are there in New York. I'm sick of being alone all the time. Right now I'm sitting in the middle of the mall on a bench whiling away the time like a well-dressed homeless person."

"Stop being dramatic," Johnny said with a slight chuckle. "Are you still having the troubles with the flowers and stuff?" Johnny always asked, but in a skeptical way that told Kendall he didn't believe how unnerving and serious it was.

"You mean other than someone breaking into my dressing room, trashing it, and leaving two roses in the mess?" Kendall said.

"Kendall, you should have called," Johnny scolded.

"I did, and you would have known if you'd called me back. I left you a message two days ago," Kendall snapped. "Look, if you don't care anymore, that's fine. You can just say so." Kendall stood up, yanked his bag off the bench, and stomped back through the mall toward where he'd come in. "I know you don't believe me, but whoever is doing this has me really scared, and being patronized isn't helping."

"I'm not patronizing you," Johnny said. "I'm sorry. I didn't realize how serious it was. And…." Johnny paused. "I sort of dropped my phone in the toilet and had to get a new one." Kendall slowed his pace as he reached the mall entrance and began to laugh.

"Okay," Kendall began, still chuckling. "It's okay. I'm sorry too. I think all this really has me on edge," he said with a sigh, his humor gone. "They've hired extra security for when we're on location, and though it's been a few days since anything happened, I'm still nervous."

"You should be," Johnny said. "Have you gone to the police?"

"No. The studio is handling it. They've had extra security on the set for the past few days, and I've had no issues," Kendall explained. "I know it isn't over, but maybe they'll get the message and move on to bother someone else."

"Okay. But be careful," Johnny said.

"I will," Kendall replied and pushed open the door to the parking garage. "I'll talk to you later."

"Okay. Jeremy and I have work to get done. I'll talk to you soon." Johnny hung up, and Kendall stopped, shaking a bit with anger as he thought about what Jeremy and Johnny might be up to. He handed the valet his ticket. While the valet got his car, Kendall wondered what Johnny had wanted to talk about. God, things were a real mess.

His phone rang as the valet braked his car to a stop. "Hey, Guy," Kendall said when he answered the call.

"I've got things I have to do for Lyman and won't be able to have dinner," Guy said. "But I'll see you on location, and maybe if we got done filming early one night, I can show you a bit of Vegas."

"That would be nice," Kendall said. The valet held his door, and Kendall tipped him. "I'll see you next week." He hung up and placed the phone on his seat, then drove to the apartment.

There was nothing outside his door when Kendall let himself inside. He set down the bag and went into the bedroom. After stripping off his clothes, Kendall took a shower and dressed comfortably, then flopped on the sofa to watch television while he waited for Juan to arrive. He wished Johnny were here to curl up with him. But then again, maybe those days were over forever.

CHAPTER
SIX

"TWO weeks," Kendall grumbled as he walked back to his trailer, desperate to get out of the infernal heat. Juan raced to catch up with him.

"Kendall," Juan said. "You know they're going to need you on the set in a few minutes."

Kendall stopped and waited for Juan to catch up.

"If you need something I can get it for you," Juan said.

"What I need is five minutes to get out of this heat," he lied. What he really needed was for them to rewrite the entire premise of the movie so he wouldn't need to spend hours inside that car. The thought made him cold even in this ungodly heat. "I'll be fine once I get a drink and can spend a few minutes where it's cool."

He could tell Juan wasn't buying it, but he kept his opinion to himself and followed behind. Over the past few weeks, Juan had made sure Kendall was rarely alone when on the set. There hadn't been any incidents at all, but Kendall passed the guard who sat in the shade near his trailer. "Hey, Carl," Kendall called as he approached. He nodded to Kendall as he passed.

The inside was cool. Thank God for air-conditioning and the nearly silent generators that powered everything out here in the middle of nowhere. Kendall got bottles of water out of the refrigerator and handed two to Juan. "Pass one to Carl too," he instructed. He sat on one of the benches and did his best to push the fear away. He'd known this part of the movie was going to be hard to make, but he'd had no idea how difficult.

Juan came back inside. "Are you going to be okay? They said they'll need you in five minutes."

Kendall swallowed. "Okay." Up to this point, they'd filmed a variety of scenes, including him being carried around by the would-be kidnapper, and even a number of the scenes in the car. Those hadn't bothered him. After all, it had been the front half, the open side, or the back half the car. But now they needed to film him in the car, the full car, with the doors closed.

"You should get back out there," Juan said gently, and Kendall nodded and stood up, then left the trailer and went where they were shooting between the hills. The sun was brutal and beat relentlessly on his skin. Kendall had taken to using an umbrella and sunscreen whenever he could, because he couldn't get tan or it would ruin the shots. His skin tone had to stay the same. He hurried to where they were shooting and stood off camera in the shade of an awning as he waited until they were ready for him.

"Kendall," Lyman said once they were done and motioned toward the car. "We've talked about this scene and what you need to do."

"Yeah, I got it," Kendall said and walked toward the car. He sat down behind the driver's seat, and Arlene, one of the production assistants, fastened his hands to the steering wheel with handcuffs.

"They're props, so don't pull too hard or they'll come off," Arlene said, and Kendall did his best to smile at her. "It'll be fine, honey," she told him. "Everyone is out here and nothing is going to happen." Kendall looked up at her, a bit confused. "My grandson doesn't like confined spaces either," she whispered, and once he was secured, she closed the door and Kendall sat inside the only slightly cooled car, trying to breathe as evenly as he could while at the same time preventing himself from passing out from the heat. "Okay, action!" Kendall heard from outside the car, and he peered out the window, darting his eyes from side to side, and then tilted his head to look up at the sky. His fear built by the second, and he opened his mouth, breathing through it. "Cut," he heard and the car door was opened. "That was pretty good, but I need more," Lyman said, and

Kendall nodded. His stomach roiled, and he hoped to God he wouldn't be sick.

"Okay," Kendall said softly, and the car door closed again. This time he watched the people move away from the car, sweeping out their footprints in the sand. Kendall listened for Lyman and then went through the same motions, this time much more frantically, and he pulled on the steering wheel. His own fear barely contained below the surface, Kendall looked out at the landscape beyond the dunes behind the film crew, opened his mouth, and let out a cry that seemed to come from the very center of his being. There was no way he could take much more of this, and he let it all out. He was still crying and gasping for breath when someone opened the door. He yanked his hands away from the steering wheel and the cuffs came apart and fell away. Kendall leaped from the car and bent over, gasping for air. "Are... you... done?" he managed to wheeze between breaths.

"That was amazing," Lyman said.

"Good," Kendall sputtered as he forced himself to stand upright. "Now leave me the fuck alone." Kendall took the first stumbling steps back toward his trailer. "And don't you dare ask me to do that again." He took a few more steps and heard someone hurrying up behind him.

It was Lyman. "It's all right," he said and guided Kendall toward a chair. "He needs some water." Someone brought over a bottle and Kendall drank it, trying to catch his breath and slow his racing heart. "You know we're not done," Lyman whispered, and Kendall nodded.

"Fine," Kendall said. "But I want this part of this thing over with. I can't take days of this, Lyman. I can't."

"We'll do what we can," Lyman told him. "It's just a car, and everyone is out here. No one is leaving you alone." Kendall nodded and drank his water, doing his best to get himself together again.

Kendall finished his water. "Just tell me when you're ready," he told Lyman as steadily as he could. This wasn't the first time he'd had to overcome fear in relation to his work.

KENDALL sat backstage in his dressing room, shaking like a leaf. He had no idea where all this fear had come from, but he was scared to death. All night long, he'd dreamed he kept falling down on stage and forgot every line of his new part. He'd just been cast in his first lead role, and the entire show rested on his shoulders. If he messed up, the show would be a disaster. He reached for his copy of the score and opened it. He knew his lines—he always knew his lines—but now they were gone and he couldn't think of a single word other than, "Shit.... Shit, shit, shit, shit, shit." He was about to toss the score across the tiny room when a knock sounded on the door.

"Forty-five minutes."

"Thanks," Kendall answered and picked up his phone, pressing his number 1 contact. "Help me. I can't remember a single line, and I don't know what to do."

"I'll be right there," Johnny said. "I'm already on my way. Tell someone to let me backstage."

"Thanks," Kendall said. He got up and pulled open his door, stopping one of the runners, a young guy whose name escaped him, along with every line from the show. "Please tell someone out front that I have someone coming and they're to let him back. His name is Johnny Harker. He should be here in a few minutes." Randy... the runner's name was Randy, Kendall remembered.

"Don't worry, Kendall," Randy said. "I'm heading out front. I know what he looks like. I saw him a couple months ago when he came to see you."

"Thanks," Kendall said and went back in the dressing room to finish getting ready. If this was going to be a complete disaster, he might as well look stunning while he crashed and burned.

A few minutes later he heard a knock and Johnny stepped inside, then closed the door right away. "You're going to be just fine," Johnny told him before Kendall could say a word.

"I don't know if I can do this," Kendall said, his leg shaking slightly.

"Of course you can. You've rehearsed this a million times, and you know every line and every move by heart. It's as automatic as breathing and as vital as air." Johnny pulled him into his arms. "You're amazing, and there isn't another person anywhere who can do this part better than you." Johnny lightly touched his chin, and Kendall

lifted his gaze. "I love you, Kendall, and that will never change, no matter what. And I'm going to be out there in the front row, cheering you on. So when you hear that first clap, know it's from me."

"But...."

"You're going to be great, and I'm going to be so proud sitting out there watching you." Johnny hugged him close again. "I love you more than anything in the world."

KENDALL snapped out of his daydream and glanced around. No one seemed to have been paying him any attention. Preparations were being made for the next shoot, and everyone was busy as hell.

"They're going to be ready for you in about twenty minutes," Juan told him, and Kendall nodded his response. He didn't feel like talking right now. "I'll let you get into character," Juan added and then stepped away. He stood nearby, and Kendall knew his friend was standing guard so he'd be left alone.

"I LOVE you more than anything in the world," Johnny whispered into Kendall's ear. "And I think you're so amazing. I want to shout to everyone in the theater that the amazingly talented and gorgeous leading man up there on the stage is mine."

Kendall chuckled softly, some of his anxiety and the tightness in his chest slipping away. "Do you mean that?"

Johnny paused and stiffened slightly. "Of course I do. You're everything to me."

"Even more than your books and your stories about dead people?" Kendall quipped.

"Yes," Johnny said, hugging him tightly. "I love you more than dead people." Kendall smacked him lightly on the arm, but he laughed. "All this is just nerves, and you've had them before. So use them in your performance—let them add energy and excitement."

"Ten minutes," someone called after a quick knock. Johnny stepped back, and Kendall looked in the mirror to make sure he was

*perfect. His makeup was slightly smeared, so he did a quick fix before
brushing a smudge off Johnny's clothes.*

*"It's okay," Johnny told him. "Just finish getting ready." He
kissed him with the promise of heat. "That's a preview of what's
waiting for you at home." Johnny stepped away, and Kendall sighed.
"I'll be waiting for you out front. Break a leg," Johnny added with a
smile and then left the dressing room. Kendall checked himself yet
again in the mirror and then stepped out of his dressing room, and
walked to the stage.*

*Multiple "break a legs" were whispered as he passed, and
Kendall acknowledged each one with a smile and whispered the
greeting in return.*

*The overture started, and Kendall got into position, then the
curtain lifted, he heard his cue, and leaped into his first dramatic move,
landing perfectly before opening his mouth and singing to the back of
the house. Beyond the lights he saw Johnny smile, eyes shining with
reflected light. After that, his mind and body took over, lines came
easily, every movement crisp and spot on, every leap and stunt just a bit
higher than in rehearsal. He gave the performance of his life… for his
Johnny.*

"KENDALL, they're ready for you," Juan said, and Kendall shook his
head, bringing his attention back to the present with a bit of regret.
"Are you okay? You seemed…."

"Far away," Kendall supplied. "Seems more like a lifetime ago,"
he added. But he felt better. He shoved his hand into his pocket to pull
out his cell phone before he remembered it wasn't there. There wasn't
any service out here, and Juan was holding all his personal things
because he refused to leave them in the trailer.

"Whatever it was must have been happy, because you were
smiling," Juan told him. Before Kendall could answer, he was called on
the set, and he walked to where they indicated and got back in the car.
This time he was much calmer, and this time when they shut the door,
it seemed like Johnny was there with him, just like it had felt like
Johnny had been with him that night all those years ago. He didn't

question or second-guess the feeling; he just went with it and got the job done.

BY THE time shooting ended well after dark, Kendall had spent much of the day in the car. His legs and back ached, and all he wanted was to get back to the hotel, have a decent meal, and crawl into bed. He got his things from Juan and walked to his car. He opened the trunk and placed his bag inside it before opening the car door and getting inside. He shifted to get out his keys and heard movement from the backseat.

A cloth was jammed over his mouth and nose…. His skin tingled, and he tried not to breathe in whatever chemical was on the rag, but he couldn't help it.

"I said you were mine," a raspy voice hissed in his ear. It might have been familiar, but he couldn't be sure. Kendall's mind was already beginning to shut down. "But you didn't cooperate, so no one will have you." Within seconds, his vision went blurry and then the entire world went black.

CHAPTER
SEVEN

KENDALL'S head ached, and even with his eyes closed, the world seemed to be spinning. He shifted and encountered resistance. What the hell was going on? He waited a bit, and slowly his mind cleared. He'd been about to drive back to the hotel. He remembered someone else being in the car and.... Kendall cracked his eyes open. He was still in the car. He moved his hands, and metal jangled. Everything was wrong. But his mind didn't seem to be able to process what was happening. Kendall closed his eyes and willed his thoughts to clear. He opened them again. This time he was less dizzy. Whatever had done this to him seemed to be wearing off, and he needed to figure out what had happened. He was inside his car, that much was obvious. He was still belted into the seat. Okay, that was normal. He was also handcuffed to the steering wheel.

It took a few seconds for his foggy mind to process that he wasn't on the movie set. This was his car, not the movie car. He was in his own car. Kendall peered out the driver's window, still half expecting to see the crew and cameras staring back at him. But all he saw was a sandy hill directly beside him, covered with brown plant remnants and a few cacti. When he tilted his head, he could look around the hill to empty land as far as the eye could see. "This can't be happening," he whispered. Panic welled up inside him, and he remembered that the stage handcuffs had come off when he pulled on them. Kendall yanked, hard, but all he got was an ache in his wrists. He tried again, his yells filling the car as he did. Nothing. These were the real thing. Almost instantly panic set in, and he squirmed and fought against the handcuffs and seat belt, trying to get the hell out of them. In the end all he got were sore wrists and an aching throat from the screams that resounded in his ears, but of course brought no one or anything of help.

Kendall sat back in the seat, breathing through his mouth, and took a look around him. He could see almost nothing out of the windshield—it was covered in sand, as was much of the back window. He could see out both sets of side windows, but that was it. Of course the keys weren't in the ignition. He could reach a few of the dashboard buttons, not that any of them worked. He was pretty much stuck where he was.

The light outside the car increased, and Kendall quickly realized that as the sun rose higher, the car would turn into an oven. The heat was already beginning to rise inside the car, and Kendall was instantly thirsty. He licked his lips and swallowed to coat his suddenly dry throat. Kendall continued looking around, racking his brain to try to think of a way out of this. But of course nothing came to mind. He reached for the latch to open the door. He could make it if he twisted his arm just right, but he paused. The only moisture he had was coming from him, his breath and his body, and at least that was trapped inside the car. If he opened the door, the heat inside the car would escape, but so would all the moisture. He was damned if he did and damned if he didn't.

"What in the hell am I going to do?" Kendall asked out loud just as the sun shone on the partially covered back window. The heat inside the car rose quickly, and Kendall closed his eyes, sat still, and did something he hadn't done in years… prayed, and hoped for a miracle.

HOURS passed, and the heat built further and further, then finally seemed to level off. Kendall's lungs began to ache from it, but at least the sun was no longer blasting directly in through the windows. That was a bit of a relief, but it appeared like the only break he'd been able to catch. His clothes and the seat were wet, and sweat ran down his forehead, threatening to run into his eyes. Kendall leaned forward and managed to wipe the sweat with his hand, and out of sheer desperation licked the moisture with his tongue. He'd had time to think and to plan, but all the paths he came up with led one place—nowhere. He couldn't get word to anyone, and he couldn't get out. All he could do was hope someone found him and that whoever had done this to him didn't come back.

Kendall had decided that the person who had kidnapped him intended for him to die out here and was unlikely to return. However, niggling in the back of his brain was the thought that his stalker might intend to return and "rescue" him. At this point, Kendall didn't care. He'd play along and pretend, do whatever he had to, as long as he could get back to civilization. From there he'd let the police handle it. But that wasn't likely. They weren't going to give themselves up like that.

There was nothing he could do. Kendall was completely helpless, and until someone found him, *if* someone ever found him, it was his job to try to stay alive, and that meant water. Of course, at the rate he was sweating, there wouldn't be much water left inside him for long. He closed his eyes and relaxed as best he could, conserving as much energy as possible.

The sun moved outside the car, the shadow from the hill beside him just out of reach of the car and then moving on. Eventually he had to keep his eyes closed or his head turned away as the sun shone on the windshield. The sand blocked much of the sun, but not all of it, and the car heated up once again.

HIS stomach began cramping from hunger and thirst as the sun finally began to set. Kendall had been hungry for hours, but the pain was the worst it had been all day. Worse, he'd had to go to the bathroom, and through plenty of wriggling around he'd managed to lift his hips to his hands and open his fly. He managed to get most of it on the floor and mostly missed his shoes, and then he'd gotten his dick back in his pants but couldn't redo the zipper. Eventually he gave up, settled back on the seat, and went back to looking around.

Once the sun went down, the heat abated and it got completely dark. He briefly saw the stars shining in the sky, and then, as the temperature dropped, the windows fogged over. Kendall licked every inch of the glass he could reach with his tongue. Then he sat back and hoped like hell the window would fog up again. His stomach eventually stopped aching, and as the heat leached out of the car and it became more comfortable, he closed his eyes.

JOHNNY came home and set his bag on the table. "What's wrong?"

"I knew I was being completely stupid," Johnny said, pulling out a pile of papers joined together by a huge paper clip and plunking it on the table.

Kendall got up from the table. His current show was dark today, and it was typically their evening to do something special together. With this show it was Monday, and he never made evening plans. This was their time together. "What's this?"

"My book," Johnny said, and Kendall widened his eyes in surprise.

"You wrote a book? You never told me you'd done that." Kendall reached for the pile of paper. "Why didn't you say something?"

"Because it's crap. I started it on a lark before I met you because I got this idea, and it took me two years between classes. I've been finishing it while you were working." Johnny plopped into one of the chairs. "I spend a lot of time alone, and I filled some of it, finishing the story. It's an adventure story about a man looking for treasures stolen by the Nazis and thought lost forever. I showed it to my doctoral advisor and he said he'd read it. He gave it back to me and said I would be better off concentrating on my classwork and thesis."

"What did he say exactly?" Kendall asked, gathering Johnny into his arms.

"He said that kind of work was beneath a true historian, and that if I wanted to make anything of myself, I should spend my time on more academically worthy endeavors," Johnny mimicked pompously, and Kendall snickered.

"Can I read it?" Kendall asked.

"If you want to," Johnny said. "Heck, you can have it, if you want. Maybe when we're old we can pull it out for a laugh."

"Hey, I bet it's great," Kendall said and kissed him.

"Of course you would say that. You love me," Johnny said.

"Okay," Kendall countered. "How about you let me read it, and I'll tell you exactly what I think."

"Even if it sucks?" Johnny asked.

"Yes," Kendall agreed and kissed him again. He'd planned to go out to dinner, but they ended up staying in that evening. Actually, Johnny made a quick dinner, and they spent the rest of the evening in bed. Once Johnny fell asleep, Kendall was wide awake, so he got out of bed, picked up Johnny's manuscript from the table, and sat in the living room to read. He didn't stop until it was nearly morning and he'd read every word. Johnny woke him up in the morning where he'd fallen asleep on the sofa, the manuscript beside him on the floor.

"Was it so bad that it put you to sleep?" Johnny asked when Kendall woke as Johnny covered him with a blanket.

"What time is it?" Kendall yawned, curling under the blanket.

"Just after seven," Johnny answered. "Why?"

"I read it straight through and couldn't put it down. My heart raced and I was on the edge of my seat for hours. Your professor is so full of shit, he'll attract flies. That is pure gold. I didn't just like it, I loved it, and I love you for writing it."

"You're not kidding?" Johnny said.

"Hell no, I'm not. I'm going to call Sal this morning and see if he knows any literary agents." Kendall yawned, and Johnny kissed him before leaving the apartment.

KENDALL jerked himself upright when he fell forward onto the horn. He blinked a few times and quickly remembered where he was and what had happened to him. It was pitch black and Kendall could see almost nothing inside or outside the car. The window near him had fogged up again and he licked it, the moisture feeling amazing on his dry tongue. Of course, the effect didn't last long. All he could think about was his primal need for water, no matter how hard he tried to push it from his mind. He wasn't getting any more water, and all he could hope for was that someone would find him before too long. His lips ached already, and he knew soon it would hurt to blink. His throat already felt like sandpaper, and swallowing hurt, but there wasn't anything he could do about it.

Kendall worked himself forward in the seat, slowly lengthening the seat belt. Once he was as far forward as he could get, Kendall licked what condensation he could off the windshield. It wasn't much, but it was better than nothing, and when he was done, his throat felt a bit better. When he'd gotten all the moisture he could, Kendall sat back down with a sigh. He hoped like hell someone was looking for him. He pushed the doubts from his mind. Hope was all he had.

The hours ticked by, the only sound reaching his ears his own breathing and the occasional soft squeak of the seat when he shifted. Kendall closed his eyes again, because if he could sleep, at least he was conserving some of the energy he had left. But of course that didn't happen, and Kendall stayed awake much of the night. He might have dozed off a bit, but he really wasn't sure.

The first rays of light lit the windows, and Kendall's fear instantly rose. He'd made it through the night, but he knew the worst was yet to come. Yesterday had been hell, but the second day in the oven the car would become would be nearly unbearable. The light increased quickly, shining in the back window and almost instantly starting to increase the temperature. Kendall licked the glass one last time before the moisture disappeared and then closed his eyes, sat back, and waited for the heat he knew was only a short way off.

Once the sun was up, Kendall pretty much lost track of time. Not that it mattered, because every hour that went by meant he was one hour closer to dying of thirst. His mind wandered and Kendall made no move to stop it. At least his wandering thoughts were an escape from the reality of sweltering heat and unending thirst.

"Johnny how could you do this to me?" Kendall moaned out loud at one point, desperate to hear something other than his own breathing. "How could you let this happen to me?" Kendall knew he wasn't thinking clearly, but he didn't care. "If you'd have come, I'd have been safe." Kendall pounded the steering wheel in a fit of rage, the handcuffs chinking. "You..." *pound* "should..." *pound* "have... been... here!" Kendall gripped the wheel and pulled on it, his frustration and anger overwhelming him. "This is all your fault. You should have loved me enough to come with me." His rage and energy were spent in a matter of seconds, and Kendall hung his head forward and softly began to cry. "You didn't love me enough."

How long he stayed that way Kendall didn't know. His neck hurt, but he ignored it along with the hunger, thirst, heat, and every other fucking thing ripping his body and mind apart.

HE AND Johnny were moving. Johnny had moved out of student housing and into Kendall's small apartment two years earlier. It had been cramped, but they were in love, so the space, or lack thereof, didn't matter. It still didn't, but Kendall had happened upon a larger apartment thanks to a friend. He was leaving for an opportunity in Seattle and had offered Kendall the apartment, a rent-control apartment, no less. He and Johnny had taken one look at the brownstone building and then seen the apartment. They smiled at one another and instantly said yes.

Kendall had rented a truck, which was parked just outside their building. Everything had been packed, and Kendall was now making what seemed like his millionth trip up and down the stairs. A friend of Johnny's was staying with the truck and loading the things as they brought them down. "That's nearly the last of it," Kendall told Steve as he took the box. "Just a few more trips and we're done." Johnny came wobbling out of the building carrying a stack of boxes. Kendall hurried over and took the top one. "How could you see?"

"Couldn't. Not really," Johnny answered a bit breathlessly. Kendall hurried to the truck with the box, and then one by one, unloaded Johnny. "There's just a few more things," Johnny said. Reluctantly they both went back inside and climbed the stairs. The apartment was largely empty, with just a few smaller boxes and some cleaning supplies left.

"I'll carry these down if you want to finish sweeping up. I'll meet you down at the truck," Kendall said, and Johnny got to work. Kendall picked up the boxes and paused, watching as Johnny worked. Then he set them on the counter and tapped Johnny on the shoulder. *"We're moving to our first apartment, yours and mine,"* Kendall whispered, and Johnny dropped the broom before pulling Kendall into his arms.

"This place was nice...," Johnny said as they hugged.

"Yes, it was. But the new apartment will have a real bedroom and kitchen," Kendall whispered back, and Johnny leaned in for a kiss.

A knock interrupted them, and they both turned as a throat cleared. "I have a package that needs to be signed for." The mail carrier appeared a bit surprised, but not shocked. Johnny released Kendall and signed the form. The carrier picked up a box he'd set just outside and handed it to Johnny. Then he smiled quickly and left.

"What's this?" Kendall asked. *Johnny seemed to vibrate as he carried the box to the small bit of counter and yanked open the top. Then he handed Kendall a hardcover book. Johnny's book.*

"Can you believe it?" Johnny asked. *"Look at the dedication."*

Kendall opened the cover and turned to the page. "To Kendall, who encouraged me to go forward when I was about to stop. Thank you for believing in me when others didn't. "

"I could never have seen this through without you," Johnny said, *and he tugged Kendall back into his arms. "I wanted to add that I loved you more than life itself, but the publisher said I shouldn't be too... 'in your face' was the term he used. But I do. I love you."* Johnny *kissed him intensely, and Kendall nearly dropped the book.*

"We'd better get the last of this done," Kendall said after *swallowing once Johnny had broken the kiss. "Steve is still downstairs." Kendall stumbled a bit, his legs unsteady. Then he lifted the boxes and started down the stairs.*

He made it to the first landing and was about to turn when the boxes he was carrying tipped. He tried to compensate, but then he was falling too, pushed off his feet. Kendall let go of the boxes and they fell down the stairs, glass breaking as they bounced.

"*Look at this,*" *a deep male voice said, and Kendall was practically lifted back onto his feet and then beyond. "It's one of the fags," a man growled.*

"*That's enough, Eddie,*" *another guy said as he climbed toward them.*

"*Come on, Hank. I've had to listen to them do God knows what kinds of disgusting things to each other for years. It's sickening!*" *Eddie shook him and dropped him onto his feet. Kendall heard rapid footsteps coming down the stairs and soon Johnny burst onto the landing and pushed Eddie against the wall.*

"*You can think what the hell you want,*" *Johnny growled, "but this is not your lucky day. Hey, Steve!" Johnny bellowed, and within seconds more footsteps sounded on the stairs. Steve stepped behind Hank, acting more like a brick wall than a person. "What happened?" Johnny asked Kendall softly.*

"*They pushed me.*"

Steve looked down at the boxes. "I hope you can pay for those," Steve growled. Eddie and Hank went white. Johnny glared at them and so did Steve.

"*Are you okay?*" *Johnny asked him, and Kendall nodded.*

"*We were only having a bit of fun,*" *Eddie said a bit shakily.*

"*Well, your fun could have hurt someone,*" *Johnny countered harshly. "You broke some of his things, and he could have fallen down the stairs." Johnny tightened his grip on Eddie, pressing him harder against the wall. "Maybe I should just give you a push. See how you like falling down the stairs." Kendall stepped back, holding the railing.*

"*You can't...,*" *Hank began, and both Johnny and Steve growled at him. "Dudes, he's a total idiot, but don't hurt him," Hank added.*

"*Johnny,*" *Kendall said quietly and touched his arm. "Let him go. He isn't worth it." Johnny looked at him and then stepped back from Eddie.*

"*Get out of here. We're leaving, and I don't want to see you again, either of you,*" *Johnny commanded, and the two men took off down the stairs. "You might want to change your pants," Johnny called after them, and then both he and Steve broke into peals of laughter.*

"He actually wet himself," Steve said as he turned and headed back down the stairs. "I'll get the boxes on my way back to the truck," he added, and his laughter reverberated off the stairwell walls until he got outside.

"Are you okay?" Johnny asked, gathering Kendall into his arms. "He didn't hurt you, did he?"

"No. He didn't get a chance," Kendall said and began to shake. "What were you thinking? He could have hurt you," Kendall said and slapped Johnny on the arm. "Don't ever do that again."

"He could...." Johnny paused. "You're angry with me? Why?"

"You could have been hurt," Kendall answered, still quivering a bit.

"So could you, and I was just protecting you," Johnny said. "I wasn't going to get hurt."

"How do you know that?" Kendall asked. "How could you possibly know that?"

"I've known Steve for a long time, and after I came out, he taught me how to fight. Not how to box, but how to kick someone's ass. I know you're scared, but I'll fight to protect you."

"You will, huh?" Kendall said.

"Oh, yeah," Johnny told him forcefully. "I'll kick anyone's ass from here to kingdom come who tries to mess with you," Johnny whispered roughly. "You're the person most important to me in the world. I will always be there to protect you, just like I know you'll always be there to protect me."

KENDALL opened his eyes, gasping for breath. He was so tired and weak he could hardly move. His mouth felt like the sand blowing around outside the car. His eyes burned, they were so dry, and his lips had begun to crack. His throat constricted occasionally, and he tried not to swallow—it only brought more pain. The sun shone through the front window, worse than the day before. The wind that whistled outside the car had blown some of the scattered sand off the glass, and the car heated up even more than it had the day before. "Where are you to protect me now?" Kendall whispered. Well, tried to whisper. He moved his lips and said the words, but no sound came out. Not that it mattered; there was no one to hear it anyway.

Kendall did his best to simply breathe. In order to pass the time, he forced his mind to try to figure out who could have done this to him. He thought about everyone he'd encountered. It couldn't have been Juan. He had been at the apartment when one of the messages was delivered. Granted, he could have had someone deliver it, but what was the point? He'd slept on Kendall's sofa and had run interference for him for weeks.

Could it have been Lyman? At first the director had been a royal pain in the ass, but they'd come to respect one another, and over time, maybe even like each other. Besides, Lyman was as straight as an arrow. Kendall tried to remember if his gaydar had ever blipped even a little bit with Lyman, and it hadn't. Besides, Lyman was the kind of man who said what he thought to your face. He yelled, insulted, screamed, and strutted, but he wasn't a schemer—at least Kendall didn't think so. It surprised him to realize he'd be hurt if Lyman had been behind this.

Was it Guy? They'd gone out a few times for drinks, but all they'd talked about was film. Guy was great, but he was boring as sin. He seemed to live for film, camera angles, and getting the perfect shot. And he talked about girls all the time. Sure, most of the time Guy was quiet, but Kendall liked him. They'd connected early on, and Kendall would hate to think Guy could do this.

Every muscle in his body ached and seemed to cramp at the same time. He figured his body must be pulling all the moisture from his muscles to try to preserve his organs. He couldn't quite put his finger on where he'd heard that. Then he remembered and smiled. Johnny had included it in the book Kendall had read before leaving for Hollywood. His legs ached and quivered. He slowly moved them back and forth, trying to limber them up a bit. Then he leaned forward and flexed his back, which ached and throbbed from his butt to his neck. Once he was done, he started over again, slowly moving one part of his body and then another. But it came at a price, because after only a few minutes, he was breathing harder. He realized he was tiring himself out and losing even more precious moisture from his body, so he sat still once again and tried to focus on figuring out who had done this. At least it gave him something to do with his mind.

Barbara. Could it be her? Kendall seriously doubted it. They'd had a bit of a rocky start, but there was no romantic tension between them whatsoever, at least not off camera. If the rumors were correct, she was dating some high-powered action star, anyway. No, he could rule her out.

Thinking about anything other than water, food, pain, and water, oh, and more water, took almost all the energy he had, but he persevered.

Could Johnny have done this? He focused on the idea, and suddenly everything became clear. He could see it all now: the stalker was just a diversion. Johnny knew where he lived because he had Kendall's address. He also knew his work schedule and could give it to whoever he'd hired to stalk and ultimately kidnap him. After all, Johnny had laughed when Kendall had first told him what he suspected. Maybe Johnny was trying to put him off the scent so that he wouldn't suspect him. Maybe this whole thing was the enactment of the plot from some book Johnny wanted to write. After all, he'd done worse things to his characters than lock them in a car. Johnny had tortured some of them, killed off his heroines, and even had some of his heroes left barely alive after their ordeals. "It can't be Johnny," Kendall whimpered. He didn't want to live if Johnny had done this. Slowly, Kendall rocked his head back and forth against the seat.

THE air around him felt a bit cooler, and Kendall opened his eyes as the sun disappeared behind the hills in the distance. The day was over and somehow he'd made it. But he knew he wouldn't last another day, so he stared out the front window and watched the sun set for what he figured was the last time. He'd probably make it through the night, but sometime tomorrow, the temperatures in the car would bake the last bit of sanity from him, and if he were lucky, he'd pass out. Then he'd die and it would be over. He was too weak to put up a fight any longer, so as darkness fell, he sat still and waited for condensation to form on the windows.

It didn't. Kendall wasn't sure why, and he didn't have the strength to try to figure it out. All he knew was that tonight there wasn't enough moisture in the air to form condensation on the windows. *Duh,* he told himself in his mind, unable to speak and no longer having the energy to actually move his lips. The car wasn't airtight; if it had been, he would have suffocated. The moisture had probably been leaching out the entire day, and he didn't have enough in his body to replace it. Well, it was over as far as Kendall was concerned. He couldn't keep his eyes open any longer and he didn't even want to try.

The air was still, with almost no sound whatsoever. Even his breathing had become quieter, or maybe he could no longer hear it. He let go of whatever conscious thought he had and simply floated. Maybe he'd fall asleep and simply wouldn't wake up. He had to be close to that point now. "Good-bye, Johnny," Kendall managed to say out loud, his throat scratching as he made the sounds. "I don't know what happened to us, but I love you. Even though you can't hear them, I want those to be my last words. I love you." Kendall closed his eyes and slumped in the seat, his head hanging forward.

CHAPTER
EIGHT

SOMETHING reached Kendall's ears, a sound he couldn't seem to process, but he didn't open his eyes—he was way too tired. If dying came with a fanfare or a bunch of angels singing like the chorus of some huge Christmas show, then bring it on, because he was ready for it. If it came on slow and silent, he was ready for that too. He only hoped that heaven wouldn't require him to move, because that he couldn't do.

There were voices in heaven, he was pretty sure of that, because he could hear them, although he wasn't sure what they were saying.

Then he heard, "Dear God in heaven," and he smiled in his feeble mind. Yeah, he was in heaven, all right.

The sound of breaking glass startled him. Somehow he didn't think that belonged in heaven.

"Kendall," he heard, but he didn't move. He was too tired. If this was heaven or hell, he didn't really care. They could come take him wherever they wanted him to go.

"Be careful," another voice said, more softly.

"Honey," he heard whispered, and then someone touched him. Kendall groaned and forced his eyes open. "Sweetheart, it's me." He turned his head and saw Johnny staring back at him. Kendall moved away and whined softly.

"Get away, you did this," he said or tried to, but nothing came out.

"It's okay, honey, don't worry, I'm here," Johnny said. "Drink some of this if you can." A bottle touched his lips, and Kendall let some of the liquid slip into his mouth and then swallowed. His throat burned, but he swallowed again. The second time it felt much better. Liquid ran down his chin, but he just kept swallowing. "That's good. Don't try to drink too much at once." Johnny pulled the bottle away, and Kendall groaned. "You'll get it back in a few seconds, I promise."

"You found me," Kendall said. "Did you do this to me?"

Johnny looked behind him, and Kendall saw Lyman standing just behind Johnny. Then Johnny turned back to him. "No, sweetheart, I didn't do this to you. I would never do anything to hurt you," Johnny said and placed the bottle to his lips once more. This time Kendall drank, gulping what he could. Johnny pulled the bottle away again after a few drinks. "I don't want you to get sick, so we need to take it easy at first." The bottle shook. "I was so worried about you."

"How?" Kendall asked.

"We'll explain everything we know once we get you out of here," Lyman told him. "Drink some more."

Kendall did and then turned toward the director. "Why does your accent come and go?" Kendall asked. He'd been dying to ask that for months.

"That's what you're concerned about?" Johnny asked.

Kendall drank and shrugged. Maybe his mind was gone.

"I grew up there but haven't lived there in a long time. It sort of pops up when I hear other Australians or watch movies with Aussies in them," Lyman answered with a bit of a smile. "I'm going to get the cutters." Lyman stepped away, and Kendall sat with Johnny, drinking more from the bottle.

"Why would you think I did this to you?" Johnny whispered.

Kendall swallowed and shook his head slightly. "My thoughts are jumbled."

The door on his side of the car opened, and Kendall saw Lyman holding a big set of bolt cutters. He snipped the chain between his left wrist and the cuff on the steering wheel. Then Kendall shifted his hand, and Lyman cut the other chain. Kendall's arm protested when he tried to move it, but he took the bottle from Johnny and drank, emptying it.

"Do you feel better?" Johnny whispered.

"A little," Kendall answered. He ached all over.

"What do you remember?" Johnny asked him.

"Someone placing a cloth over my mouth, and then I woke up here. I don't know who it was except that it was a man," Kendall said and slowly shifted his gaze from Johnny to Lyman. They knew something. He could tell by the way they wouldn't meet his gaze for a few seconds. "What is it?"

Johnny looked at Lyman. "We'll tell you all about it later," Johnny promised. Lyman left, and Kendall turned to Johnny.

"Let's get you out of here," Johnny said as he unsnapped the seat belt and carefully retracted it. Then he backed out of the passenger door and a few moments later, leaned in through the opening created by the driver's door and gathered Kendall into his arms.

Kendall held on and stifled the groan that threatened. All his muscles ached, and moving or being jostled was painful. Johnny carefully carried him across the sandy ground to a huge SUV. Lyman opened the back door, and Johnny gently set him on the seat and then climbed in after him. Lyman closed the door but opened it again a few seconds later and handed Kendall another bottle of water. Johnny opened it for him, and Kendall drank some more. With each sip he felt a bit more alive. "Where are you taking me?"

"Back to the set," Lyman told him. "Your trailer is air-conditioned and you can get some rest there. We could try to get you to Las Vegas, though."

"Maybe we should take him to a hospital," Johnny said.

"No. Just let me drink and get something to eat. Then I need to sleep. That's all they'll have me do at the hospital anyway, and…." Kendall paused. "Lyman, tomorrow I want to film."

"What?" Johnny demanded. "No way in hell!"

Kendall ignored him. "We need to film the way I look. There's no way anyone could ever recreate this. Also, we have the movie wrong.

We've been concentrating on the heat, but over time I began to question everything, including my own sanity. By the end of the day yesterday, I could barely think."

"Okay." Lyman chuckled. "You're the expert."

"Are you crazy?" Johnny asked, holding him a bit tighter. "I nearly lost you. There is no fucking way in hell you are going anywhere near any cars in the desert ever again."

"So you do love me?" Kendall asked quietly. Johnny buried his head in Kendall's shoulder, and for only the second time in all the years he'd known his partner, Kendall saw Johnny cry. He closed his eyes and held Johnny in return, feeling his own tears well to the surface.

"Of course I love you," Johnny said. The engine started, and within seconds cool air began blowing inside the vehicle. Kendall drank some more of his water and held onto Johnny as Lyman put the SUV in gear.

The drive to where they'd been filming didn't take very long. Some of the crew milled around. "Where is everyone?"

"Out looking for you," Johnny said.

"What about the police?" Kendall asked, and Lyman scoffed.

"You left a note saying you were quitting and going back to New York," Lyman said. "The police used that as an excuse not to look for you. Out here, they really don't care much unless you're a casino owner."

"But I didn't leave a note," Kendall said.

"We know that," Johnny said lightly. "Your friend Juan didn't believe it either, and he called me." Johnny shifted and pulled Kendall's phone out of his pocket and handed it to him. "You forgot to get it from him before you left for the night. When he saw the note in your trailer he called me, and with this stalker thing going on, he and I put together what we thought happened. I caught the first plane out here, and Juan got Lyman involved." Johnny hugged him closer. "You have one hell of a friend there."

"He was like a pit bull," Lyman said as he pulled to a stop and put the vehicle in gear. "I bought the note, I'm sorry to say, and he read me the riot act—called me every name in the book and threatened to beat the crap out of me if I didn't listen." Lyman turned around and peered into the backseat. "I think I might have fired him, and he flipped me the bird, told me I was full of shit, and then said he didn't care if he was fired, he was going out to look for you. Then Johnny arrived a while later, and he laid into me like no one's business. We've been out looking for you ever since." Lyman turned off the engine and opened his door. Kendall's door opened a few seconds later.

Johnny got out and then reached for him. "I'm okay." Kendall slowly slid off the seat. He wobbled a bit and leaned on Johnny as he made his way toward his trailer. The crew gathered around as he gingerly put one foot in front of the other. One of the crew members applauded and soon all of them were clapping and cheering. Kendall smiled. "Thank you," he said a bit breathlessly as Johnny opened the trailer door and helped him climb inside.

Kendall collapsed into a chair and closed his eyes.

"Here, you need to keep drinking a little at a time," Johnny said.

Kendall took the bottle and drank.

"It's Gatorade. You need more than just the water."

Kendall drank. His stomach protested for a bit, but then settled down. Johnny had pulled all the curtains, and it was cool and relatively dark. "Let's get these clothes off, and I'll help you clean up. Then we'll get you in bed."

Kendall nodded and continued drinking. He was too tired to open his eyes. Johnny helped Kendall to his feet and removed his clothes, then shoved them in a plastic bag. Kendall practically fell back into the chair. Johnny ran some water, and Kendall didn't resist or help as Johnny washed him. "You're going to be fine now," Johnny told him as he cleaned him up, emptying the pan of water a few times and getting more. When Johnny was done, he took away the final pan of water, and when he returned he helped Kendall into underwear and a T-shirt, and then guided him back to the bed.

"Will you stay with me?" Kendall asked as he settled on the mattress. He sighed as he relaxed on the bedding. Such comfort was almost unreal after the last few days.

"I want you to drink a bit more before you go to sleep," Johnny said, and he helped Kendall sit up.

Kendall drank the rest of the Gatorade and then reclined back on the bedding. Johnny lay down next to him, and Kendall curled close. "I'm sorry," he mumbled over and over until he fell asleep.

Kendall woke alone. But he felt better, if really thirsty. He parted one of the curtains, squinting at the bright sunlight before letting the curtain fall back into place. After carefully getting out of bed, he stumbled to the refrigerator and grabbed another bottle of Gatorade, downed half of it in a few gulps and then took a break before drinking the rest of it. Then he opened the bathroom door and used the toilet with much relief. At least his body still seemed to be working. When he was done, he flushed and got a bottle of water from the refrigerator and then returned to bed. He drank most of the water before setting the bottle on the small counter beside the bed and closing his eyes once more.

When he woke again, there was no light coming through the windows, and Johnny was sitting at the small table in the front, his laptop open, typing away. Kendall groaned and slowly sat up.

"Are you thirsty?" Johnny asked, and after a few seconds he closed the lid of his laptop, stood up, and walked to where Kendall sat on the side of the bed. "Do you want something to eat?" Kendall nodded, and Johnny handed him a bottle of Gatorade.

Johnny hunted around in the cupboards until he found a toaster. He plugged it in and slid in two slices of bread. Then he got some butter out of the refrigerator. When the toast was done, he buttered it and added some cinnamon sugar—where that had come from Kendall had no idea, and he was too out of it to care. "Is that all I get?"

"Go ahead and make sure you can keep it down. Then I can make you something heartier," Johnny explained, and Kendall ate the toast in a matter of a few bites.

"That was good," he said, handing Johnny back the plate. Then he drank some more of the Gatorade before heading to the bathroom again. He took care of business and then joined Johnny at the table. "I'm still tired but feeling a lot better." His muscles didn't ache, and his mind seemed clear once he began to wake up. "So what is it you aren't telling me?"

Johnny shook his head. "It's nothing important, at least not right now." Johnny stood up. "Why don't you get dressed and I'll drive you to your hotel. We can get something to eat there, and then you can go to bed." Johnny moved to where Kendall was sitting, and he scooted over. "What matters is that you're all right."

"Johnny, do you know who did this to me?" Kendall asked.

Johnny shook his head. "No. I don't, and I don't think Lyman does either. I think he suspects someone, but he hasn't said who it is." Johnny put his arm around him, and Kendall leaned into the comfort of his embrace. "You had me so scared. I thought I'd lost you forever."

Kendall swallowed and moved away. "I didn't think you cared anymore," he told him softly.

"Of course I care," Johnny countered indignantly.

"Then why wouldn't you come with me?" Kendall asked. "I had this stalker who wouldn't leave me alone, and he kidnapped me and left me in a car in the middle of the desert to die. Is that what it took to get you out here? For me to nearly die?"

"You know that's not true," Johnny countered.

"Isn't it? If you'd been here, like you promised, none of this would have happened," Kendall said and squirmed to get away.

"Like I promised?" Johnny asked softly.

"Yeah. Don't you remember, when we moved into the brownstone and you took down the guy from downstairs? You promised you'd always be there to protect me, but you weren't," Kendall said. "I remembered all of it while I was locked in that damned car. I remembered a lot of things. Like how we used to really care for each other and how we were there for each other. Stuff that's gone now." Johnny stood up, and Kendall jumped out of bed and hurried to the back, pulling the curtain so Johnny couldn't see him, and conversely, so he couldn't see Johnny's face. He hadn't kept much in the trailer, but managed to find a pair of jeans and a shirt. "And I don't know if we can get that back."

Kendall yanked on the jeans and was about to pull on the T-shirt when Johnny tore at the curtain, ripping it down from its track. "That's not fair—how could you say that?" Johnny grabbed him by the shoulders and manhandled him forward, crashing their mouths together in a show of passion Kendall hadn't felt from him for a long time.

Kendall moaned softly and closed his eyes. "Johnny, do you—" The words were cut off when Johnny kissed him again, this time harder, and held him closer. Kendall held on as he returned the kiss, reveling in the taste of his lover like he'd just rediscovered a long-lost delicacy he thought he'd never be able to have again.

Then Johnny gentled the kiss and slowly pulled away. "Did that feel like anything was gone to you?" he asked as he held Kendall's gaze. "Things may have been a bit difficult with distance...."

"It started long before that," Kendall said.

"I know," Johnny told him. "But it ends now."

Kendall stepped back. "Okay, if that's what you want. You can go back to New York, and when I'm done with the film, I'll get my stuff from the apartment and find another place to live." Kendall turned around and continued getting dressed. "When we get to the hotel, I'm sure they can get you a room of your own."

Johnny placed his hands on Kendall's shoulders and spun him around. "What are you talking about?" he snapped.

Kendall shrugged away from him. "You said it ends now, so I figured you meant us."

"Is that what you want?" Johnny asked, and Kendall shrugged again. "Because that wasn't what I meant." Johnny moved closer. "What I meant was that I want the excitement back in our lives. I want us to be closer and to be passionate." Johnny leaned into him, his lips close to Kendall's ear. "I want to make you scream the way you used to. Remember? That poor neighbor pushed your boxes because you treated him to a screaming love fest every night. Do you remember that?"

Kendall swallowed and nodded. "Then you aren't having an affair?" Kendall asked, and Johnny's eyes widened.

"No," Johnny answered, but he looked a bit guilty. "Jeremy made his interest known, and"—Johnny turned away—"in a moment of weakness I kissed him. He wanted more, but...." Johnny didn't turn around. "But there was a problem—he wasn't you." Johnny finally turned back to him. "I've never been interested in anyone but you."

"Then why didn't you come with me? I missed you every day...."

Johnny sighed. "I should have. If I had it to do again, I'd come with you instead of being selfish. I should have been your partner and supported you the way you've always supported me." Johnny tugged him into his arms. "Do you remember? Because I certainly do." Kendall smiled and leaned his head against Johnny's shoulder. "I've had lots of time to think over the past few months."

"So have I," Kendall said, closing his eyes, the knots that had been in his stomach for months unwinding. He hadn't realized they'd been there until they were gone. "You make me happy, Johnny. You always have, and it hurt when I thought you might have found someone else."

"No way, sweetheart. I may be an old grump who spends way too much time in his own head, but you mean the world to me, and I can't imagine my life or my world without you in it." Johnny held him tighter, and they stood together quietly for a long while. "Have you noticed in my books that there's always a man, young and talented, who goes with his heart each and every time?"

"Yeah. I wondered about that."

"Those characters are you. Each and every one of them is you." Johnny paused. "I can't write a single book without you—it just doesn't work."

Kendall shook his head slightly. "You haven't been able to write?" The thought made a small part of him happy.

"Not one of my stories," Johnny said. "The entire time you were gone, I was working on something else, something different from anything I've ever written. It was almost done when I got the call about you and I rushed out here. See, the story I've been working on is for you. It's our story. I wrote it for you."

"You did?"

"Yeah. After I kissed Jeremy, I realized what was really important. When I finished the last book, nothing came. The ideas dried up, and then I started thinking and dreaming about us, about how we met and our first date."

"The carriage ride through the park," Kendall supplied, and Johnny nodded.

"Yeah, and then moving in together and getting our first apartment together. The story wasn't high adventure, but it was definitely one of love. After I started writing it, other ideas came, and I've had Jeremy researching for those, but nothing happened between us other than the kiss, which opened my eyes to what I had. Can you forgive me?"

"Honey," Kendall said, burying his face in Johnny's neck, inhaling the richest, warmest, most masculine scent on earth, "there's nothing to forgive." Then Kendall kissed Johnny hard.

"Should we go back to the hotel?" Johnny asked.

Kendall shook his head. "Are we safe here?" he asked.

"Yeah. Lyman has people here guarding the equipment, and right now there are two men, huge guys, outside the trailer making sure no one comes near you who shouldn't. Why?"

"Then let's find something to eat here and then go to bed," Kendall said.

"I don't want you to get too tired," Johnny cautioned, and Kendall kissed him, communicating everything he was feeling without saying a single word. When he broke the kiss, Johnny stared back at him and then took off for the door. The trailer rocked a bit as he left, and then the door slammed closed. Kendall had no idea what was going on, but about five minutes later, Johnny returned with a plate of sandwiches and more bottles of water. Johnny set the plate on the table and closed the door. "Are you hungry?"

Kendall sat at the table, and Johnny slid in next to him. He took a sandwich and began eating slowly. Johnny did the same. They shared looks and smiles while they ate. "I think I'm going to need my energy," Kendall said as he finished the first half of his sandwich and started on the second.

"Somehow I think we both are," Johnny said, and he moved a bit closer, wrapping an arm around his waist. "But you have to promise me no screaming, and if you get too tired, you have to promise to tell me. I nearly lost you once. I'm not going to go through that again." The care in Johnny's voice reassured Kendall more than anything Johnny had actually told him. As an actor, he knew sincerity and care when he heard it, especially from his Johnny. "Let me take care of this," Johnny said, motioning toward the debris on the table. "I want you to get undressed and climb into bed. I'll be there in just a few minutes." Johnny kissed him gently and then slid out of the bench seat. He began cleaning up, and Kendall slid out as well, moving past him to the bed in back.

Now that he'd eaten, the ordeal of the last few days really began to catch up with him. Kendall undressed and climbed beneath the covers, closing his eyes almost immediately. He felt Johnny join him a few minutes later.

"Sweetheart, you need to drink a bit more before you sleep," Johnny told him, and Kendall sat up without opening his eyes. He drank some water and then lay back down. Johnny chuckled softly, and Kendall didn't have the energy to ask what he found funny. The last thing he remembered was Johnny settling next to him, holding him tight as he fell asleep.

Almost instantly Kendall was back inside the car. He knew he shouldn't be there, but he was. This time the heat inside the car was even more intense. Kendall pulled on the handcuffs, trying to free himself so he could get out. In his dream, he managed to lower the window in an effort to let some of the heat escape, but more just poured in. He had nowhere to go and he prepared to die. But then night fell and the heat vanished. He breathed a sigh of relief, and then the sun rose again and the heat was back. Over and over, this cycle repeated until Kendall couldn't stand it any longer. "Help me" was all he could seem to mutter.

"Shhh," he heard someone say, and Kendall opened his eyes. "You're okay. You're here with me and not in the car."

"Johnny?" Kendall asked and blinked a few times.

"It's me, I'm here," Johnny told him gently and soothed him back down on the bed. "You're fine, and no one is ever going to be able to do something like that to you again." Johnny held Kendall close. "You're in bed with me and there's no car."

"I know," Kendall said with a relieved sigh. His heart was still pounding as Johnny slid his hand under Kendall's T-shirt and rubbed small circles on his belly.

"Lie back down and close your eyes," Johnny whispered. "You're just fine. I have you, and there's nothing to worry about." Kendall did as Johnny said, hoping he wouldn't end up back in that car every time he closed his eyes. "It'll fade. You know it will. The memories, the experience, it will fade."

"What if it doesn't?" Kendall asked without opening his eyes.

"You're strong, and what happened to you was hurtful and cruel, but it will fade with time," Johnny said calmly. Kendall wasn't so sure. "You need to trust me," Johnny told him, and then Kendall felt Johnny's weight shift as he climbed on top of him. Johnny kissed him gently, softly, but with heat, passion, and love that went straight to Kendall's soul, rekindling the care and rebuilding the deep connection they'd always had. It was that connection he'd always counted on, and the one he'd feared might be gone forever, but with a kiss and a reassuring touch, Johnny brought it roaring back.

Kendall moaned and almost desperately clutched Johnny to him. They broke their kiss only long enough for Johnny to tug off Kendall's T-shirt and to get off what he was wearing. Kendall sighed softly when Johnny's skin pressed to his. He needed that intimacy so badly. "Johnny," Kendall moaned, very near tears. He'd missed him so much. Kendall placed his hands on Johnny's cheeks, stilling him. "What happened to us? I've missed you so much, and not just since I've been here. I think I've missed you for months, maybe years. I was always so busy, and then you got busy too, and we never seemed to be together much, and…."

"Hey, I said all that stops and I meant it. We're going to change our schedules, and that means if you're shooting a movie, then I'll be out here, staying with you. I'll work when you're working, and when you're not, we'll spend our time together. If you're working in New York, then I'll be there too. I thought I couldn't write if I wasn't in our home in New York, but I was wrong. I can't write if I'm not home with *you*. That's where I was wrong—it wasn't the place that gave me inspiration—it was you." Johnny kissed him hard, nibbling a bit on his lower lip. Johnny slid his hands down Kendall's side and continued lower over his hips, pushing his underwear down.

"I…," Kendall whined, and he almost immediately forgot what he wanted to say.

"I know. It's been far too long," Johnny said, and Kendall gasped when Johnny grabbed him, wrapping his cock in the warmth of his hand and talented fingers. "It should never be so long again." Johnny stroked slowly, and Kendall clamped his eyes shut, reveling in a sensation he'd almost considered lost to him.

Johnny took off the last of his clothes, and then they were skin to skin, warmth to warmth. Kendall moaned and writhed under Johnny's expert ministrations. He tried to reciprocate, but Johnny held him still, kissing and touching him all over. "I need to be sure you're in one piece."

"Does that mean licking me everywhere?" Kendall asked playfully.

"Yup," Johnny reassured him. "I need to be sure you aren't hurt in any way, and that means verifying that you still taste right." Johnny licked and kissed his way down Kendall's neck. "Yes, you still taste sweet and rich there. But how about here?"

Johnny licked one of Kendall's nipples, and he groaned softly. "Yup, still the same, still mine." Johnny stroked lightly down Kendall's chest, kissing a trail behind his hand. "Everything's okay so far." Johnny was obviously loving this, and so was Kendall. Johnny mumbled something as he swirled his tongue in Kendall's belly button, and when Johnny kept going, Kendall stilled, silently pleading for Johnny not to stop. His mind filled with supplications and entreaties. "I know what you want," Johnny said.

Kendall whined softly, waiting, tingling where Johnny touched him, his cock jumping in anticipation. Finally, Johnny tilted his head and licked slowly up his length. "Oh God," Kendall moaned softly as his legs throbbed against the bedding. He lolled his head back as his entire body zinged with passionate energy.

"Yes, you're still the same as I remembered," Johnny told him, and Kendall was about to make a smart quip when Johnny sucked him into his mouth and he forgot about everything except the way Johnny felt around him.

"Jesus," Kendall swore softly, and Johnny hummed as he sucked and licked him. It had been so long and Kendall was already so keyed up, he nearly lost it completely. "Johnny," Kendall moaned, closing his eyes and going with the feeling. "I missed you so much."

Johnny stopped, then his lips slipped away, and Kendall's cock bounced against his belly. "I missed you too," Johnny told him, and then he was there, kissing and pressing Kendall against the mattress. "The day I met you, I knew you were someone special and someone I wanted in my life forever. I wanted to show you how special I thought you were, and I'm sorry I lost sight of that."

"We lost sight of that," Kendall corrected and then guided Johnny back into a kiss. Kendall wrapped his legs around Johnny's waist, communicating exactly what he wanted, what he needed.

"I don't have... stuff," Johnny said. "And I will not hurt you." Johnny kissed him again and then shifted on the bed, surrounding Kendall once again in his wet heat. Johnny bobbed his head, and Kendall thrust upward, needing his lover so badly he could hardly think straight. Within moments, pressure built inside. Kendall gasped a warning, but Johnny continued, pulling him over the edge until he soared into space, gliding and floating, before settling in Johnny's arms.

Kendall opened his eyes, and Johnny grinned at him. He barely noticed Johnny shifting on the mattress. "Johnny, I...," Kendall began as he attempted to move, but Johnny held him still.

"Relax. Everything is fine. Just go to sleep, and I'll be here when you wake up," Johnny soothed.

"But...," Kendall protested, not understanding.

"I'm fine. Just close your eyes and think happy, relaxing thoughts," Johnny said as he stroked his forehead. Kendall's eyelids became heavy, and his worries and cares slipped away as sleep, a deep contented sleep, came over him. Johnny was here and he would protect him. That was all that mattered for now.

CHAPTER
NINE

KENDALL woke to a tapping that was definitely out of place with his dream. He opened his eyes and looked around, expecting to be back in that damned car, but he was in the trailer with Johnny asleep next to him. Kendall carefully got up and pulled on a pair of pants. He yawned as he shuffled to the door. Juan's smiling face greeted him.

"They're ready for you in wardrobe," Juan said.

"Shit," Kendall swore softly. "I'll be right there." He held the door open, and Juan climbed inside. "Please make some coffee," Kendall mumbled as he shuffled to the back and carefully closed the clothespin-repaired curtain. He pulled on a shirt and shoved his feet into a pair of tennis shoes. He heard Juan moving around and then smelled coffee.

"What's going on?" Johnny mumbled.

"It's all right. Go back to sleep. I need to get to wardrobe," Kendall whispered and kissed Johnny on the cheek. Then he cleaned up quickly and used the facilities before joining Juan, who had the coffee made and in a travel mug. Juan practically shooed him out of the trailer. Once he was outside, Kendall realized it wasn't yet light. "What time is it?"

"Just after five," Juan said, escorting Kendall to the wardrobe trailer at one end of the encampment.

"Are you sure you're up for this?" Lyman asked as he strode up beside him. "No one will blame you if you want to wait."

Kendall paused outside the trailer. "Everything inside me says that if we don't do this now, it'll take a bulldozer to get me inside a car again."

"Okay," Lyman agreed. "You look like hell, by the way." Lyman studied him in the light that shone out of the trailer. "It's absolutely perfect for the scenes."

"Thank you, I think," Kendall said, and Lyman chuckled softly.

"We're all glad you're back and doing okay," Lyman said and then poked his head inside the trailer. "Make sure he drinks lots of water," he told the wardrobe mistress and then looked at Juan before striding off. Kendall climbed inside, and Juan took his mug.

"Hey," Kendall said.

"You heard the boss. I'll bring you some water, but no coffee. It makes you pee." Juan hurried away, and damned if Kendall didn't see him sipping his coffee.

"Come on, let's get you in these clothes," Diane, an older lady, tough as nails on the surface, but sweet once Kendall got to know her, told him gruffly. Kendall stripped down, and she handed him the soiled shirt and pants he needed for the scene.

"You need to create a stain around the crotch," Kendall instructed, and she raised her eyebrows. "Trust me, after a day or two in that car, there will definitely be a stain, if you get my drift." Diane raised her eyebrows and looked as if she were about to ask a question, but she stopped herself and found a spray bottle. She added a bit of yellow to the water and sprayed it on the pants. The moisture dried instantly. "Perfect. Now the other thing we need is a bit of white where sweat has repeatedly dried. Mild salt stains and things like that."

She worked her magic, and Kendall put on the clothes, very pleased it was fake dirt rather than the real clothes he'd worn in the car. He never wanted to see those again as long as he lived. Once Diane pronounced him ready, Kendall thanked her and headed over to makeup.

"Good God," Denny said dramatically as he sat in the chair. "I'm never going to make you look right."

"Don't. Make me look worse," Kendall said. "I should look emaciated and sallow."

"Even more than you do now?" Denny asked, and Kendall nodded.

"Cracked lips and a nose that looks like I've had a cold for a week, because it felt like it when I was in the car. Also, a bit of dried blood under my nose and redness around the eyes. They felt like sandpaper after a day or so." Kendall was quiet while Denny worked, and once they were both satisfied, he placed his hands on the table. "Make them look as bad as my face."

Denny worked and Kendall tried not to think about what he was about to do. He had to get through these scenes now or he would never be able to do them. Once Denny was done, Kendall thanked him and left the trailer, then headed toward the set. Everyone stopped to look, and Juan handed him a bottle of water with a straw. Kendall drank what he could and got into position.

"Let's do this, Lyman," Kendall said. He didn't have much in him. He took another drink of water and sat in the car seat, allowing himself to be handcuffed. He tamped down the panic that threatened to rise from inside him and took a deep breath.

Then everyone moved away from him, and Kendall peered out at the assembled crew just as the sun began to rise. "Quiet," someone yelled, and Kendall began to shake and pull on the cuffs. He had to get the fuck out of there.

Johnny's voice broke the silence. "It's okay, Kendall, I'm right here, and you're going to be okay."

Kendall stilled and closed his eyes like he'd just dozed off. Lyman said, "Action," and Kendall played the scene.

"Okay, use it," Lyman said eventually. Kendall had continued long after the script had ended, and no one had made a sound. In his mind, he let himself go back to his car. Despair and hopelessness reigned inside him as he tried to figure out who had done this to him. The hours of doubt as hope dwindled away came back to him, and he used it… all of it. "Can you continue?" Lyman asked as he walked to where Kendall sat with Johnny right behind him.

"Yeah, but I'm starting to sweat," Kendall said. "At this point, I shouldn't be able to sweat. There wasn't enough moisture in my body."

"Get something over here to cool him off," Lyman said, and people scurried around. One of the windows was lowered and a portable air conditioner placed through it. They were working with a whole car with the one side removed. A tarp was thrown over the opening and almost immediately, the heat began to dissipate. The passenger door opened, and Johnny sat down next to him and shut the door.

"How are you doing?" Johnny asked as he took Kendall's hand. "Drink this," he added, thrusting a bottle into Kendall's hand.

"I'm fine," Kendall lied. He wasn't fine. He was barely holding on, but he knew he had to get this done.

"No, you're not. I can tell, so don't try to lie to me. You can tell them whatever you like, but I know different. That's why I'm here, and I'll be out here all day just behind the camera. Know that and remember this isn't real."

Kendall shifted in the seat. "I know it's not real, but it has to look and feel real. When they watch this, the viewer has to think they're here with me. This is hard as hell, and it scares the shit out of me, but that's why I have to do it now. You were right last night. It will fade and mute. But right now I need everything to be sharp."

"Five minutes," someone called, and Johnny got out and closed the door.

"Remember I'm just out here," Johnny said through the tarp, and Kendall breathed deeply and did his best to relax while others worked around him.

"It's going to be a few more minutes," Lyman said, his voice drifting through the blue plastic. "I need the light just a bit higher in the sky. We got the sunrise, now I need midday. We can simulate some of it with camera angle, but it needs to be a little higher."

"It's okay, Lyman. Do what you need to," Kendall said and turned his head away as the sun shone brightly through the windshield. After a few more minutes, they removed the tarp and the air conditioner, and Kendall once again descended into character.

They filmed for much of the day, and Kendall rarely got out of the car. He added all the discomfort and pain that crept into his body into his performance, stretching his muscles and trying to keep his shackled arms from cramping. Lyman gave very little direction, and after every take simply said, "Use it." The only time they reshot was when a breeze blew Kendall's clothes, making them move in what was supposed to be a closed car.

"That's it for the day," Lyman called eventually.

"Just a second," Kendall said, getting out of the car slowly, wincing in pain before walking to Lyman. "There's another scene you need to film," he explained, and Lyman's mouth fell open, but he nodded.

"Okay, we have one more short scene after the sun goes down," Lyman said. "Be back here in an hour and leave all the equipment right where it is."

Kendall walked back toward his trailer and climbed inside without saying a word. Johnny followed right behind him and immediately held him once the door had closed.

"Don't," Kendall said. "Not right now." Johnny looked hurt. "I need to stay in character until this next scene is done. Then I'll need all the comfort you can give me."

"Okay," Johnny said, and he grabbed his laptop and left him alone.

The light through the windows faded, and Kendall was called back to the set.

"We did what you wanted," Lyman said. "I'm giving you leeway here."

"Trust me. You're going to want this," Kendall said. The driver's door had been put back on the car, and Kendall got inside. They cuffed him to the steering wheel again and fogged up the windows. Lyman called for action, and Kendall licked the areas of the windows he could reach. Then he licked the little bit of the windshield he could get to before flopping back into the seat in total exhaustion that didn't have to be faked. He didn't hear the call to end filming. He only knew it was over when the car door opened.

Johnny was there, and Kendall waited until the cuffs had been removed before unfastening the seat belt. Kendall stepped out of the car and nearly tumbled to the ground. Before he could catch himself, Johnny lifted him into his arms and carried him off the set.

"Johnny, I'm fine. Put me down." Johnny complied reluctantly. "I need to check with Lyman and make sure we're done for the day, then you can drive me back to the hotel and go as caveman as you like."

Kendall stretched his muscles and found Lyman and Guy talking together about the shots they'd gotten. "Do you need me anymore this evening?"

"No," Lyman said softly. "We'll review what we have, and hopefully in the next few days, we can fill in any shots we need and get the hell out of here. The only scene we need to film is the rescue scene, and I have some changes I want to discuss with you in the morning." Lyman went back to talking to Guy, and Kendall turned back toward where Johnny was waiting.

He'd taken a few steps when he swore he could almost feel someone staring holes in him. His spine prickled and he turned around, looking over the entire crew, but no one seemed to be watching him. He turned back around and walked to where Johnny waited by the car. "I need to get out of these clothes and then we can go. Give me ten minutes."

Johnny nodded, and Kendall hurried to the wardrobe trailer. He changed and then headed to makeup to have the heavier stuff removed. Finally, he was back at the car with Johnny, and they headed away from the set toward the lights of Las Vegas and the comfort of the hotel room he hadn't seen in days.

Kendall fell asleep during the trip and woke with the lights of Vegas shining in his eyes. "I'm at the—" Kendall began, but Johnny drove by the turnoff to his hotel.

"I have all your things in the trunk. I had Juan drive in and get them," Johnny said as he continued driving. He then turned into the drive for the Bellagio. "There are things we still need to talk about, but no one has been able to figure out who kidnapped you, so there's no way you're going back to that hellhole they put you up in." Johnny drove beneath the portico to the valet parking. "I made a reservation here under my name."

Johnny stopped the car, got out, and told one of the attendants his name, and Kendall didn't quite know what happened from there. He and Johnny were escorted through the casino to the desk, where they were checked in and then escorted up to their huge room. "I don't understand," Kendall said, looking around the luxurious space once the escort left and their bags were brought in.

"I've been making money on my books hand over fist for years, and we've always lived simply, but I figured it was time I spent some of that money," Johnny told him and pulled the curtains aside. The fountains danced below them, and the Las Vegas Strip stretched in both directions. "You deserve this. To be treated like this," Johnny said.

Kendall shook his head and moved away from the windows. "First thing, the view is gorgeous, but I don't need that." He moved closer to Johnny. "All I really need is you. We live simply because it fits who we are."

Johnny sighed. "It does, but you know that as soon as your movie is released, those days will be over. There isn't enough security at our apartment in New York, and when you're here, you're going to need protection. We've been lucky up till now and have been able to remain under the radar. That won't continue for much longer." Johnny wrapped his arms around him, and they stood gazing out the windows.

"So what do you want to do?" Kendall whispered.

"I'm not sure. Lyman and I talked a lot while you were sleeping yesterday. He'd like to turn one of my books into a movie. It seems he's a huge fan and said he'd maintain the character and flavor of the book. He also wants me to help write the script and act as associate producer."

"Are you going to do it?"

Johnny shrugged. "That depends on you." Johnny held him tighter. "I'm not going to be out here working on some movie while you're doing a show in New York any more than I'm going to allow you to be out here making a movie again while I stay in New York to write."

"I want to go back to the theater. I like movies, but I love the stage," Kendall said.

"Then I'll tell Lyman no deal."

"Or you could tell him the writing team will be based in New York," Kendall suggested and turned in Johnny's arms. "Enough talk for now. I want to get dinner, maybe spend a few minutes in the casino, and then come up here and have loud screaming fun that will scare the straight people."

Johnny checked his watch. "We have a reservation for dinner in half an hour." Kendall stared. "I called while you were asleep." Kendall yawned, and Johnny picked up the phone. "How about room service, no casino, and we see about the screaming."

Kendall nodded slowly. "The room service is fine, and I can do without the casino," he agreed. After pausing dramatically, he promised, "But there will be screaming," and then he headed toward the bathroom while Johnny took care of the arrangements. He started the water and stepped beneath a shower with jets coming from every direction. By the time he was done, it felt like he'd had a massage. Johnny had placed light sweatpants and a T-shirt on the counter. Kendall changed into them and left the bathroom. Johnny waited for him on the sofa, and he sat next to him, relaxing as they watched television while waiting for their dinner.

Johnny answered the knock on the door, and the waiter wheeled a cart into the room. Johnny tipped him, and the waiter left, leaving them alone once again. They ate in front of the television without much conversation. Kendall was tired, and Johnny seemed deep in contemplation.

"What is it?" Kendall asked once he'd eaten all he wanted.

"I told you they don't know who put you in the car," Johnny said, and Kendall nodded. "Well, it's definitely someone in the film crew." Kendall agreed. "They left a note that you were quitting and going back to New York."

"You told me that already," Kendall said, and Johnny seemed a bit scattered.

"I did? Well, it's the rest of the note that was so disturbing. It said you weren't happy, and no one was paying enough attention to you.

The note said you were going back to New York, where you could be the center of attention. It was a little disjointed."

"Whoever wrote the note was probably projecting their emotions onto me," Kendall said thoughtfully. "The whole stalker thing had me pretty scared, but…." Kendall shivered. "The guy's a real nutcase."

"And a dangerous nutcase," Johnny said. "As soon as this movie's over, we're heading back to New York where I can keep you safe."

"What are you going to do? Hire bodyguards?" Kendall asked.

"I don't know. But I do know we're not staying here until I know you're safe." Johnny moved closer and held Kendall tighter. "Are you ready for bed? I've told hotel security about your problem, and they've put us on a secured floor. Not just anyone can get off the elevator at this floor. I've also been assured that security will be making regular rounds all night long."

Kendall nodded slowly and stood up. "What did I do to deserve this?" he asked. He slipped out of his clothes and climbed under the covers. "I've been trying to figure out what I did to make someone want me dead. I've been nice and respectful to everyone. Why does someone hate me so much?"

Johnny joined him in bed and turned out the light. He then got up and pulled the draperies closed before returning. "I don't think whoever is doing this hates you. I think they're in love with you, and when you didn't return those feelings, they got more and more desperate."

Kendall didn't reply right away. "But it was so creepy," he said.

"Yeah. But what you saw as creepy, they probably thought was romantic. You were given flowers, right? And at first you thought they were from me, so you were happy to get them." Johnny held him, and Kendall rested his head on Johnny's shoulder. "They probably thought you were pleased with the flowers and that made them bolder."

"This sounds like a subplot for one of your books," Kendall said and then yawned.

"It could be," Johnny admitted. "Once you figured out the flowers weren't from me, you started rejecting the gifts, and they got more insistent."

"Hence breaking into my car and coming to the apartment," Kendall said. "And when that didn't work, they destroyed my dressing room."

"Frustration and violence," Johnny added. "But that still didn't get them what they wanted, and by then they couldn't come forward or otherwise you'd know and they'd be in trouble. And by then security had been alerted and more was added to the location shoot, so they waited until they could get you alone." Johnny swallowed and held him closer while Kendall wrapped his arms around Johnny's waist. "Why were you apologizing so much the other day?"

Kendall lifted his gaze to Johnny's. "When I was in the car, I blamed you. I actually thought you might have done everything. I wasn't thinking clearly and I blamed you for not coming out here with me to keep me safe. I might have hallucinated things. I really don't know." Kendall tried not to think about it too much. "I shouldn't have doubted you."

"And I shouldn't have stayed away," Johnny whispered and slowly shifted until he was on top, his reassuring weight and warmth pressing Kendall into the soft, luxurious bedding. "I never should have let you go, even temporarily." Johnny kissed him, and instantly Kendall's passion rose, his cock throbbing as he shimmied his hips slightly to get a bit of friction from Johnny's hip. Johnny stroked Kendall's cheek and then kissed him. "You're everything to me," Johnny whispered.

"So are you," Kendall said, and then their kisses cut off further conversation. Their bodies remembered and knew each other deep down. Johnny had set his kit near the bed when he unpacked, and in the darkness Kendall heard a soft snick. He rolled over, thinking it had been way too long since he and Johnny had been together like this.

Johnny swirled his slick fingers around Kendall's opening, teasing his skin. He added more slick, and Kendall groaned long and low when Johnny breached him with a long, slender finger.

"Been too long," Kendall moaned.

"Yes," Johnny hissed and slowly moved his finger in and out. Then he added another, the burn exquisite and unexpected. Kendall breathed shallow and fast, his heart thundering in his ears as he anticipated what would happen next.

Kendall stretched out, parting his legs wide, silently issuing his invitation. "Make me yours, Johnny, like I was before."

Johnny slowly stroked down his back. "You were always mine, and you're not broken," Johnny said, and Kendall felt him press for entrance. Kendall pushed back, and Johnny eased inside him. "You're perfect and stronger than anyone I know." Johnny sank deeper and deeper, pulled out a bit, and then went deeper still, joining them together. "I love you," Johnny whispered when he pressed his hips to Kendall's butt. He waited for a minute and then slowly began to move. Kendall ground his hips against the bedding, moaning softly with each loving thrust.

Johnny withdrew, and Kendall rolled onto his back and lifted his legs, and Johnny sank back into him. Their bodies pressed together, gazes locked in the dim light, they made love, soul-deep love that rekindled the banked flames of their relationship. Kendall had always needed Johnny, but being with him, connected to him, he realized how much he'd been missing, how much they'd both been missing.

"How did we let this happen?" Kendall whispered, arching his back as Johnny drove into him, rubbing the spot that damned near sent him into orbit.

Johnny paused. "You want to talk now?"

Kendall pressed back against him. "No. Fuck now, talk later," Kendall said, and Johnny moved again. Groans changed to moans, which morphed to cries and turned into yells that could probably be heard for miles, but Kendall didn't care any more than he could stop it. Johnny loved him, and he went with it, each scream a cry of joy from the depths of his soul. "Johnny, I can't take much more," Kendall moaned, arching his back, desperate for more.

"Yes, you can, and you will," Johnny gritted between his teeth as he snapped his hips like a madman. "You're mine," he said.

"And you're mine," Kendall replied. Johnny stroked him hard and firm, just the way he liked. Kendall gasped for air as his release built and built. He wouldn't have been surprised if he exploded, but instead his release bloomed like a tropical flower, showy, full, and bright in the jungle sunlight. Kendall groaned and floated as Johnny came deep inside him. His lover, his friend, his world, everything he had and wanted wrapped into one package that was honestly and truly his. There was nothing in the entire world that meant more or was better than his Johnny. Nothing. "Love you," Kendall whispered, and Johnny kissed him.

"Love you too," he said, and then all was still and it was just the two of them. Kendall didn't remember Johnny cleaning them up or him tucking him in, but Johnny must have because Kendall was soon warm and comfortable, with Johnny holding him as he sank into a restful sleep.

TWO very busy days later, Lyman wrapped up shooting, and everyone packed up their gear to head back to the city. They checked out of their hotel, and Kendall said good-bye to Juan, Guy, Lyman, and the crew who'd helped him through the shooting process. Lyman and Johnny seemed to have hit it off, with the director showing Johnny how movies were made. It seemed he was really interested in turning Johnny's stories into films.

"We'll probably need you to come out in a few weeks to make some sound edits, and I'd like it if you were able to come and see the first draft edit. You have an eye for the theatrical that would really help," Lyman said to Kendall. "I truly hope we get to work together again."

"Same here," Kendall said, and they shook hands. Once the good-byes had been said, they got into the car, and Johnny drove them back toward the city.

"What do you have to do before we can go home?" Johnny asked as they rode.

"Make sure the insurance company has everything set for the car, empty out the few things in the apartment, and get plane tickets." Kendall sat back and closed his eyes, basking in the cool air that blew from the vents. "I'll never be able to sit in a car and not think about what happened."

"I know," Johnny said gently. "If I get my hands on whoever did that to you...."

"If we find out, we'll call the police, and they'll take care of everything," Kendall said, and he saw some of Johnny's anger slip away. Johnny rested his hand on Kendall's leg.

He had finally put his foot down and made Lyman call the police. They'd explained everything that had happened and showed the investigators the car. Of course, the police were pissed as hell, but when Lyman explained what had happened when they'd reported the missing person, and that they had gotten no support, the police had changed their tune pretty quickly. Of course, there wasn't much for them to find by that point, but at least a report had been made, and that was about all Kendall cared about for right now. At least he'd gotten out alive. He was with Johnny, and they were on their way home.

CHAPTER
TEN

IT TOOK them three days to wrap everything up, and then he and Johnny were on a plane back to New York. It touched down at LaGuardia, and after getting their luggage, Johnny hailed a cab and they rode to their building. As they crossed the bridge into Manhattan, Kendall sighed deeply as tension he'd been holding for days seemed to slip away. "I never thought seeing New York could be relaxing."

Johnny chuckled. "It's home." Kendall moved closer and leaned against Johnny as they rode through Manhattan traffic to their building. Johnny paid the driver, and Kendall hauled bags up the stairs and inside. He returned for another load, and together they got the last of the bags into the apartment. The place was stuffy, and Kendall threw open the windows and let the breeze and city air flow into the room. Kendall flopped down on the sofa and immediately put his feet up while Johnny bustled to start getting things put away.

"That can wait a few minutes," Kendall said. "Come sit with me."

"I will, but I have something for you," Johnny said as he carried some of the bags into the other room. He returned with a large envelope and handed it to Kendall. "This is for you. I've called it *Johnny Loves Kendall*—not very original, I'm afraid." Kendall opened the envelope and slowly turned the pages. Johnny had had it bound together for him. "I was planning to tell you about it when you got home, but... well, things happened."

Kendall read the dedication out loud. "'To Kendall, the real Kendall—I love you forever and always.' That's very sweet, but couldn't you have said something like, 'To Kendall, the super stud of the entire world. I love you more than anything. You're my amazingly hot superhero', or something like that?" Kendall dodged a pillow, and then Johnny leaped onto the sofa, tickling his ribs until Kendall squealed like a girl and squirmed so hard he nearly fell onto the floor along with the manuscript.

"I should, huh," Johnny teased as he continued tickling, and Kendall curled up to try to block potential access to his ticklish parts. "Oh super stud of the entire world."

"So you agree," Kendall said, and Johnny eased up on the tickling. "I'll take that as a no on the dedication change," Kendall said as he picked the manuscript off the floor, then sat back up.

"You're such a goof," Johnny said as he sat down next to him. "I fictionalized the story, but it's based on our romance." Johnny grinned, and Kendall set the manuscript on the table.

"I do love you, and I love that you wrote a story about us. Are you going to have it published?" Kendall asked.

"I don't know. I mean, it's rather personal. I did change details and add some things to make the story readable. I also added bits of drama and a conflict that didn't exist in our relationship for tension and to move the story along. But it's still our story, and I didn't want to do anything until you read it and agreed."

"Okay," Kendall said. He picked up the manuscript and then leaned against Johnny. He opened the pages and began to read.

"What's this?" Johnny asked, shifting slightly.

"You're my comfy reading pillow," Kendall said, and he made a show of "adjusting" Johnny so he'd be more comfortable.

"How about if I bring you a pillow," Johnny offered. "I have another story that's been pushing its way forward, and I need to get started on it." Kendall sat up, and Johnny returned with a pillow. Kendall got comfortable, and soon he heard Johnny typing away at the table.

He stopped reading to eat and get a drink of water. Otherwise he read the book all the way through. It wasn't as long as one of Johnny's adventure stories, but it was definitely a page-turner. "Am I as hot as you describe the Kendall in the book?" he asked as he set the completed manuscript on the table.

"Yes. You always were. I can remember waiting outside that theater that first night. I wasn't sure which way you'd come out, and I tried to keep an eye on all the possible exits. I thought you were so incredibly beautiful and spent the entire time I waited wondering what you saw in me. I told myself a million times I was being a fool, but then you came out and smiled at me. I was a goner from that moment on. You were this talented actor, and I was just a poor graduate student, yet you seemed to like me, and...."

"Like you?" Kendall stood up and walked to where Johnny sat in front of his computer. Leaning over Johnny's shoulders, he slid his hands down his chest and belly. "You were sweet and kind. You didn't seem as interested in the fact that I was a performer as much as you were interested in me, the person." Kendall kissed Johnny's cheek and then nibbled lightly on his ear. "If you want the truth, you had me at the buggy ride through the park in the snow. And yes, I want you to publish the story. I think it's beautiful."

"Okay, I'll let Elizabeth know to accept the offer from Penguin," Johnny said.

"You already have an offer?" Kendall confirmed.

"Yup, but I didn't want to accept until you read it. I'll use a pen name for this one, but I don't plan to keep it a secret. I just don't want to mislead my regular readers. Because if I use my real name, they're going to pick it up and wonder why Johnny isn't dodging a hail of bullets and Kendall doesn't have ninja powers." Johnny smiled. "I'm very pleased with it," he said as he turned around and tugged Kendall to him.

"I love it," Kendall said softly, and they kissed gently, languidly.

"Do you want to finish unpacking while I run to the store and find something for us to eat?" Johnny asked. Kendall agreed, and Johnny grabbed his keys and left the apartment, but only after snagging another kiss.

Kendall carried the last of the bags into the bedroom and began the unpacking. His phone rang just after he started, and he almost let it go to voice mail, but peeked at the display and grabbed it just before it shifted. "Hey, Sal," he said brightly. "What have you got for me?"

"Your pick of shows, if you want them," Sal told him. "It seems being gone for a few months has increased your value."

"Go ahead and send the offers over, but I'm not sure what I want to do right now. The filming was grueling. More than any show I've ever done, and there was a bit of an incident." He told Sal what happened in the desert.

"Was it that bad?" Sal asked.

"I'm not being dramatic. I wouldn't have made it through another day if Johnny and Lyman hadn't rescued me. So yeah, it was that bad. No one ever figured out who the stalker was, but afterwards the gifts stopped, and I'm very grateful. I hope whoever it was stays the hell away from me." Kendall shivered at the thought and sat down on the edge of the bed. Then he stood up and checked that the doors were locked. He wished Johnny were there.

"Okay, I'll send the offers over," Sal said a bit softly. "I'll talk to you real soon."

"Don't you dare hang up until Johnny gets home," Kendall said, nearly panicking. He hadn't spent much time alone since the incident. He hadn't realized it, but Johnny had been there almost constantly.

"Kendall, of course I'll stay on the line," Sal said, and he heard papers shuffling in the background. "Is it still that difficult?" Sal asked in this rather fatherly way he had sometimes.

"Sal," Kendall whispered, beginning to shake like a leaf, "I was knocked out and handcuffed inside a car in the desert. It took more than two days for them to find me." Kendall gasped for breath, and it took a concerted effort on his part to keep the panic from completely taking over. "You read the script they sent me. That's almost exactly what happened. I thought I was going to go out of my mind. In fact, I probably did." Kendall took a deep breath and listened for Johnny. God, Kendall hoped he got back soon. "When they found me I could barely walk, and Johnny had to carry me to the truck." Then the tears came, and Kendall couldn't stop them. "Sal, I wet myself, and worse, I think." He tried to stop crying, but all that came out were gasps and sniffles. "I licked the car windows so I could get water. That's all I had for two days." Kendall gasped and finally caught a breath. "I licked the windows, Sal!"

"It's okay, my boy," Sal said gently. "It's over, and you're home with Johnny. Nothing is going to happen here."

"I know that. I know I'm fine and that I'm safe. But it doesn't feel like it. I wake up almost every night thinking I'm back in that damned car. Sometimes it's just for a few seconds, but it happens night after night." Kendall took a deep breath, then let it out very slowly before taking another. He had to calm down. "To make matters worse, after all that, I had to get back into the fucking movie car and shoot almost identical scenes. I don't know how I did it."

"You did it because you're strong and because you're damned good at what you do," Sal told him calmly, and Kendall felt some of that calm come through to him. "I've been around actors all my life. My folks were in vaudeville and then they ran a small theater once they retired. I know actors, and you got through it because you had to and because you compartmentalized what happened and what you needed to do. It's what we do to keep ourselves sane when performing difficult parts. Now that you're home, those compartments are breaking down, and believe it or not, that's a good thing. It means you're dealing with it."

"I know," Kendall said. He just hated that it was happening now and Johnny wasn't here to help him. "They don't know who did that to me, Sal. The police weren't helpful when I went missing, and when they found me, Johnny and Lyman were just interested in getting me back safe."

"They didn't call the police?" Sal asked, horrified.

"We did, but by then there wasn't much for them to find," Kendall explained. "So this freak is still out there somewhere." And he was now afraid to be alone.

"It's going to be all right," Sal said gently. "It isn't likely they'll go to New York, but I can help you with security if you need it. I've helped arrange this sort of thing before. You remember that incident with Hugh Jackman a few years ago...." Sal didn't need to go into details. "I helped with that situation."

Members of the cast were accepting donations for Equity Fights AIDS, and Kendall dropped a bill into one of the buckets.

"Kendall?" one of the nearby ladies asked tentatively, and when he turned, a woman he knew named Cherie practically leaped into his arms. "You're back. I heard you made a movie," she said.

"Yes. I got back a few days ago," he told her. "Cherie, this is Johnny. Cherie and I were in the chorus together ages ago." He shifted his gaze back to her. "I recognized that kick of yours on stage. You were great," he said, and she thanked him before turning back to let exiting patrons make donations.

"Are you back for good? Or has Hollywood stolen you away from us?" Cherie asked.

"I'm back for now, assessing my options. I think I'd like to do another film, but they're going to want to see how this one does," Kendall said as the crowd began to thin around them. "We'd better let you get back to work, but call me and we'll have coffee." Kendall kissed her on the cheek, and then he and Johnny walked down the sidewalk, away from Times Square so they'd have a better chance of catching a taxi to take them home.

"You're really feeling better?" Johnny asked again.

"Yes, why?" Kendall asked, and Johnny stepped closer as they waited to cross the street. Kendall felt Johnny slide his hand down his back and then lightly cup one of his butt cheeks and squeeze gently. "Oh, that's why," Kendall said dramatically as he pressed back slightly into Johnny's touch. It was good and felt right to have that portion of their relationship back.

Johnny managed to hail a cab, and they got inside and rode back to their building. For some reason, traffic was a bit backed up on their street, so they had the cab stop on the corner, and after paying the driver, walked the half block.

Kendall stopped as soon as they got close. "Jesus," he whispered.

"What is it?" Johnny asked. Kendall slowly walked up to the stairs and stared at two pink roses. "Someone left flowers."

"They're from him," Kendall said, his insides quivering, and for a second he thought he might throw up. "Those are the exact same kind

"Can I have Johnny call you? He's been handling that part of things," Kendall said.

"Of course," Sal answered. "I'll have the copies of those books and music sent over to you today. Look them over and see if anything catches your fancy."

Kendall heard noise in the hallway and he stilled. Keys sounded in the lock, and Kendall peered through the peephole before opening the door. "Johnny's here," he said with relief. "Thanks, Sal."

"No problem, and let me know what you'd like to do." Sal hung up, and Kendall put the phone on the counter and practically launched himself at Johnny, who'd just managed to get the groceries set down.

"You're shaking," Johnny said as he reached around to close the door, and then he held Kendall tight. "Did something happen?" Kendall shook his head. "You're okay."

"I was alone, and Sal stayed on the phone until you came home." Kendall rested his head against Johnny's chest. "What the hell am I going to do? I'm afraid to be alone, and the thought of being on a stage in front of a crowd scares the shit out of me. What if he's in the audience?" Kendall shook again, and Johnny held him tighter.

"Just relax as best you can. You don't have to go back to work until you're ready. Give yourself some time." Johnny soothed him and lightly stroked Kendall's hair. Some of the tension eased. "You love the theater way too much to let some stalker take that away from you." Kendall lifted his gaze. "You can't let that happen, ever. Part of you will die, and I could never bear to see that."

"I feel like part of me has already died," Kendall admitted.

"No, it hasn't. Part of you is exhausted, scared, and nervous, but it hasn't died. You need to give yourself time. Read whatever Sal is going to send over and don't let anyone pressure you into anything."

Kendall nodded. "Would you call him? He said he could help with security or something."

"He seems to be able to do everything," Johnny quipped.

"The man's older than dirt. He's seen everything and probably done everything. That's part of why I love him," Kendall said with a sigh.

"Do you know what I think will help?" Johnny didn't wait for an answer. "Doing normal things, like going for coffee, visiting your family. Maybe find a theater to haunt, and seeing familiar places and faces. This is New York, our home, where we have a full life together. So let's reconnect with that."

"But I don't want to go out alone, at least not yet."

"Then I'll go with you. I'll bring my laptop. You and Gina can chat until you're hoarse, and I'll work." Johnny smiled and instantly disarmed all of Kendall's arguments. "So call your mother and arrange to go out for a visit. Call friends and we'll meet them for coffee. Do what you'd normally do." Johnny got a wicked look in his eyes. "Call and get tickets for a show you'd like to see. We'll go to the theater together. We haven't done that in a long time."

That was true. When Kendall was performing, he never got the chance to see anything. "You're sure?" he asked with more excitement than he thought possible under the circumstances. "Let me call a friend. Maybe I can get tickets to *Book of Mormon*. I've wanted to see that for years." Kendall hugged Johnny and then grabbed his phone. He called a contact about tickets, who said he'd call him back. Then he called his mother, and they were both commanded to come out the following weekend.

"It's lovely out here right now, so pack your suitcase and stay a few days," his mother had said. "I never get to see you for very long, so I intend to take advantage." He wouldn't say no to a weekend in the Hamptons. He then called friends and set up afternoons for coffee and conversation. Kendall even got Johnny to call some of his friends—equal time, or punishment, as the case might be. By the time he was done, his theater contact had called back and said there would be tickets waiting for them at the box office the following night.

"You're going to be fine," Johnny reassured him once Kendall hung up the phone.

"I think you're right," Kendall agreed with what he hoped was more sincerity than he felt. Johnny was being so supportive, and he felt like such a wet blanket. But Johnny was right—getting to a normal routine would help, as long as Johnny was there with him.

"Good," Johnny said and kissed him lightly. "Let me make some dinner, and you can finish unpacking." Kendall sighed softly. "You didn't think I was going to let you get out of that little task, did you?"

Kendall reluctantly let go of Johnny and returned to the bedroom. He got his suitcases unpacked, put the dirty clothes in the laundry, and put away his clean clothes. "We should think about hiring a valet," Kendall called from the bedroom.

"Either that or a maid," Johnny called back, and Kendall jumped as pans clattered to the floor in the other room. "Maybe just a larger apartment," Johnny added.

Kendall closed the suitcase and slid it under the bed. "You know, we could look for a house," he called, but he didn't hear a response. Kendall stepped back from the bed and peered out into the other room. Johnny stood still. "Did you hear me?"

"You'd move outside the city?" Johnny asked softly.

"Yeah. I think so. We could look for a house on Long Island or in New Jersey. Someplace within commute distance."

"You realize you'd be coming home after the curtain most nights," Johnny said and then shook his head. "I don't think that's practical."

"Okay," Kendall said softly. "But maybe we could look at buying a bigger apartment. A place of our own."

Johnny set down the knife he was holding. "Yeah, I think I'd like that."

"So how much do you think we can afford?" Kendall asked as he went back to work.

"Honey," Johnny said from behind him, and Kendall started again. "We have a lot of money." Johnny sat on the edge of the bed and patted the mattress next to him. "You remember how we talked early on about how both of our careers could be hot one day and ice cold the next?"

"Yeah," Kendall said.

"Well, we've been hot for years. Your career has been a steady climb, and, well, I figured the books would cool off, but they haven't. The thing is, we haven't spent a lot of it," Johnny told him. Kendall had been happy to let Johnny manage the money. He'd never had a good head for it, so they'd set up an allowance system for both of them years ago, and he'd always lived within it. The rest went to savings and investments. Rent for their place was still reasonable even if some of the rent control had started to expire.

"What are you saying?"

"With our investments and things, we have millions. I'm not saying we should spend it all on an apartment, but we can afford a mortgage." Johnny sighed. "But I think before we make any decisions, you need to find out what you want to do in the long term. Once your movie comes out, you're going to be in demand and Hollywood is going to come calling again. Do you want to stay in the city or work out there? Do you want to do both? If you do, then we could keep the apartment here and buy a house in LA."

"Johnny, I can't...," Kendall said as the walls threatened to close in.

"You don't have to make any decisions, not right away. See what offers come and decide what you want to do. There's no rush, and I'll be there the whole way." Johnny held him tight, and Kendall huffed as he tried to let the stress slide away.

The door buzzer sounded, and Johnny got up. Kendall heard him answer it and then the door close. Johnny returned a few minutes later and returned to the bedroom, handing Kendall a thick package. "It's from Sal."

"I know," Kendall whispered, making no move to open it.

"Like I said, take your time." Johnny left the room and returned to the kitchen. Kendall set the package on his dresser and finished unpacking. He wasn't ready to look at anything like that, not yet.

THE following evening, Kendall was undeniably excited. "If you don't stop pacing, I'm going to have to tie you down," Johnny said and then grabbed him as he walked by the sofa. "You know, I could tie you down and have my way with you." Kendall squirmed and tried to get away. "Hey, it's me," Johnny said in a whisper and began gently stroking Kendall's back.

"Sorry," Kendall said. "Sometimes I forget, and little things make me remember what happened. I know you were just playing, but for a second I was back there."

"No, I'm the one who should be sorry," Johnny told him. "Go on and get ready. I made dinner reservations, but I think we can show up early." Johnny patted his butt. "I'll be right behind you."

Kendall walked to the bedroom, and Johnny closed the lid on his laptop. Kendall stripped out of his comfortable "lounge around the house" clothes and pulled out a pair of dress pants and a crisp shirt. Johnny joined him, and Kendall finished dressing and then watched Johnny. "Do you have any idea how handsome you are?" Kendall asked quietly and then stood up and adjusted Johnny's collar.

"It's why you love me. Because I'm cute," Johnny said, giving him a jaunty smile.

"No. I love you because you're you. I'm hot for your bod because you're cute," Kendall corrected with a wink. "You look great," he said, stepping back a bit.

"So do you," Johnny said with a grin and then looked over at the dresser. The unopened envelope still sat there. Then he returned his gaze to Kendall, and Kendall walked toward the bedroom door. "Are you going to look at them?"

"Eventually," Kendall said with a shrug and then he headed for the door. He didn't want to look at the envelope or think about being in front of a house full of people. He wasn't sure he could ever do that again. What if that part of his life was over? That thought scared him almost as much.

"I wasn't pushing, and I told you to take your time." Johnny was right behind him. "Give yourself time. Sal knows you aren't going to get back to him right away."

Kendall nodded. "What if I'm never ready? What if I can't do it anymore?"

"I know you can," Johnny said. "You can do anything you set your mind to. Now let's leave that for a while and go to dinner and then the theater. I bet as soon as you sit down and the overture starts, you'll wish you were up on stage with everyone else."

"Is that what you're doing? Theater therapy?" Kendall asked as he grabbed an umbrella. It had been raining all day, and while it seemed to have stopped for the moment, he wasn't taking any chances.

"I guess that depends," Johnny answered, and Kendall tilted his head slightly waiting for more. "On whether it works." Johnny chuckled. "Let's go."

Johnny guided him out the door and locked the apartment behind them. They descended the stairs and stepped out on the street. Kendall realized this was the first time he'd been outside since they got home. The rain had made everything seem fresh, the scent of the city muted. Kendall stood still and took a deep breath, closing his eyes.

"I bet it's good to be out," Johnny said softly.

Kendall nodded. "Yeah, it is," he said. "I think I've been a bit of a fool."

"No, just a bit unnerved, but I knew you'd feel better once you went out to places that were familiar."

"So where are we going for dinner?" Kendall asked, intrigued.

"No place fancy. Just the little Italian place we always go to. But I bet they'll be glad to see you," Johnny said with a smile. They opened their umbrellas as the rain began again and slowly walked the couple blocks to the restaurant.

Of course Johnny was right. As soon as they walked in, the couple who owned the place hurried over, and they were both hugged and kissed. "It isn't every day we have a movie star in the place," Mrs. Gianetti said as she fussed over them.

"He's not a movie star yet," Johnny countered before leaning close to the short rotund woman who'd obviously spent years eating her own incredible cooking. "I don't want him to get a big head," Johnny stage-whispered, and Mrs. Gianetti laughed warmly before taking Kendall's arm and guiding him toward the best table in the place.

"You're way too nice to get that way," she said to Kendall as she patted him gently on the arm. They took their seats, and Kendall expected to be handed a menu. "You two just sit, and I'll cook for you." She smiled and then bustled away. Within minutes they were poured glasses of white wine.

"Feeling better?" Johnny asked with a grin. "I knew familiar places and people would be just the ticket."

"Now who's getting a big head?" Kendall quipped, and Johnny squeezed his knee under the table. "Okay, I do feel better and I'm glad you're right." Kendall looked around at the familiar little restaurant, seeing the older couple in the corner with the bowls of what had to be minestrone. They were a fixture in the place, always eating the same thing, and from their expressions, having the same argument they always had. The servers they always saw waited on the tables and talked with the patrons like old friends, which most of them were. "It's good to be home."

"It's good that you're home," Mrs. Gianetti said, surprising him, but he didn't start the way he had the past few days. "It's always good when you come home again." She smiled at Kendall. "We really missed our darling boys." Kendall thought there might have been a tear in her eye for a second. "I'm sending over some nice antipasti and then a little pesto, and for you I'm making my special veal and then a bit of tiramisu. I made some of Johnny's favorite, and there's just a bit left for you." She patted Kendall's shoulder. "Not to worry, I will not overfeed you so you can keep your movie star looks." She pretended to swoon, and Kendall laughed, a deep sincere laugh he hadn't felt in a while.

"Thank you," Kendall said. "That's just what I needed. Good home cooking. We're going out to see my mother soon, and she'll feed me until I can't move."

"Well, this will tide you over until your mama can feed you properly. I promise," she said and then hurried away. The servers brought a plate of appetizers, and then the scent of rich pesto filled the entire restaurant. Kendall smelled one of his favorites well before their plates arrived. Thankfully, Mrs. Gianetti kept her word and didn't make the portions enormous, just huge, and Kendall dug in, forgetting about his diet for one night.

"Maybe tomorrow we can go to the gym for a few hours," Johnny said as they ate.

Kendall leaned close and lowered his voice. "I think we'll need to do that for the next week to work this off," he said. But every calorie was worth it, and Kendall would walk the treadmill, ride a bike, use the elliptical, and lift weights until he couldn't see straight for food like this. "But who cares?"

Mr. Gianetti stopped by the table and talked for a few minutes. He was the polar opposite of his wife, tall and thin with a shock of white hair. "How was Hollywood?"

Kendall laughed. "Fine, Mr. G. In some ways as fake as you'd expect, but by and large, the people were wonderful." He thought about Juan and Barbara, both of whom had turned out as good friends. Both of them had called at least twice since he got home to see how he was. Even Lyman had turned out to be a much more upstanding guy than their first meeting had indicated. "But there's no place like home." Kendall did his best Judy Garland, and Mr. Gianetti laughed.

"I did commercials when I was young and handsome," he told them.

"You did one commercial for hair tonic," his wife teased as she brought plates to the table. She motioned to one of the servers, and their pasta bowls were cleared before she set plates down in front of each of them. "That was before I met him, but I remembered the commercial. That's why I agreed to go out with him." She glanced at her husband and giggled. "Sometimes I still see him like that. Young, a real looker, with scads of dark hair, standing in nothing but a towel in front of the mirror." She grinned. "Then I wake up and wonder who the old man is in my bed." She scooted away with her husband right behind her, both of them laughing until the kitchen door cut off their mirth.

Kendall's laughter shifted to a smile that lasted a long time. He sighed for no reason other than sheer contentment. With their dinners before them, veal in a richly scented sauce that made Kendall's pasta-filled stomach rumble as if he hadn't eaten in days, they finished their wine, and Mr. G brought fresh glasses and poured them a rich red wine. They ate and talked for the rest of the meal, and by the time they were done, neither of them felt much like moving.

"I'll have dessert for you in just a few minutes," Mrs. G told them.

"I can't eat another bite," Kendall told her.

"Then I'll make it to go for you," she said and hurried away, returning a few minutes later with a small container in a bag for each of them.

"Thank you so much," Kendall said as he stood up and hugged Mrs. G. "You have no idea how much this meant."

She hugged him back and then stepped away. "Go on with you," she said and guided them toward the door. They were both on the street before they realized they had never been given a bill.

"I'll wait for you," Kendall said, and Johnny went back inside. He came out a few minutes later.

"They wouldn't take anything," Johnny said, and Kendall nodded, not surprised.

"Of course they wouldn't," Kendall said as they started back toward the apartment. It had stopped raining, but they were careful on the wet pavement. "Mrs. G once said she loved Abba. I don't know how that came up, but it did. I'll see if I can get them tickets to *Mamma Mia*. She'll be thrilled." They arrived at their building, and Kendall waited in the lobby while Johnny raced upstairs to put the food away. After he came back down, they hailed a cab and made it to the theater five minutes before the curtain rose.

Kendall's contact had managed to get them good seats, so they were right down front. They settled in, and Kendall relaxed as he waited. The overture began, the curtain rose, and Kendall spent the next two and a half hours laughing so hard his sides ached, and then he laughed some more. At the end of the performance, Kendall was the first person on his feet, clapping and grinning as the actors took their bows. The cast did one more quick number, took a final bow, and then the curtain came down for the final time. Kendall gathered his things, and they waited for the others to filter out before walking toward the exits.

"So did it work?" Johnny asked with a grin.

"Yes," Kendall said. "You were right. I'm energized and ready to read through scores and figure out what I want to do next," he declared as they stepped out into a throng of people gathered by the sidewalk.

of flowers he left me all the time." The traffic had cleared out once the light changed, and Kendall looked around. "He's around here somewhere, I can feel it. He's watching me."

"Are you sure?" Johnny asked as he untied the flowers, freeing the small note wrapped around the stems. "*You're mine*," Johnny read.

"That's the exact same note I got in LA just before my dressing room was destroyed," Kendall took the flowers from Johnny and ripped off the heads, then threw them and the stems into the wet street. He then took the note, crumpled it, dropped it onto the concrete, and stomped it to oblivion. "If you're watching, go away," Kendall said and then unlocked the door and went inside. Johnny followed, and Kendall made sure the door was closed and locked before stomping up the stairs.

In the stairwell of each floor, there was a small window, and Kendall pulled the shades on each one of them as they climbed. He even went up further, making sure they were all pulled before coming back down. Then he and Johnny unlocked their door and went inside. "Don't turn on the lights," Kendall said. "If he's watching, he's probably trying to figure out which apartment is mine, and I'll be damned if I'm going to give him the satisfaction." Kendall heard others coming and going, and he peeked out, waiting until one of the other tenants had gone to the floor above theirs. Then he turned on one of the lights and the light in their bedroom.

"I'm sorry," Johnny said, and Kendall nervously stayed away from the windows.

"I thought changing coasts would discourage him, but obviously not."

"We'll keep our eyes out and not leave you alone, and tomorrow I'm calling Sal to see what he can do to help," Johnny said. "For now, I want you to get ready for bed. I'm going to sit up for a while. I'll probably work and make sure nothing happens."

"Are you sure?" Kendall asked.

"It's okay. Go to bed, and I'll join you in a while." Johnny kissed him, and Kendall went into the bedroom. He cleaned up and then turned out the lights, getting undressed in the dark. Then he sat on the edge of the bed, staring at the lump on the top of his dresser. He knew it was the scores, but the excitement he'd had an hour earlier was gone. The lights in the other room dimmed, and he heard the gentle clicking of Johnny's keyboard. Then nothing.

"Are you okay?" Johnny asked, and when Kendall didn't answer, the sofa springs squeaked slightly and then footsteps sounded, getting closer. "Honey, I'm here, and I'm not going to let anything happen to you."

"But what if something happens to you?" Kendall asked. "He already kidnapped me, presumably because I spurned him. What will he do to you if he thinks you stand in his way?" Johnny came into the bedroom, and Kendall clutched him around the waist. "What if he hurts you?"

"Should we call the police?"

Kendall laughed. "I destroyed the evidence. They're really going to appreciate that." He shook his head. "We will next time." Kendall wanted to cry, because he knew there would be a next time. Something was going to happen; he could feel it.

"And we'll be a lot more careful," Johnny said.

"How?" Kendall asked painfully. "We were having such a good night. For a few hours I even managed to forget about all that crap, and then he shows up again. I don't know what to do."

"For one thing, you're going to get into bed and get some sleep," Johnny said firmly as he pulled down the covers, and then he waited for Kendall to lie down. "I still have some work I have to get done, but I'll listen for anything and come to bed in a few hours. In the morning I'm going to go down and talk to Mrs. Miller on the first floor. That woman knows everything going on everywhere. I swear, she never sleeps. I'll find out if she saw anything. Don't worry. No one is going to get to you on my watch." Johnny pulled up the covers. Kendall half expected a kiss on the forehead and for Johnny to ruffle his hair, but instead Johnny kissed him hard. "I love you very much, and I'll be up all night if it means you'll sleep better, so get some rest."

"Okay," Kendall sighed, and Johnny left the room after giving him another kiss. Kendall heard him typing a few moments later and he closed his eyes. He tossed, dozed, and listened for any strange sounds, but all he heard was the soft clicking of Johnny's computer keys as he typed. After a while, he heard Johnny's footsteps. The lights switched off, and Johnny cleaned up before joining him in bed. Kendall curled close to him and was finally able to relax. Kendall must have fallen asleep eventually, because the next thing he knew sunlight was streaming through the windows. Johnny was still asleep next to him, and Kendall rolled over and went back to sleep.

When he woke again, Johnny was gone and the apartment was quiet. Kendall got up and pulled on his robe before peering out of the bedroom. The apartment seemed empty. The door was closed, and he made sure it was locked before making coffee and looked out the front windows. He wasn't sure what he was expecting, maybe to see someone familiar standing on the sidewalk across the street watching the place. Of course there was no one there, and Kendall wasn't sure if that reassured him or not.

He didn't like being alone, but he couldn't expect Johnny to be with him every second, so he poured his cup of coffee and set about finding something for breakfast. He needed something to do. Before he could open the refrigerator, he heard footsteps on the stairs and tensed. The knob on their door rattled and then a knock sounded. "Kendall, it's me."

He hurried over and unlocked the door, letting Johnny in. "Sorry."

"Me too," Johnny said as he shut the door. "I talked to Mrs. Miller, and she saw a man hanging around the front of the building last night. She saw him pace up and down the sidewalk. She said he tried to get in behind someone else, but she put a stop to that." Johnny smiled. "She told me she gave him a good tongue-lashing, and he went away. She didn't see him leave anything."

"Did she get a good look at him?"

"Well, she said he was tall, a bit broad, and paunchy, which describes a quarter of the men in the city. She did say he seemed to be walking with a bit of a stiff leg, though. Do you know anyone like that?"

Kendall thought for a few minutes and then shook his head. "Not that I can think of." Kendall poured Johnny a mug of coffee and handed it to him. "I guess we're back to square one."

"Not exactly. She saw him, and she said she'd be able to recognize him again. I told her if she saw him to call the police. Mrs. Miller said she would and that she'd be very vocal about it."

That made Kendall chuckle. He couldn't imagine Mrs. Miller being quiet about anything. She was very sweet, but persnickety, and liked things just the way she wanted them. She also made sure no one left a mess in the entryway, and the hallways were always spotless, even though he never saw her clean them. "If you say so," Kendall said.

"I know you're worried, but we'll get to the bottom of this whole mess. I can promise you that. I also called Sal, and he's going to contact a friend of his in the security business and have them call you today."

"I don't want a stranger around," Kendall said.

"Yes, you do," Johnny said firmly, taking Kendall by surprise. "Look, I know you're scared, and I don't blame you. I know this guy took you and stranded you in the desert, but I won't allow you to strand yourself inside this apartment. We need to make sure we can keep you safe, and then we need to find out who this guy is and stop him. You're sure it's a guy, right?"

Kendall huffed. "It was a man's voice I heard when I was taken, so I'm assuming it's a guy."

"Okay, so we're getting you some protection," Johnny said. "Now let me make some breakfast." Johnny got to work, attacking the pans like they were weapons. Kendall went back into the bedroom. He got his clothes and went into the bathroom, where he showered and then dressed before joining Johnny in the kitchen. Kendall's stomach had started to rumble at the scent of bacon and eggs when his phone rang. It was Sal.

"The security man should be calling you this morning," Sal began as soon as Kendall answered the phone. "He's very good."

"Thanks," Kendall said softly.

"Have you looked at those scores?" Sal asked.

"Not yet," Kendall said with a sigh. "I will, I just…."

"It's okay. If you aren't interested, just say so, but there are some great shows in there. Some I think will become legendary."

"I'm not up to it right now," Kendall admitted.

"I know all this stalker stuff has you unnerved, and I can understand it, but you know people will only wait so long. You can't let this lock you in fear," Sal said.

"You sound like Johnny," Kendall said with a light scoff.

"I always knew Johnny was brilliant," Sal retorted, and Kendall chuckled. "But we're right and you know it." Kendall did know it, but he wasn't ready to admit it, at least not yet. "I also got a phone call from Lyman Davidson this morning. He's in New York and wants to meet with both of us to talk about a deal for a future project he's working on. He loved working with you and he said the part he has in mind is perfect for you. Can I go ahead and set it up?"

Kendall didn't answer. He'd gone cold and was shaking like a leaf. "Yeah, okay," he said automatically.

"I'll set it up, then, and let you know the details," Sal said. "Take care, my boy, and try not to worry." Sal disconnected, and Kendall stared at the walls.

"What is it?" Johnny asked, but Kendall barely heard him. It took a few seconds before he realized Johnny was talking to him.

"Lyman is in town and wants to meet about a movie deal," Kendall said.

"That's great," Johnny said, setting the plates on the table.

"You don't understand. Lyman is in New York," Kendall said. "He shows up and suddenly I'm getting flowers and the stalker shows up. I think that's maybe too much of a coincidence. Don't you?"

Johnny paused. "You think Lyman is behind all this? No way. He helped me find you. The man was relentless and refused to stop. He...."

"Think about it. He kidnapped me and left me in the desert, and then helps you find me. He gets to be the hero." Kendall sat down, but the food didn't look good anymore. "He also got a better movie out of it." Johnny sat as well, but he didn't touch his food either. "I'm not saying this is rational, because clearly whoever is doing this isn't rational."

"Could Lyman have trashed your dressing room?" Johnny asked, and Kendall shook his head slowly. He had to admit that wasn't possible. "He could have had someone do it, though."

"I don't want it to be him. I like him. He's a pain in the ass, but he's also an upstanding guy and I like him. But he shows up in New York and suddenly so does the stalker. It's too coincidental to ignore. I don't know what to think, except we have to accept that Lyman is a possibility."

"If it's him, and I'm not saying it is," Johnny began, "then he's one sick, twisted guy, and I'd like to think I'd recognize that kind of person. But then again, he's also an actor."

Kendall held his head in his hands. "I don't know what to think. Sal wants me to meet with Lyman, and I don't want to go anywhere near him. I don't want to step foot outside the apartment." Kendall groaned and felt about two seconds from crying. He'd just begun to think he could leave some of what had happened behind him. They'd done familiar things, and he'd been comfortable. Now the crap was starting all over again. "I know that's not possible and I know you're right, I can't let him strand me here, but I don't know what to do." Kendall breathed deeply to calm himself, but it wasn't working, not one bit.

"I don't know either, but if you decide to go to the meeting with Sal and Lyman, I'm going too," Johnny said.

"You don't have to," Kendall said. "This is my problem, and it isn't as though I'm going to be alone. Sal will be there. This can't affect your life too."

Johnny got up and walked over to where Kendall sat. "It already does, because it affects you." He lightly stroked Kendall's shoulders. "I almost lost you once because of this guy." Kendall turned around when Johnny's voice broke. "I nearly lost you because I wasn't there for you. That won't happen again." Johnny closed his eyes and held Kendall close. "I know that sometimes it takes nearly losing someone to realize what they mean to you, and I'm sorry that had to happen to you. I took you for granted for a long time, and I won't do that again."

"You weren't the only one. I did the same thing," Kendall whispered. He closed his eyes and leaned back into Johnny's embrace.

"Have been for a while, so maybe that's the one good thing to come out of this."

Eventually they returned to their food. It was mostly cold, but Kendall wasn't hungry anyway. He nibbled a bit at his bacon and ate a few bites of egg before giving up. He carried his plate into the kitchen and took care of the dishes. His phone rang, and Johnny answered it before handing it to Kendall.

"Hello," Kendall said hesitantly.

"Good morning," a deep voice said. "I'm Henry Gold with Gold and Marks security, and I wondered if I could speak with you about the problem you've been having. Sal gave me this number and said it was urgent I contact you."

"How do you know Sal?" Kendall asked.

"I've helped some of his other clients over the years. I've known Sal for quite some time. When I was a kid, we went to the same temple," Henry said.

"Okay. Tell me something about Sal. What does he look like?"

Henry laughed. "Short, old, Jewish guy. Smokes way too many of those stinky cigars and wears expensive suits and carries a pocket watch."

"Okay, you know Sal. Where do you want to meet?" Kendall asked.

"I'm outside your building now, and I'd like to come up to meet with you." Kendall walked toward the front of the apartment. He pulled the curtain slightly and peered down to the sidewalk. He saw no one. "I'll be up in five minutes. You won't need to let me in the building." Henry hung up, and Kendall stared at the phone.

"That was the security guy," Kendall said.

"I gathered," Johnny said. "Is he coming over?"

"He'll be here in five minutes," Kendall said and wondered what was going to happen next. A soft knock paused Kendall's train of thought, and Johnny peered through the peephole.

"Who is it?" Johnny asked.

"Henry Gold," Kendall heard through the door, and he nodded. Johnny unlocked the door and a medium-sized man stepped inside.

"Your building is incredibly insecure. I picked the front door lock in a matter of seconds, and I knew exactly which apartment was yours, because as soon as I called, you peered out the front window," Henry said, taking off his jacket. "Sorry, I tend to get right down to business. I'm Henry."

"Kendall," he said, shaking Henry's hand, "and this is my partner Johnny."

"Johnny Harker, yes, I know, I love your books," Henry said with a smile as they shook hands. "So what can I do for you?" Henry asked, and Johnny closed the door and locked it again. Kendall motioned toward a chair, and Henry sat down. He wasn't at all what Kendall had been expecting. He wasn't particularly huge, but he had a commanding manner, and deep-set eyes that had obviously seen a lot, if the hint of pain in them was any indication. He was handsome with his short clipped hair and the manicured stubble around his chin.

Kendall sat on the sofa with Johnny next to him and told Henry everything that had happened in California as well as what had prompted the call here in New York. He also told him his suspicions about Lyman. When he got to that part, Henry's black eyebrows knitted together, but he said nothing until Kendall was done.

"Okay," Henry began, "let's start at the beginning from a security standpoint. We'll make sure your home is secure, and then we'll move from there. First thing, you aren't on the ground floor. That's both good and bad. It's good because it limits the way anyone can get in, and it's bad because you have fewer exit strategies."

"There's a fire ladder in our bedroom, and there's a fire escape in back. That door has a fire latch on it and no outside knob or lock," Kendall said.

"That's pretty good, then, and in a building as old as this one, there's only so much that can be done. I do suggest you contact the landlord and ask to have the front door replaced and the locks changed." Kendall looked at Johnny. "If you give me the contact information, I'll have an associate make the call. She's very good at getting even the most reluctant landlord to do what needs to be done." Kendall wondered how she did that, but kept the question to himself.

"Neither of you should go out alone," Henry continued.

"We haven't. The problem we have is that Kendall doesn't want to leave the apartment at all," Johnny said, and Kendall colored as Henry turned his attention to him.

"There's nothing to be ashamed of. A lot of my clients feel the same way in this kind of situation." Henry leaned forward and looked Kendall in the eyes. "But for your own sanity and peace of mind, you mustn't allow that to happen, and that's part of why I'm here—to help give you peace of mind so you can live your life." Henry's confidence was infectious.

"What do you want us to do?" Johnny asked.

"Live your lives as much as you can, but let me know when you're planning to go out and where you expect to be going." Henry handed them each a card.

"Will you be staying here?" Kendall asked, and Henry shook his head. "Then what's your plan?"

"I'll be around when you go places. If you go to a coffee shop, I'll be the guy who walks in a few minutes later and sits at a different table or someone who strolls by the windows. You'll hardly ever know I'm there, and I can almost guarantee you won't recognize me. I'll be looking at faces and people who are looking at you. I'll also spend time outside the building when you're home to see who comes and goes. If someone leaves something like flowers or tries to break in, I'll call the police and stop them. It won't take long for me to know every person who lives in this building. I already recognize some of them and even know which apartment is theirs."

Kendall was impressed. "So we should call you if we need to go out?"

"Yes. I won't be able to follow you everywhere, particularly during the day, because I'm going to concentrate on the evening and early nighttime hours. Believe it or not, though it may sound like a cliché, that's the time most people like this are active. They need some sort of cover, and darkness works."

"How long will we have to keep this up?"

Henry sighed softly. "People like this are obsessed, and based on what you described, the guy we want is probably in New York for a limited time. I doubt they've relocated here, so they're under a time crunch. They aren't going to wait weeks or even days, so I'm hoping not too long. As for your friend Lyman...." Henry paused. "My gut is really mixed on him. He doesn't seem like the type, because stalkers are usually repressed, and Lyman seems like the kind of person who would go for what he wanted full bore, not manipulate to get what he wants. But then there's the fact that he's in town and this just started again. That could be a coincidence, but I don't tend to believe in them."

"Me either," Kendall said, and Henry stood up.

"I'll be around, and like I said, just call if either of you need to go somewhere alone." Henry walked toward the door and then paused. "I need the information on your landlord." Johnny got it for him. "This shouldn't be a problem."

"Thank you," Johnny said, and he and Kendall joined Henry at the door.

"You're welcome." He opened the door but then closed it again. "One more thing. Always assume when you're outside the apartment that someone is watching you. Whoever is doing this has most assuredly been watching to see where you live and when you're home. Get some timers to turn lights on and off in another room when you're home. Keep them guessing. If the two of you are out, set the lights to go on and off periodically so it looks like you're moving around the apartment. If he doesn't see you leave, then maybe he can't be sure if you're home or not. The more he doesn't know, the safer you are."

"Okay," Johnny said. "I'll go out and get some today."

"Bring them home in a grocery bag," Henry suggested. "Like I said, assume someone is always watching." Henry opened the door and left the apartment. Johnny closed and locked the door behind him.

"Well, I...," Johnny began and trailed off.

Kendall sat back on the sofa. "I know. I'm not sure if I feel better or worse."

"Hey, at least someone is watching out for us and looking for him," Johnny said, and Kendall had to agree. Johnny stood up and extended his hand, tugging Kendall to his feet. "Come on, I think we need to get our mind off all this, and I need to take a shower."

"But I already took one," Kendall said, and Johnny stopped and turned to him, a smoldering look in his eyes. "I need another one," Kendall said with a smile. In their bedroom, Kendall undressed, and Johnny started the water in the bathroom. Kendall joined him a minute later, just in time to see a naked Johnny step under the water. He followed behind him, and Johnny pulled the curtain closed and then pressed Kendall back against the tile. Johnny pressed his chest to Kendall's, and Kendall was kissed within an inch of his life. All the worry and cares he'd had when he stepped into the bathroom seemed miles away when Johnny was holding him, his slick skin sliding against him. "God, I love you," Kendall moaned softly, and Johnny grinned before leaning down to suck lightly on a nipple. Kendall whimpered and thrust his chest forward. Johnny suckled harder before licking and nibbling gently at his skin.

"I love you too," Johnny whispered as he slowly went down on his knees, and Kendall's cock pointed directly at Johnny's lips. Kendall held his breath and closed his eyes, sighing softly, legs shaking in anticipatory excitement. Then Johnny slid his lips down Kendall's cock, sucking him deep before sliding back.

Kendall's head thunked back on the tile. It should have hurt, but Kendall felt so good, he hardly noticed. Johnny's wet mouth sliding up and down him was too damned amazing for him to think about anything else. "That's so good," Kendall moaned, closing his eyes and letting the sensation wash over him. "Johnny," he cried as a warning, and Johnny sucked harder, taking him deeper. Kendall's legs throbbed and threatened to collapse from under him, and he tried to stave off the impending climax as long as he could. "I can't...."

Johnny paused, and Kendall whimpered. "Baby, I just want to make you happy," Johnny said, then he sucked him deep once again, and within seconds Kendall was balancing on the edge of a knife. This time Johnny sucked hard, and Kendall tumbled over, coming hard with a cry that echoed off the tile.

Kendall pressed to the wall to keep upright and let the bliss float over him. When he opened his eyes, Johnny smiled at him, eyes shining. Kendall hugged him close, kissing him, tasting himself on Johnny's lips. Johnny stood still, and Kendall kissed down his torso, sucking and licking until he reached Johnny's thick cock. It bobbed in front of him for a few seconds, and then he sucked it hard. Johnny was usually pretty quiet during sex, but this time he nearly screamed. At first Kendall thought something was wrong, but the cry morphed into a deep, throaty moan, and Kendall smiled around Johnny's cock and sucked harder.

He loved when Johnny came apart, and that was exactly what he did. Johnny slapped the tile and moaned deep and long as Kendall sucked him. He swirled his tongue around the bulbous head and tickled the sensitive spot with his tongue. That made Johnny's legs shake and his moans turned to high-pitched whines. Kendall loved Johnny's rich flavor and reveled in it, sucking harder to get more and more of his lover. He stroked up Johnny's inner thighs to his balls, stroking the smooth skin, and then slid his fingers back along his perineum and tapped at his opening. Johnny gasped, and Kendall knew just from the pitch that Johnny wouldn't last much longer. Sure enough, within seconds, Johnny came.

Kendall swallowed everything Johnny could give him and then let Johnny's cock slip from his lips. Then he smiled at the expression of bliss on Johnny's face. He hadn't seen that in a while, and Kendall realized that no matter what was happening, as long as he had Johnny with him, happiness and bliss were only a touch or a kiss away.

CHAPTER
ELEVEN

THE following morning Johnny had an appointment at the Columbia University library. Jeremy met him at the apartment, and the two of them planned to travel to the library together. As soon as Kendall met Jeremy, he had to keep himself from snickering. He'd pictured a strapping college-age man going after Johnny, but what he met was a kid of about twenty-three who looked maybe twelve. He was attractive in his own way, but Kendall felt like a fool for thinking Johnny had been having an affair with him.

"I've seen many of your shows," Jeremy told him as they shook hands. "I must confess I'm a fan." Jeremy rocked back on his heels with what appeared to be excitement.

"Thank you for going with him," Kendall said, shifting his gaze to Johnny.

"It's no problem. I'm starting my graduate work in history, and Johnny is really helping me with my research techniques." Jeremy looked at Johnny, and Kendall saw a definite bit of hero worship.

"I'll call you when we're ready to come back," Johnny promised and leaned in close for a quick kiss. Then he and Jeremy left the apartment, and Kendall locked the door behind them.

For the past day or so, he hadn't seen Henry at all. They'd had a telephone call from him at one point with questions about someone going inside the building, so they knew he was around, but other than that, there had been no contact. Nothing had been left at his door and no one had tried to contact him, so some of Kendall's nervousness had subsided. Admittedly, knowing Henry was around and watching made him feel much more secure.

He hadn't made plans for the day, so he picked up a little around the apartment. He also got the laundry together and trooped it down to the laundry area in the basement. He got the machines running and went back upstairs. In the apartment, he finally picked up the envelope of scores and sat down to look them over. The first one he read didn't speak to him and he set it aside before trudging to the basement to shift the laundry. Then he returned and looked over another one.

By the time the laundry was done and he was back in the apartment, much of the morning was gone. He'd also looked over all the scores, but hadn't come to any decisions. One interested him, but Kendall wasn't sure he was ready to go back on the stage yet. The thought of being in front of people again, especially with his stalker still out there, scared the crap out of him. The problem was he didn't know how to tell Sal. His agent was going to think him crazy for turning down what could very well be the next mega-hit show. It had that kind of feeling to Kendall and he would probably kick himself later for making this decision. But he didn't see another way.

His phone rang and Kendall looked at the display. "Sal, I was just about to call you."

"So you've come to a decision, then," Sal said.

"Yes, I have," Kendall said with gravity.

"Oh no," Sal told him firmly. "I know that tone. I've heard it enough in my career, and don't you think I'm going to let you throw everything away."

"Sal—" Kendall began.

"Don't 'Sal' me. You've read all the scores and you like *The Devil with Love*, but this whole stalker thing has you so unnerved you don't want to do it."

"Yeah, I guess...."

"Welcome to the big time," Sal told him, and Kendall was speechless. "What were you expecting—to be coddled and pampered? Think again, bucko. Every celebrity gets a stalker at some point.

Granted, they don't usually do what yours did, but you can't let that stop your career." Papers rustled in the background and Sal shuffled the phone. "I've already scheduled a sit-down with the producers. They want to meet you badly. They say you're the only man they want to play their Lucifer. It's the role of a lifetime, and you know it."

"Okay," Kendall said, caving. "When do you want me to meet with them?"

"They're taking you to lunch, two o'clock at the Four Seasons."

"Today?" Kendall asked in disbelief.

"Yes. Today as in an hour and a half." Sal sounded gruff, but Kendall knew he was pleased. "It was the only time they had, and you have to do this. They can't wait, and while they want you, they won't hold up the entire production."

"Okay," Kendall said, girding himself. He could do this. "I'll be there. Will you send a car around for me?"

"Of course. They'll be out front in an hour," Sal told him, and Kendall relaxed. "They'll have your number, and it's my usual driver, Ivan, so you shouldn't feel nervous."

"Thanks, Sal," Kendall said and hung up the phone so he could begin getting ready.

KENDALL was dressed and waiting well before the car was scheduled to arrive. He dug the card out of his wallet and called Henry. "It's Kendall. I have an appointment at the Four Seasons for a late lunch."

"All right," Henry said. "How are you going?"

"My agent is sending a car. I know his driver, so I should be fine. But I wanted to let you know. I'm not sure quite how I'm getting back, though. I'm hoping Sal will let me use the car and driver to get home, but he's a busy man, so...."

"You call me as soon as you know," Henry said. "I'll be around."

"Thanks," Kendall said and then hung up and finished getting ready. When the call came, Kendall left the apartment, locked up behind him, and then hurried out to the car. He made sure the door to the building locked behind him and then checked the driver. Ivan smiled at him as he held the door, and Kendall got in back. Ivan closed the door and walked around the car, then got back in and drove him to the restaurant.

At the restaurant, Kendall was shown through the elegant dining room directly to the table. Two men stood up, and Kendall shook hands with both of them as greetings were exchanged. Kendall knew both Derrick Hanson and Izzy Leftwich fairly well. He'd worked on one of their shows earlier in his career. They talked a bit, ordered drinks, and then discussed business over lunch for the next two hours.

The lunch must have cost a fortune, but Izzy paid the bill without looking at it once they were finished. "Can we count on you?" he asked across the table.

Kendall swallowed, and both men shared a glance. "I think the show is amazing, and if you do what you say you're planning, it will be a spectacle that will be remembered."

Izzy cleared his throat. "Sal was kind enough to tell us about your current problem. If you decide to join the cast, we will employ extra security and we'll provide transportation to and from your apartment. Your safety is important to all of us."

"Thank you, gentlemen." Kendall knew better than to commit to anything on the spur of the moment. "Your offer is generous, and I'll give it very serious consideration. I know time is of the essence, so I'll give you my answer no later than tomorrow evening." Izzy and Derrick shared another brief look. "I don't jerk people around, but I need to make a sound decision."

"Of course," Derrick said. "We'll be thrilled to have you."

The three of them stood up, and Kendall phoned Sal, but got his assistant, who said he'd been called away. He wasn't about to bum a ride from Izzy or Derrick, so he phoned Henry. "Have the doorman get you a taxi and come right home. I'll be watching when you arrive," Henry said.

"Okay," Kendall said. He followed Henry's instructions, looking around him for anyone paying extra attention. During the ride home, he called Johnny for reassurance.

"I'm on my way home too. Jeremy and I gathered a lot of material, and I figured we could organize and review it at home. I should be there in fifteen minutes or so," Johnny said.

"We're almost home now. I'll see you when you get home," Kendall said as the taxi turned onto their street and drove the few blocks to the building. Kendall paid the driver and got out of the cab. He hurried up the walk, digging out his keys as he moved.

"Hi, Kendall," he heard from behind him. Kendall turned as Guy bounded up the stairs behind him. "Unlock the door and step inside," he said gruffly, and Kendall's heart pounded.

"You?" Kendall asked, and Guy pushed him toward the door.

"Just unlock the door," Guy repeated, pressing his hand into the base of Kendall's back. Somehow Kendall got the key inserted into the lock with his shaking hand, wondering where Henry was. "Don't make me hurt you."

The key went in and Kendall pushed open the door, trying to stall as much as he could. As soon as the door opened Guy pushed him inside and closed the door behind them. "Why?" Kendall repeated. "I thought you were my friend."

"And I thought you were mine. But after having drinks a few times, you were more interested in that twink kid than me. You even spent the night with him. I wonder what your Johnny would think about that if he knew. Maybe once you're gone, I'll make sure he finds out. Then he can find out just what a little shit you are." Guy pushed him toward the stairs, and Kendall stumbled on the first step before catching himself.

"I was your friend, but that's all," Kendall said, trying to think of something to keep Guy talking. "Why would you hurt me if you wanted to be friends?"

They reached the first landing, and Guy pushed him again. Kendall hit the wall with a thud. "I loved you. I sent you flowers, but you gave them to that bitch Barbara. That's when I knew what I meant to you. Nothing! I even asked you for drinks, but you invited your bit of ass to come along. Why Juan and not me? I could have made you happy. I would have given you everything. But you had your chance, and now you're going to regret it." Kendall listened for footsteps, the door opening… anything. But he heard nothing.

Henry, where are you?

Kendall kept climbing the stairs, going past their apartment door. When Guy made no move to stop him, he continued climbing. At least Guy didn't know which apartment was theirs. That might be some advantage if he could figure out how to use it. He continued slowly climbing the stairs. When he got to the third and final floor, he stopped.

"Unlock your apartment," Guy said.

Kendall went to the door of one of the people he knew on this floor. He only hoped Martin was home. He fiddled with the knob and worked at inserting his key into the lock he knew it wouldn't fit. Then he switched keys on his ring. "I need to get the right one."

"Don't screw with me," Guy hissed and light glinted off the blade of a small knife Guy drew out of his pocket. "Now open the door," Guy said very deliberately.

"I can't," Kendall said honestly. "It's not my apartment."

Guy grabbed him around the throat, and Kendall felt the knife against his back, a single pinpoint of pressure that if it grew…. "I said not to fuck with me," Guy whispered menacingly. Then he licked along Kendall's neck and sucked on his ear. Kendall did his best not to shiver with revulsion, though all he wanted was to get as far away as he could. "You like that, don't you?" Guy said, doing it again. "You could have had all that and more. I would have made you scream with ecstasy, and now… I'm just going to make you scream, but that's after you beg. Now, you're going to slowly go down the stairs and right to your apartment. No sudden moves and no sound or I'll push this knife just under your ribs and you'll bleed out like a stuck pig."

"Okay," Kendall said, slowly moving back toward the stairs. He took a few steps, and the pinprick from the knife eased. All he kept thinking was that he couldn't let Guy into the apartment. If he did, when Johnny came home, both of them would be in danger. Out here, people could come to his aid, but inside, there wasn't much anyone could do for them. They made it to the landing, and Kendall turned. He heard the door below open.

"Kendall, is that you?" Henry called up in a deep voice.

Before he could answer, Kendall felt Guy shift. Kendall stepped to the side and turned around, sliding out of Guy's grip. Without stopping or thinking, he pushed Guy backward. Guy stumbled back and hit the railing. Just reacting, Kendall pushed again, and Guy flailed his arms. Kendall jumped away, almost falling down the stairs. He regained his balance and hurried down the stairs. He expected Guy to come after him, but all he heard was a cry and a thud.

"Kendall," Henry cried, followed immediately by Johnny. Rapid footsteps sounded on the stairs, and within seconds Johnny was there.

"Are you all right?" Johnny asked. "You're bleeding."

Kendall looked down at his arm and saw blood on his sleeve. Then the pain hit and he pulled his shirt away. The cut didn't appear too bad, and Johnny helped him down the stairs.

"It was Guy," Kendall said as Johnny unlocked the door and led him through the apartment to the bathroom.

"I know. I saw him," Johnny said. "Sit down so I can look at it," Johnny said gently.

"Is he okay? I think he fell," Kendall said, a little shaken.

"He did, and I doubt he's okay," Johnny told him levelly. He wet a cloth and gently dabbed the blood off Kendall's arm. "It looks like you were really lucky." The cut had already stopped bleeding. "I want to clean it and then get a bandage on it. I'll have someone look at it once the ambulance gets here."

"What ambulance?" Kendall asked.

"Henry called the police. Guy fell over the rail and landed on the first floor." Johnny's voice was totally absent of any emotion.

"Is he—?" Kendall asked, wincing as Johnny put some antiseptic on the cut.

"I sure as hell hope so," Johnny swore, and Kendall tensed. "He did this to you, and he could have done worse."

Kendall swallowed. He'd never heard such malice from Johnny before. "I'm okay." Johnny wrapped a bandage around Kendall's wound. "I pushed him and then ran. Then you found me." Sirens sounded, getting closer by the second and then really loud as they stopped outside the building. "I killed someone," Kendall whispered. Johnny stilled and after a few seconds pulled Kendall into his arms.

"No, you didn't. You defended yourself. That's all you did, and... and I'm so proud of you." Johnny held him tighter. "You did so good." Johnny slowly rocked him back and forth, crying on his shoulder. "I almost lost you again." Kendall hugged Johnny as tightly as he could, closing his eyes as his tears came too.

"Guys." Kendall lifted his gaze. Henry stood in the bathroom doorway. "The police want to speak to you," Henry told Kendall, and he nodded.

"We'll be right down," Kendall said, and Henry turned. "Wait," he said, and Johnny released him. "Is he... gone?" Kendall swallowed. Henry nodded slowly once and then left. He turned back to Johnny and gently cupped his cheeks in his hands. "I'm okay. I promise." Kendall slowly stood up and took Johnny's hand. "Come on. I need to tell them what happened." He took two steps and Johnny grabbed him, embracing him tightly around the waist.

"I love you," Johnny said, his words choked.

"I love you too," Kendall said with a sigh. "It's over, Johnny. At least I know who was doing this, and he'll never be able to do it again." Kendall leaned back against Johnny. "It's over," he repeated. Kendall felt as though he could breathe again and maybe he could have his life back. "Come on, let's go face the music and tell them everything they want to know." Kendall sighed. *It's over.*

CHAPTER
TWELVE

IT WASN'T that easy. Yes, part of the ordeal was over, but a man was dead, and Kendall spent hours explaining to the police what had happened in the stairwell. In desperation, he ended up telephoning Lyman, and he came down and spoke with the police. For most of that time, Kendall was in a daze. He answered all of the officers' questions in as much detail as he could. Johnny apparently filled in details, as did Henry. Finally, after hours of questions, the police were satisfied. Kendall's case was helped by the presence of Guy's knife with Kendall's blood on it as well as the marks on his neck and throat from Guy's hands.

"Thank you for your cooperation," Detective Boutcher said as they were getting ready to leave. Kendall sipped from a glass of water. "I know this has been difficult, but we needed a clear explanation."

Kendall nodded slowly. "Of course."

"We'll be in touch if we need additional information." He handed Kendall one of his cards. "How well did you know him?"

Kendall sighed. "I thought we were friends. He worked on the movie I did, but I guess I really didn't know that much about him." Johnny took Kendall's hand and squeezed it reassuringly.

"He didn't want you to. I've seen other cases like this." Detective Boutcher paused at the door and then slowly walked back to where Kendall sat looking up at him. "For some people, figuring out who they are is easy. It comes naturally, and they burst out of the closet at fourteen. For others, it takes much longer, with struggles and pain, but eventually, once they accept themselves for who they are, they realize that they can be happy." Detective Boutcher glanced toward the open door. "Some people are never able to accept who they are. It eats at them, and they vacillate between self-loathing and lashing out at the world." Detective Boutcher sighed sadly. "I think this guy may have been one of those. Hopefully, as we work to wrap this up, we'll be able to figure that out."

"Will you let me know what you find?" Kendall asked.

"If you like. Of course. But there's something you need to know—none of this was your fault. You couldn't have changed his feelings. If my suspicions are correct, he was a ticking time bomb, and it's unfortunate he went off on you, but that's probably what happened. There was nothing you did to lead him on other than be kind to him. You couldn't have known." He stepped toward the doorway. "Please don't hesitate to call if there's anything I can do, but...." He paused as Johnny slid closer, placing his arms around Kendall's waist. "Something tells me you have all the support and care you're going to need."

"I'll take good care of him. You can be sure of that," Johnny said, and Detective Boutcher smiled quickly before leaving.

Kendall sighed loudly, releasing some of the tension that had built in every muscle. "I'm sorry I ever doubted you," Kendall whispered.

"Hey, I think we were both at fault there," Johnny said, nuzzling Kendall's neck.

"Okay," Lyman said from the doorway. "I know this is your place and all, mates, but you should probably shut the door." Kendall grinned at Lyman's accent. It hadn't made an appearance for most of the day. "They seem to have cleaned up the mess, and none of us have eaten, so grab your kit and we'll get some tucker."

"Lyman, cut the crap," Kendall said. "The accent doesn't suit you, and you don't need it." Kendall rolled his eyes, and all three of them laughed. "The Crocodile Dundee fad is most definitely over." Kendall's stomach rumbled, and both he and Johnny chuckled nervously.

Lyman humphed a bit and then smiled. "The car will be out front in a few minutes."

"We'll meet you there," Johnny said. Lyman left, and Kendall and Johnny released each other. They changed their clothes quickly.

"You realize Lyman is going to try to talk business," Kendall said, pulling on his shirt.

"I know what he wants and he isn't getting an answer, at least not now," Johnny said as he buttoned up his shirt. "Although it's tempting."

"I know." Kendall checked himself in the mirror and straightened his collar before checking Johnny's. "It seems strange going to dinner like this after what happened today."

"Yeah, it does," Johnny said, grabbing his keys and wallet. "But life goes on." Johnny turned and lightly stroked Kendall's cheek. "I know this will hit us a bit later." Kendall nodded and sighed. That was quite evident.

They left the apartment and met Henry coming up the stairs. "I'm so sorry," he said right away. "Someone called the police on me, and I was talking to them...."

Kendall nodded. "I think it could have been Guy who called them. He'd obviously been watching, like you said, and might have caught sight of you. Not that we'll ever really know, but I'm okay and that's because of what you told me. I kept my options open, kept him in the dark as much as I could, and when he gave me an opening, I took it." Kendall shivered at the thought that the opening he'd taken had cost Guy his life.

"No second-guessing," Henry said. "You did what you had to and stood up for yourself. Remember, he was the man who left you to die. Don't let your compassion make you feel guilty. He didn't show you any." Henry shifted his weight slightly. "Again, I'm sorry. I should have been there."

"No guilt or regrets," Kendall said, placing a hand on Henry's shoulder. "Can we call you if we need your services again?"

Henry flashed a surprised smile. "I'd be honored."

They shook hands and then they all stepped out of the building. Lyman's big-ass limo pulled up in front, and when the driver opened the door, Kendall and Johnny joined Lyman in the back.

"So it's finally over," Lyman said as the car began to move. "I never would have guessed it was Guy. I've worked with Guy for years. He was one of the people I...." Lyman's eyes widened, and he swore under his breath. "I discussed security arrangements with him while we were on location. No wonder you disappeared. He knew of any holes and where to exploit them."

"Hey, as you said, it's over," Kendall said.

Lyman pulled a bottle out of the bar and opened it, then poured three glasses and handed them around. "This is thirty-year-old scotch," he said as he sniffed from the top of the glass. "To better days and a productive and rewarding future." He raised his glass, and Kendall followed suit, then sipped the potent liquor. "So what do you have planned next?"

Kendall looked at Johnny with a smile. "Actually, I think I'm going to be playing the devil on Broadway." Johnny lightly squeezed his knee. "After that, I haven't given it much thought. I'd like to do another film, but this time without being handcuffed to a car."

"I'll keep that in mind," Lyman said before taking another sip. He and Johnny talked some business as they rode through traffic. Kendall sat quietly, sipping from his glass. The limousine hit a bump, and Kendall slid closer to Johnny.

"You're awfully quiet," Johnny whispered.

"I'm happy," Kendall whispered back.

"Good. Me too," Johnny said, and he then leaned close, kissing him lightly. The limo stopped, and Johnny got out. Kendall followed, tripping on the curb. Johnny caught him and held Kendall in his arms far longer than was necessary. "I came close to losing you twice. Let's try not to make it three times. I don't know if my heart can handle it."

"We can handle anything," Kendall whispered, and Johnny smiled.

EPILOGUE

… AND the nominees for Best Actor are….." Kendall barely heard the names, including his own.

When the nominations had been announced earlier in the year, Kendall had been at the theater in New York, rehearsing and then performing in a show. As Sal had predicted, *The Devil with Love* had turned into a huge hit. The ultimate bad-boy story had captured the imagination of the theater-going public in a huge way. Funny, dramatic, rich, sumptuous, and majorly romantic, it had something for everyone, and people flocked to see it. That evening, just as the cast was about to make their announcement regarding Equity Fights AIDS, one of his fellow cast members stepped forward to the front of the stage.

"Ladies and gentlemen, we truly hope you enjoyed the show." Applause broke out from throughout the house. "Before we get to our bit of business this evening, we have some news to share. Today, the nominations for the Oscars were announced, and we are proud to tell you that our very own devil, Kendall Monroe, has been nominated for Best Actor."

Kendall stepped forward and bowed. The theater had erupted. Everyone was on their feet. The applause, cheering, and stomping reverberated off the walls. He bowed again and then stepped back, rejoining hands with his fellow cast members. Once the cheering subsided, the evening's business concluded. The cast took one more final bow and then the curtain fell. What a feeling that had been. When he'd gotten home, he and Johnny had celebrated in a much more intimate way, though not much less quiet. That was all he could have hoped for.

As the actress on stage opened the envelope containing the winner's name, Johnny lightly patted his leg. They'd already discussed that it wasn't likely he would win. He was up against Hollywood royalty, for God's sake. "And the Oscar goes to… Kendall Monroe for *Stranded.*"

At first, Kendall couldn't move, but then he stood up and leaned over to Johnny, who squeezed his hand and motioned toward the stage. Kendall turned and walked down the aisle and up onto the stage, where he shook hands with both presenters and accepted his statuette. Then he stepped to the podium. "There are too many people to thank. My parents, the rest of the cast and crew, Lyman, of course, the most talented pain in the ass I've ever had the pleasure to work with." Chuckles floated through the crowd. "I also want to thank Johnny, my partner, my rock, and the reason I can do what I do. Thank you."

The audience applauded and the music began as Kendall walked off stage with the presenters. The statuette was taken from him and placed on a table with the other props. He waited for what he figured was a commercial break and then was led back out to his seat. A seat filler got up as he approached, and Kendall sat down next to Johnny.

"That was beautiful, sweetheart, thank you," Johnny said, trying his best to hide that he'd been wiping his eyes.

"I meant every word. You are my rock. Without you, I couldn't do anything." Kendall held Johnny's hand as the music began to play, indicating that they were returning to the telecast, and heedless of whether there were cameras on them or not, Kendall leaned over to Johnny and kissed him. "I love you more than anything."

"I love you too," Johnny mouthed.

"Guys, please," Lyman said from the row just behind them. Kendall turned, and the two Oscar winners shared a huge grin. "Next year, Johnny, it'll be your turn to win one for screenwriting," Lyman whispered; he was still trying to get Johnny to adapt one of his books.

"One's enough," Johnny said, and Kendall shifted in his seat to get a little closer to Johnny. One was more than enough, as far as he was concerned. One Johnny, one love, and one amazing life for the two of them—what more could he possibly want?

ANDREW GREY grew up in western Michigan with a father who loved to tell stories and a mother who loved to read them. Since then he has lived throughout the country and traveled throughout the world. He has a master's degree from the University of Wisconsin-Milwaukee and works in information systems for a large corporation. Andrew's hobbies include collecting antiques, gardening, and leaving his dirty dishes anywhere but in the sink (particularly when writing). He considers himself blessed with an accepting family, fantastic friends, and the world's most supportive and loving partner. Andrew currently lives in beautiful historic Carlisle, Pennsylvania.

Visit Andrew's website at http://www.andrewgreybooks.com and blog at http://andrewgreybooks.livejournal.com/.

E-mail him at andrewgrey@comcast.net.

A Senses Story from ANDREW GREY

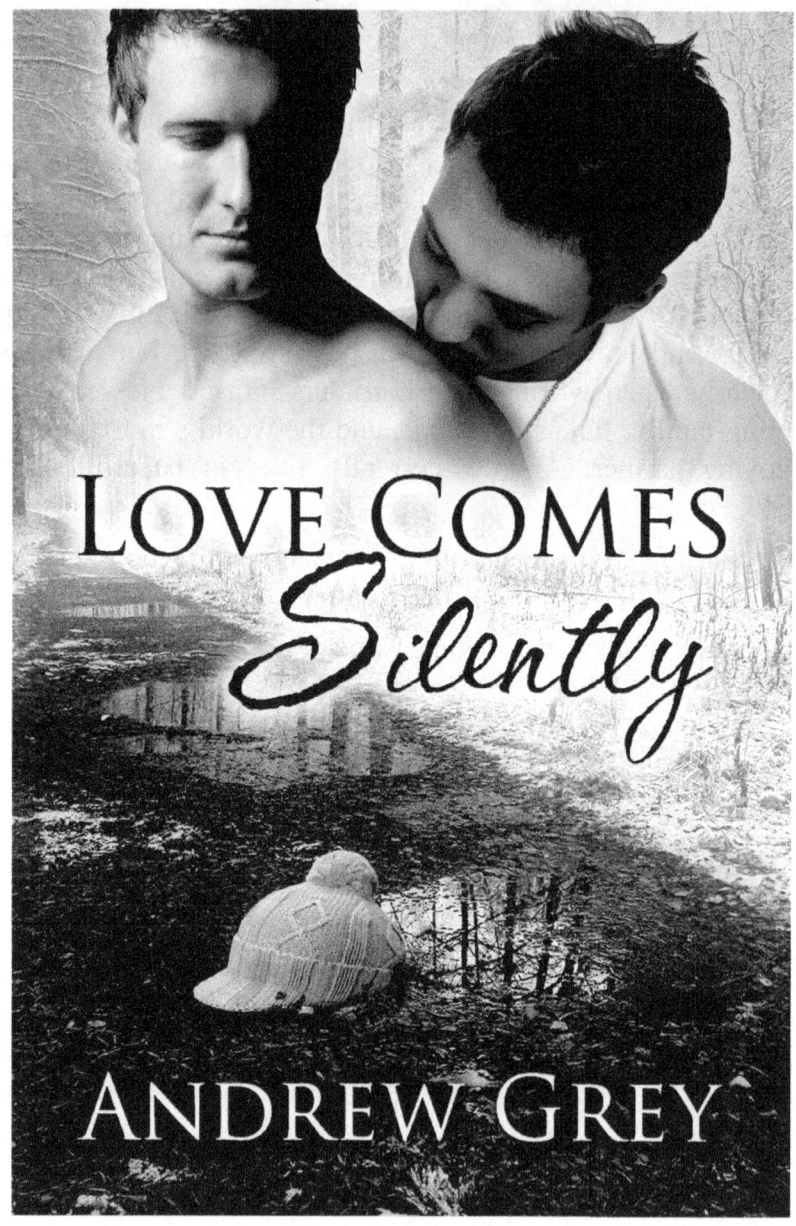

LOVE COMES
Silently

ANDREW GREY

http://www.dreamspinnerpress.com

Also from ANDREW GREY

http://www.dreamspinnerpress.com

Romance from ANDREW GREY

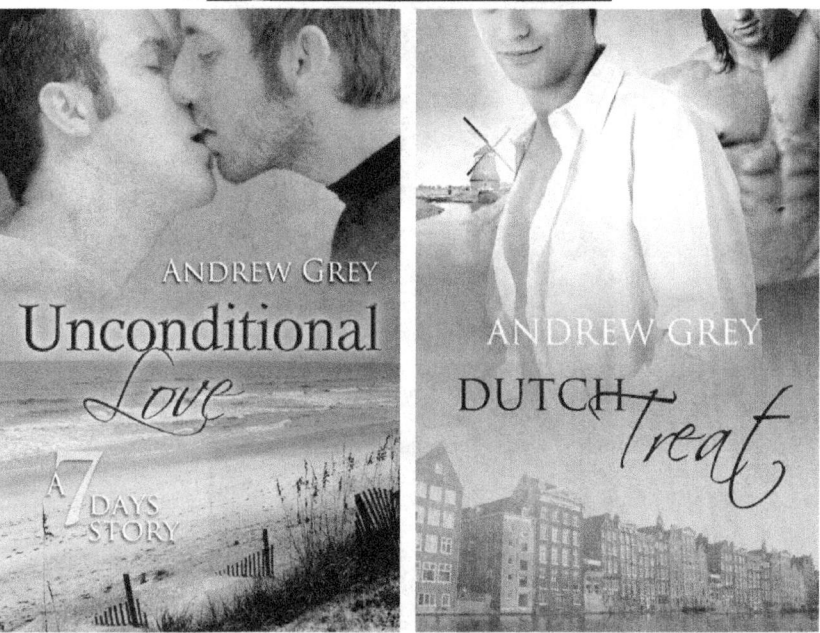

http://www.dreamspinnerpress.com

Also from ANDREW GREY

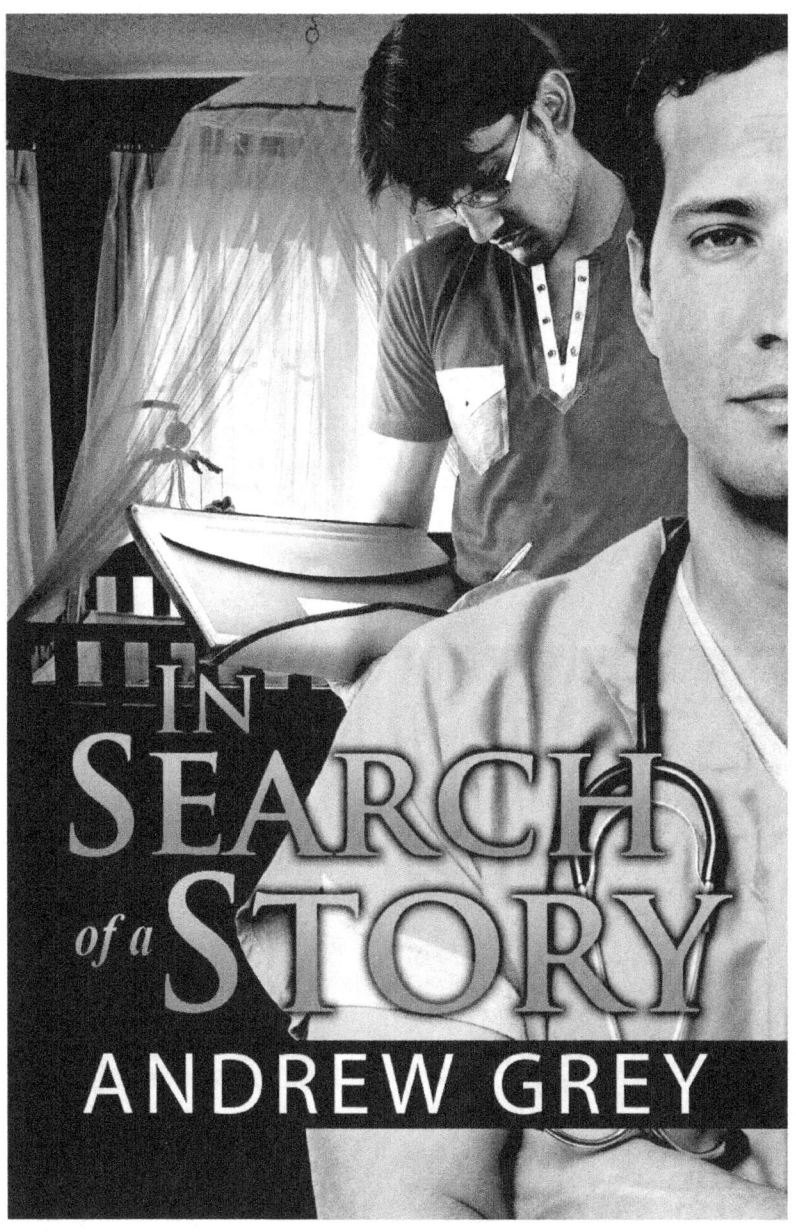

http://www.dreamspinnerpress.com

Also from ANDREW GREY

http://www.dreamspinnerpress.com

BOTTLED UP STORIES

http://www.dreamspinnerpress.com

LOVE MEANS…

http://www.dreamspinnerpress.com

LOVE MEANS…

http://www.dreamspinnerpress.com

Now in French, Italian, and Spanish

http://www.dreamspinnerpress.com

THE ART SERIES

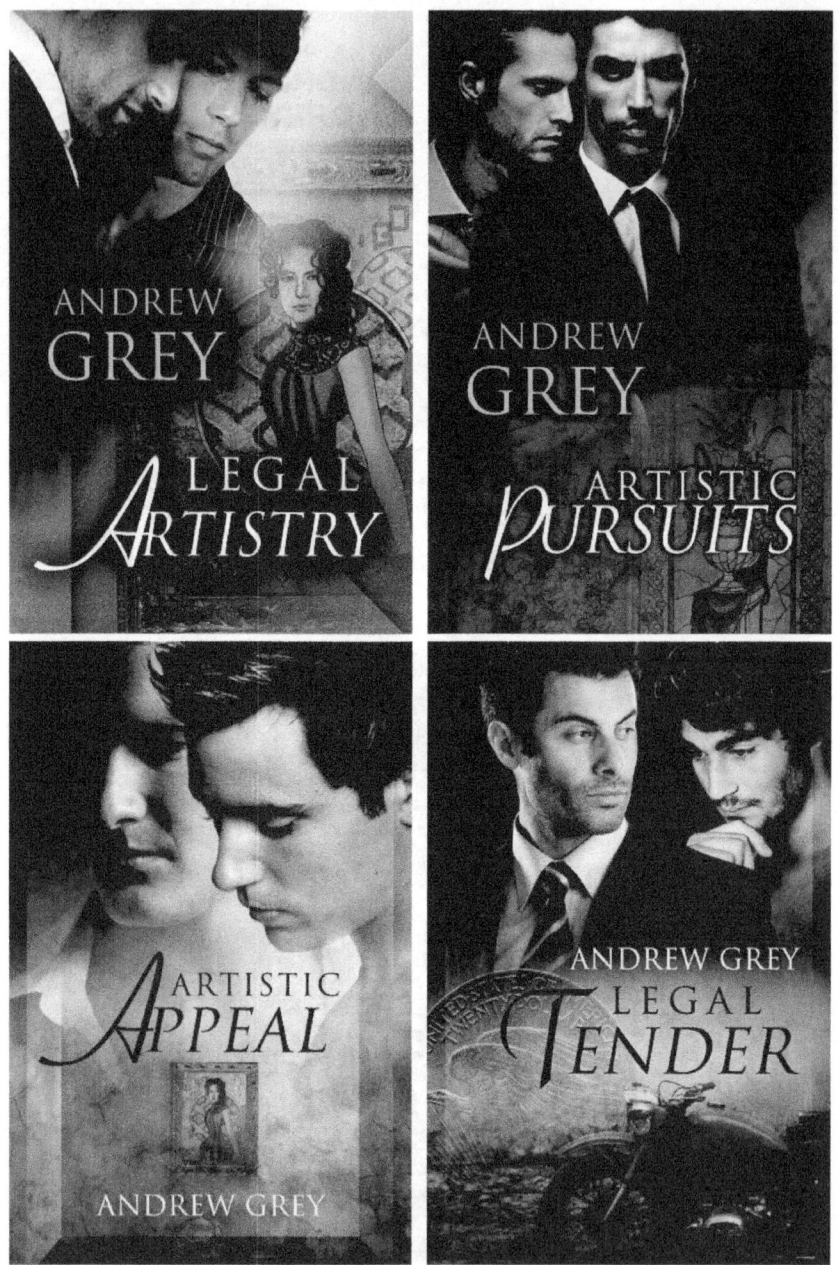

ANDREW GREY — LEGAL ARTISTRY

ANDREW GREY — ARTISTIC PURSUITS

ARTISTIC APPEAL — ANDREW GREY

ANDREW GREY — LEGAL TENDER

Also from ANDREW GREY

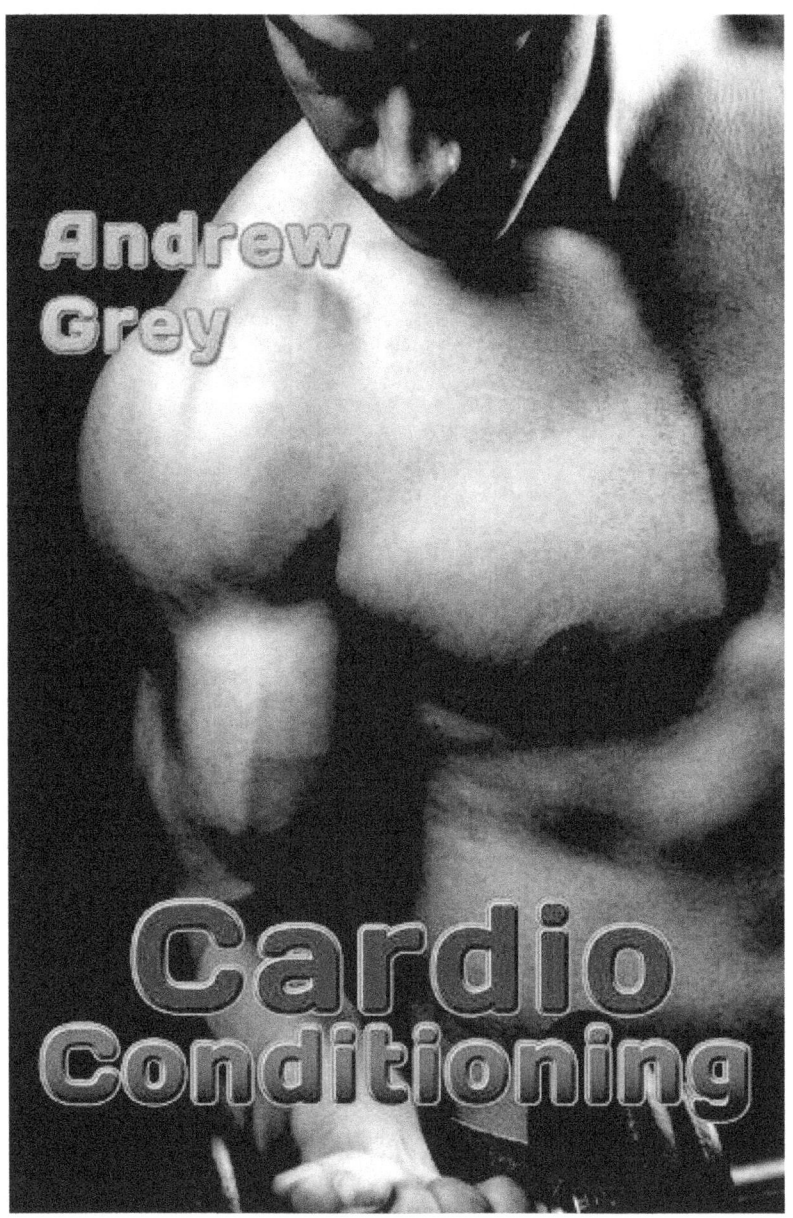

Andrew
Grey

Cardio
Conditioning

http://www.dreamspinnerpress.com

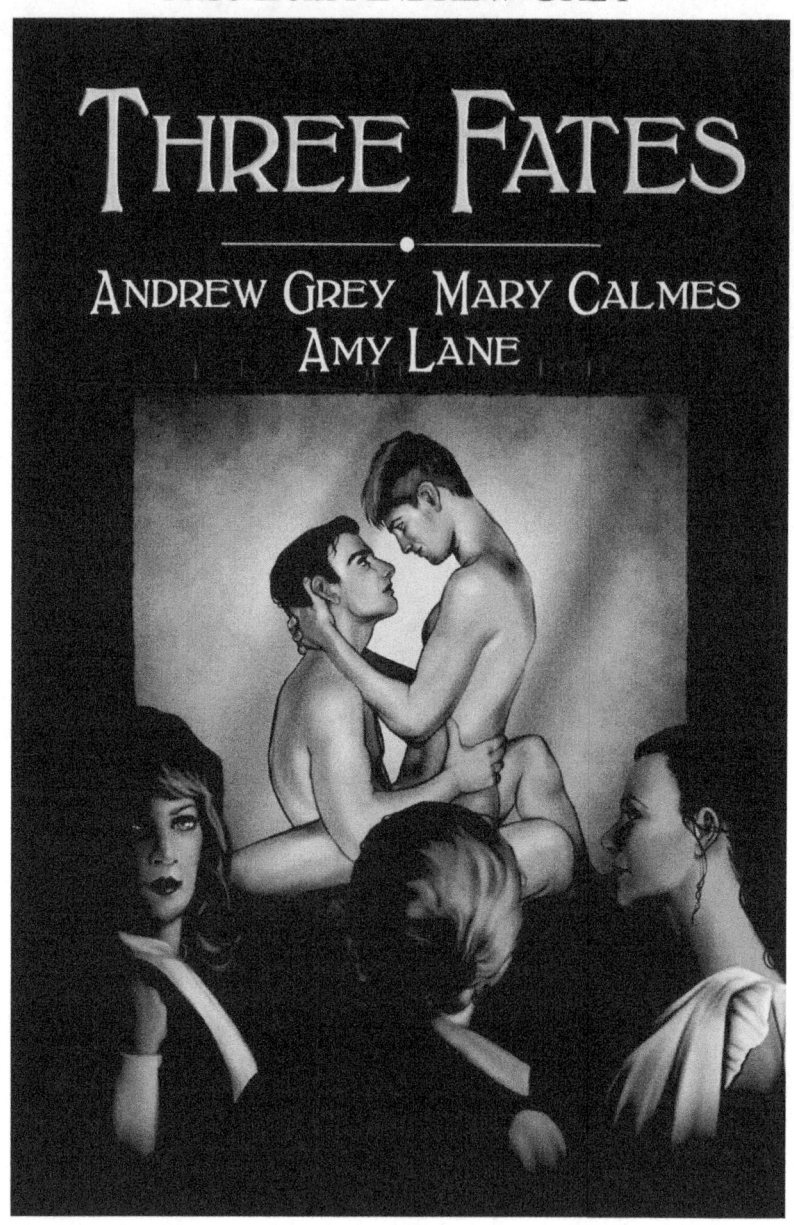

CHILDREN OF BACCHUS SERIES

http://www.dreamspinnerpress.com

Made in United States
Orlando, FL
22 March 2026